SO-AFR-339

PR
6.058
1983

...ary
... University
... 77341

WITHDRAWN

The Bright Blue Sky

02118006269813

Books by Max Hennessy

MAX HENNESSY, 1916-

The Bright Blue Sky

NEW YORK

ATHENEUM

1983

Library of Congress Cataloging in Publication Data

Hennessy, Max.
The bright blue sky.

1. World War, 1914-1918—Fiction. I. Title.
PR6058.A6886B7   1983   823'.914   82-73019
ISBN 0-689-11352-8

Copyright ©1982 by Max Hennessy
All rights reserved
Manufactured by Fairfield Graphics, Fairfield, Pennsylvania
First American Edition

Part One

I

Nicholas Dicken Quinney always considered that his career sprang from the fact that he fell in love twice in the same day – once with a girl and once with flying.

It had been his intention that Saturday in the early summer of 1914 to watch the cricket at Brighton but he missed the train and decided instead to go to Shoreham where he'd heard some idiot was going to try to fly.

At that point in his life he had no interest whatsoever in aviation beyond the intriguing discovery that men had learned to get off the ground, and almost until his voice had broken he had remained faithful to a youthful wish to be an engine driver. The man at Shoreham, however, was not one of the well-known aviators – Hawker, Sopwith, De Havilland or A. V. Roe – and, you never knew, there was always the possibility that he would crash.

The aeroplane, remarkably fragile-looking as it trembled in the breeze, had a pusher propeller, front and rear elevators and flat planes without camber. Its ailerons were without compensating cables to keep them in position so that on the ground, without the passage of air beneath them, they drooped like the tail feathers of a cockerel in wet weather. It looked, in fact, as elementary as the box-kites Dicken had been flying on the Downs not very many years before, and the doubts that it would ever get off the ground seemed implicit in the fact that the onlookers numbered no more than thirty. Dicken decided that perhaps he'd made a mistake, and ought to have gone to watch the cricket after all.

'It's got a four-cylinder ENV engine,' a voice alongside him said and he turned to see a girl of roughly his own age staring intently at the machine. Beyond her was another girl,

3

taller, blue-eyed, perhaps a little older than he was, and of an electrifying beauty. She wore a large tam o'shanter with a red bobble and had her dark hair done in a large bun at the back of her head. With them was a youth of Dicken's own age, plump, pale-haired, pale-eyed, with a bulging forehead that spoke of brains, and ears that stuck out high in his skull.

'It's Arnold Vickery's,' the boy said, indicating the air-craft. 'He's my father's cousin. He asked me to go up with him once.'

'But you didn't.' The girl who had first spoken turned to Dicken, a smaller plainer version of the other girl, her hair in plaits, her eyes green instead of luminous blue. 'This is Arthur Diplock. Cecil Arthur Diplock.' She made it sound like an insult. 'He's doing modern languages at Oxford. His father's the Rector of our village – Deane. He's thinking of following him into the Church.'

Dicken was polite but uninterested. His eyes were entirely on the older girl.

'He's been to the Rectory more than once.' Diplock seemed to sense his interest in his companion and pushed into the conversation. 'I came for a bit of a laugh.'

'I don't see why we should laugh,' the younger girl said hotly. 'It'll fly. Even if not very well.'

The tall girl smiled. 'This,' she pointed out, 'is my little sister, Zoë. I'm Annys Toshack.'

'Dicken Quinney.'

'What do you do?' Zoë Toshack asked.

Dicken hesitated. It needed, he felt, something important, well-paid or highly intelligent to impress them with his skill and the will to succeed. But, though officially he was a second class wireless operator – just! – since he was only seventeen and still legally a minor and his mother had refused to sign the form that would permit him to go to sea, he had had to find a job as a clerk at the gasworks at Brighton, and that was something he wasn't prepared to admit.

'I'm in wireless,'' he said.

'One of the coming things,' Zoë agreed.

'It must be very exciting,' her sister commented.

Dicken didn't know what to reply. The fact that this

4

goddess had deigned to speak to him staggered him.

Diplock seemed to have noticed her interest in Dicken, too, and moved closer, making the most of his relationship to the pilot of the aeroplane. It was Dicken's interest in her sister that the younger girl seemed to resent and she kept interrupting with facts about aviation which were considerably less fascinating than her sister's chatter.

'He calls it The White Ghost,' Diplock said. 'All that bed linen on the wings, I suppose. My father think he's mad.'

'I think so, too,' Zöe Toshack said. 'Aeroplanes are being built these days with camber to help the lift.'

'Zoë,' Annys Toshack said, 'is a bit odd, as you've probably noticed. Her ambition is to be a chauffeur of a motor car.'

Her sister responded vigorously. 'Women motor car drivers are the coming thing these days,' she said sharply. 'Pa has a stable,' she explained to Dicken. 'And traps which he hires out. He also owns a motor and a man's employed to take commercial travellers and doctors round the countryside. He's promised when I'm older I can take over when he's on holiday. I've already learned to drive it.'

'By observation rather than tuition,' Annys pointed out coolly. 'And in Father's style. Once round the village then foot on the accelerator instead of the brake. He's just opened a garage.'

'He says it'll eventually make more money than his stables,' Zoë observed.

The man who owned the aeroplane was standing by the machine now, gesturing. He was hardly anybody's idea of an intrepid birdman. He didn't have the lean good looks of De Havilland or the brisk energy of Harry Hawker. He didn't even have Cody's magnificent waxed moustachios. He was pale, stooping, wore spectacles and smoked non-stop, as if to calm his nerves.

'He's so short-sighted,' Diplock said, 'that when he's coming in to land, his mechanic has to run alongside and blow a whistle when he's about two feet off the ground so he'll know when to put it down.'

'One of these days,' Zoë observed, 'someone's going to lose it and then there'll be trouble.' She gestured. 'He's a musi-

5

cian,' she added. 'Did you know? Plays the fiddle. They tune the motor to the note of G.'

Dicken looked bewildered and she explained.

'He noticed that when the engine was running really well it gave out a note of G, so he bought a tuning fork and the mechanic tunes it up accordingly. When it's going at full speed they all hum the note and get the engine to match. If it agrees, everything's all right. If it's a semi-tone out, they take out all the sparking plugs for a clean and start again.'

Dicken felt she was pulling his leg and, anyway, he had eyes for no one but Annys. The fact that she lived in Deane, which was the next village to Willys Green, where he lived himself, was hard to believe. How could he possibly have missed such a creature?

'He nearly ended in the river the other week,' Zoë said.

'Who?' Nick wrenched his attention away.

'Vickery, silly,' Zoë gave him a hard look, as if she were used to young men's attention wandering from what she was saying when her sister was around.

'He hasn't learned to turn yet,' Diplock explained. 'He sideslipped into the ground. Fortunately he was only a few feet up. Half the struts and spars were broken, as well as one of the propeller blades.'

'They glued and screwed it together again.' Zoë took up the story. 'But when they came to do the propeller they had to use three bolts and that put it all out of balance, so they put three bolts in the other blade and balanced it by glueing pieces of the mechanic's dungarees to it until they'd got it right. But don't ever stand in line with it when the engine's running. It'll probably come loose and take your head off.'

While they were talking, Vickery himself approached. He nodded to the two girls and turned to Diplock.

'I need a passenger,' he announced. 'How about it, Arthur?'

'What's wrong with the mechanics?' Diplock asked.

'Taggart's too heavy and Green's scared. I need someone lighter.'

To Dicken, Diplock appeared less unwilling to go flying than to disappear from Annys Toshack's sphere of influence. 'I'm heavy, too,' he said. 'Nearly as heavy as Taggart.'

'I'll go,' Zoë volunteered.

'You're too young,' Diplock said. He indicated Dicken. 'How about him? He's lighter than me. Not so well-built.'

Dicken glared. Arthur Diplock, in his view was not so much well-built as fat.

Vickery had turned and was looking at him.

'This is Dicken Quinney, 'Annys said. 'A friend of ours.'

Dicken's heart thumped. To be called a friend was almost too much for him.

Vickery smiled for the first time. It seemed ingratiating. 'Ever been up before?' he asked.

Dicken had never quite seen himself as an intrepid bird-man. Suddenly, now, he did. At least it would be something to talk about in the office on Monday. Normally, he spent as long as he could in the lavatory reading the newspaper to avoid the job of copying gas meter numbers from one dreary ledger to another.

'No,' he said. 'I've never been up.'

'Well,' Diplock pointed out, 'you'll never get another chance like this.'

'I'm not going to turn,' Vickery said. 'Just one side of the field to the other.'

Dicken glanced at Annys who was regarding him warmly with those luminous blue eyes of hers.

'All right,' he said. 'I'll go.'

Feeling ten feet tall because he knew Annys Toshack was watching, he followed Vickery towards the aircraft. The two men in dungarees standing by it turned as they approached.

'This is George Taggart, my fitter,' Vickery said. 'And Frank Green, my rigger.'

The two men studied Dicken. As he turned away, he saw Taggart whisper something to the other man, and he suspected they'd decided he was mad.

Putting his cap on backwards like Vickery, he climbed to the passenger's seat through the maze of wires that held the machine together. He wasn't sure what to expect. The engine was being run up as they made themselves comfortable and he was startled to see the mechanics standing with their heads cocked, listening. What Zoë Toshack had said about them tuning the engine with a G tuning fork appeared to be true.

Vickery handed Taggart a whistle. 'Don't forget to blow,' he said.

'And don't you forget to stay within reach,' Taggart advised, setting off across the turf. 'I can't run alongside you all the way across the field.'

Turning to Dicken, who was beginning to wonder by this time what he'd let himself in for, Vickery gestured. 'Sit still and don't fidget,' he advised. 'You could have her over.'

The motor sounded like a sewing machine gone mad, its note high and thin, and as Green let go the wing the machine began to move forward. Dicken was startled at the rattling and the rumbling noise the wheels made over the turf but, almost before he was aware of it, the noise stopped and it sank in that he was airborne. He was about to look down when he remembered what Vickery had told him and sat as if set in plaster of Paris, trying to breathe shallowly in case deep breaths disturbed the equilibrium.

It reminded him of sliding face-forward down the banister at home, something which required nerve and a good sense of balance, and, without moving his head, he carefully rolled his eyes sideways to see that he was actually higher than the sheds where machines were repaired and business was done. It was hard to believe. He was hardly Icarus but he *was* flying!

In the field next to the aerodrome, a couple of horses, startled by the high buzz of the motor, galloped away, their tails in the air, and it amazed him that he could actually see them beyond the hedge. Still afraid to upset the balance of the aeroplane, still rigid in his seat, he peeped fascinated down his nose over the wing.

The flight ended almost before they started. They began to sink, lower and lower until they were floating over the turf and it was possible to pick out daisies drifting back beneath them. Vickery was looking anxious.

'The whistle,' he shouted above the noise of the engine. 'Where's the whistle?'

Remembering what Zoë had told him about Vickery's short-sightedness, Dicken was caught by a sudden panic, but

8

then he saw Taggart running towards them and heard the blast of a whistle. Satisfied, Vickery closed the throttle and the machine settled and they were rolling to a stop.

As the engine coughed and died, Vickery turned to Dicken. He seemed pleased with himself. 'Enjoy it?' he asked.

Dicken didn't answer for a moment. At one point in the flight, short as it was, he had actually been looking down on a seagull planing in to land. It had been too short to be called exciting, too brief to be anything more than a momentary occurrence, but he sensed he had been on the brink of something tremendous. He wasn't certain what it was, but somehow, just beyond his reach, he felt, had been an experience of incredible beauty that he couldn't describe.

'Terrific,' he said. 'But couldn't we have gone up a bit more? Really high. They say Geoffrey de Havilland can get up to five hundred feet.'

Vickery went pink. 'Some days are difficult,' he muttered. 'Today there was no lift in the air.'

Zoë appeared alongside the machine as Dicken climbed down, jumping up and down in feverish excitement. 'What was it like?' she yelled. 'Tell me before I burst!'

Dicken tried to look experienced. 'There wasn't much lift in the air,' he said. He looked around. He'd been hoping to describe his adventure not to Zoë but to her beautiful elder sister. 'Where's Annys?' he asked.

Zoë grinned. 'Arthur took her over to the sheds to see the other aeroplanes,' she said. 'He's eighteen and he has his father's motor car.'

2

It was only later that the importance of what he'd done dawned on Dicken and he was suddenly in the grip of an immediate and violent infatuation with the sky. He'd flown! Only a few other men had! Men who got their names in the paper and were already achieving an ephemeral fame. He'd joined their ranks! He was a flier! Or, at least, he'd flown! It was unbelievable.

Suddenly able to impress people with the fact that he'd been up in the air, flying took hold of him in a way he wouldn't have believed possible a few weeks before and he was eager to learn all about the pioneers – the Americans, Wilbur and Orville Wright, Hawker, De Havilland and the others, even a few new ones he'd not heard of before like Fairey and Dunne and Wilfred Parke – and about the new machines they flew – Cody's Flying Cathedral, A. V. Roe's triplane, the BE2, the RE1, the Handley Page monoplane, the Tabloid that had won the Schneider Trophy for Britain. He began to take *Aeroplane*, absorbing information eagerly, and even make the models of Blériots and Farmans he'd once despised.

Yet, at that moment, he couldn't tell just which was the more important – flying or Annys Toshack – and, because he considered flying with its inevitable expense entirely beyond him, he could only think of it in the way of distant dreams, while Annys Toshack lived in the next village which was only a bicycle ride away. A long bicycle ride, to be sure, and on a windy day an exhausting one that left him coated with sweat, with his trousers clinging to his legs and his collar like a wet rag round his neck, but it *was* only a bicycle ride and could be performed at no cost to himself, something of great moment when you were virtually penniless.

The need for money made him once more approach his mother. He wasn't sure how going to sea would work out with Annys Toshack at home, but he had vague romantic dreams about hot countries and returning, bronzed, manly and experienced, to her embraces.

'I'm a qualified second class operator,' he pointed out. 'I took the course and passed the examination. I *ought* to go to sea. So I can get experience to become a *first* class operator.'

His mother avoided his eyes. 'People get drowned going to sea,' she said.

Since the heroism of the operators of the *Titanic*, who had sent out signals for help until the very end, had been the one thing that had prompted him to go in for wireless, and since his mother had paid for his course, it seemed a little unfair.

'A lot of people go to sea who don't get drowned,' he pointed out.

It made no difference. Dicken's father had been a solicitor's clerk who had run off with one of the lady typists, and his mother had no wish to see her son also disappear abruptly from her ken. It looked as though he was going to have to resign himself to continuing to do what he did.

'After all,' his mother pointed out, 'it's a safe job. After fifty years you get a pension.'

It was an irrefutable argument but, looking round at the other people in the gasworks office, Dicken decided that if he looked like they did after fifty years, he was better off without a pension. He decided to bide his time. After all, if nothing else, not going to sea meant more meetings with Annys Toshack.

He was in a seventh heaven of delight, aware only of her flawless skin and those large blue eyes on him. It was as though he'd known her for years, and when she finally allowed him to kiss her behind the bushes near her front gate it was as if his whole life had been leading up to that one moment.

That summer was extraordinary. There seemed to be no rain at all. The scorching sun brought out the plums and the plums brought out the wasps, and Dicken was so head over heels in love he barely noticed what was happening anywhere else in the world.

He'd never been a political type and never bothered to read much in the newspapers beyond the sports page. His chief concern was Annys Toshack's unexpected interest in him and the joy he got from watching Diplock glowering from the side lines. Despite his father's motor car, Diplock didn't seem to be making much headway and Dicken started looking at himself in the mirror, wondering what it was that gave him the edge over his rival. All he could see was a normal sort of face topped with a thatch of unruly dark hair. His eyes seemed normal enough, too, and though his nose was straight it didn't appear to have any special qualities. The only advantage he could see was that his face already looked stronger and more mature than Diplock's doughy features and the high-set ears that made him look like a worried terrier. Only vaguely aware that internationally things were warming up, he was conscious of trouble in the Balkans, but it didn't worry him too much because there was always trouble in the Balkans, and the fact that an Austrian archduke had been assassinated with his wife in Serbia didn't seem of much moment because assassination was one of the occupational hazards of middle-European princelings.

But then, suddenly, there was talk of war on the Continent and wealthy travellers started rushing homewards and, to everyone's surprise, the whole of Europe seemed to be aiming for a colossal head-on crash that seemed to involve every country except Britain.

Having just discovered the twin delights of flying and Annys Toshack, however, it remained way above Dicken's head. Despite his youth, he began to think of marriage. Notwithstanding the fact that his mother lived in a perfectly normal row of red-brick dwellings, marriage to a girl you loved, he felt, was a blissful existence in a cottage with roses round the door and a garden full of hollyhocks, the two of them sitting by the fire in the evening, one with sewing, the other with a book, with occasional moments of tender love which – all in good time – produced a family. He could think of nothing else and came under severe censure at the office for dreaming when he should have been working.

'There's a dance,' Annys told him. 'At the village hall. On August Bank Holiday Monday. Mother says I can go.'

'I'll take you,' Dicken said. 'I'll come on my bike.' The idea of cycling seven miles home in the dark after a dance wasn't exactly to his taste, but the thought of holding the adorable Annys in his arms for the evening, with a short session in the bushes by her front gate as he took her home, more than made up for it.

'Arthur Diplock asked me to go with him,' Annys said.

'Cecil Arthur,' Zoë said from the settee where she was reading the *Daily Mail* sports page. 'C. A. Diplock. C.A.D. Cad. I can't see what you ever saw in him.'

Bank Holiday Monday seemed a lifetime away. When it finally arrived, Dicken rose early and laid his best suit and tallest stiffest collar on the bed ready for the evening. If he spent the afternoon doing nothing, he felt, he might not find the ride home too exhausting, and he was just established at the breakfast table with the *Daily Mail* propped up on the marmalade when the doorbell rang. He had just got to the headlines, 'Germany Demanding Free Passage Through Belgium,' when his mother appeared, to tell him someone wanted to speak to him.

It was Taggart, Vickery's mechanic, and he had an old Model T Ford in the road, the tonneau cut away and replaced with a box-like structure to make a truck.

'It's Arnold,' he said. 'He wants to know if you'll come over and be his passenger. He's going to try long distance. No turns.'

Dicken's jaw had dropped. He'd forgotten about Vickery lately and the chance of another flight excited him. 'Will he be going higher this time?' he asked.

'Have to, won't he?' Taggart said. 'Going to try to break his own record. It's a perfect day for it.'

Dicken was suddenly almost choking with excitement. 'And he wants *me*?' he said. Was there something special about him? Had he shown a particular skill? Had he a particular instinct for sitting still or leaning the right way?

Taggart disillusioned him quickly. 'The chap he arranged for let him down,' he pointed out. 'You're the only other chap he could think of.'

It was a knock to Dicken's self-esteem but he accepted it. After all, a flight, for whatever reason, was worth having.

'I'd arranged to go out tonight,' he explained. 'Can I get back in time?'

Taggart indicated the Ford. 'I can get you home in the old whizz-bang easy. Only half an hour door-to-door.'

'Can you promise? It's important. I have this date tonight you see.'

'That dark girl?' Taggart's eyebrows rose. 'Well, I see the problem. All right, kid, I'll get you back, I promise.'

Dicken was tingling with nerves as they drove off. He was so excited, he barely noticed which way they were going. If record-breaking didn't impress Annys, nothing would. Then he noticed that the signs pointed to Chichester and Southampton and woke up abruptly.

'Aren't we going to Shoreham?' he said.

'Not this time,' Taggart said. 'He's got the machine in a field at Wick near Southampton. We took it over in bits a week ago. He's going to *fly* to Shoreham.'

'From Southampton?'

'Forty miles, we reckon. Further than Blériot flew across the Channel.'

Vickery was waiting impatiently alongside his machine. The engine was warmed up ready and there were two or three other men with stop watches who looked important and official.

'You?' Vickery said, as if he were surprised to see Dicken. He glanced at Taggart who shrugged, then smiled. 'Oh, well, you're much lighter. Much better for a long distance flight.'

'We're going to need machines that will fly long distances,' one of the waiting officials observed grimly. 'These things are going to make the cavalry obsolete when it comes to scouting and bringing back information about the enemy.'

'Why?' Dicken said. 'Is there going to be a war?'

'Where've you been, lad? China or somewhere? Austria's gone into the Balkans, haven't they? That archduke of theirs who was murdered. They said it was Serbia's fault. Unfortunately, Russia's got a pact to protect Serbia and that's brought in Germany who's got a pact with Austria. And that's brought in France who has a pact with Russia. The only country that isn't involved is Britain.'

As they climbed to their places, Vickery handed over an ordnance survey map and a notebook and pencil. 'I'm going to fly along the Brighton road,' he said. 'Your job will be to make sure we don't lose it by identifying the places we see. Note down anything important.'

'Such as what?'

'Rivers. The castle at Arundel. Together with the time we pass over them. If this war they're talking about comes, two months from now aeroplanes will be doing that sort of thing all over Europe. That's why this flight's important. Forty miles is bound to set the War Office thinking. They'll buy my machines.'

Dicken wasn't so sure they would. There seemed to be too much that was hit or miss about Vickery's aeroplanes and he felt the War Office would surely demand more exact details of performance than that the engines could be considered tuned when their note matched that of a G tuning fork.

'You ready?'

Dicken nodded, despite his doubts so excited he could barely speak. Vickery leaned over the side and spoke to Taggart.

'Green's at Shoreham with the whistle, is he?'

Taggart nodded. 'He'll be waiting for you to come in.'

The engine was started. It still sounded like a sewing machine with something wrong inside but it was the most exciting sound Dicken had ever heard.

The tail of the machine was swung for it to face the wind, Vickery listening with his head cocked to the engine note. As far as Dicken could tell it was G but he didn't have much of an ear for music. Then Vickery waved his hand and Taggart and one of the other men dragged away the triangular blocks of wood from under the wheels. Lurching slightly, the machine began to move forward over the uneven ground. The sewing machine went faster and the forest of struts and piano wire began to rattle and creak. Dicken was so busy wondering why the tall, uncut grass didn't halt them he barely noticed that the rumbling had stopped and they were in the air.

The climb seemed very uncertain and Dicken was reminded once again how much the business of flying seemed to depend on balance. They rose a few inches, then a few more, then Vickery dipped the nose to gain a little extra speed and managed to lift the machine by the skin of his teeth over the trees at the end of the field.

'All that petrol,' he announced in a shout. 'Got a reserve tank on board!'

He seemed either to have gone mad or suddenly to have discovered an enormous confidence in his machine, because he was climbing rapidly. Perhaps it was the thought of all those contracts he was seeking from the War Office, but for once he seemed more than willing to take chances, and in a dream Dicken realised they were a hundred feet up and he could see the English Channel. As Vickery edged nervously south to pick up the Brighton road, he became aware of the inlets on either side of Portsmouth, the sun burnishing them like sheets of gold. Then he saw the trail of steam from a train moving almost alongside them below as it headed east. It seemed to be going faster than they were, then gradually it began to drop back and he realised the tremendous speed they were making.

'Must be nearly fifty miles an hour,' Vickery yelled delightedly. 'They do at least forty-five on that stretch. Make a note of it.'

Aware that he'd forgotten his duties, Dicken began to write. The wind flipping the pages of the notebook, his body rigid in his seat in case movement sent the machine crashing to the ground, he set down his impressions of the sea and Chichester Harbour in the distance. Just beyond the entrance, two warships were heading south-east towards Selsey Bill. The spire of Chichester Cathedral came up, a long flèche in the sunshine, then Bognor on his right and Arundel Castle on his left. When Worthing appeared, he realised the flight was almost over and felt he never wanted to go down. Below him he could see cattle in the fields like small white dots, and human beings peering up at them from the groups of houses.

When Shoreham came in sight, Vickery steadied the machine. They were still flying at what seemed a tremendous speed and height and Vickery lifted the nose. But not too far, in case they stalled. The speed dropped and Vickery lowered the nose, but very gently because wings had been known to fall off in dives. The possibility of danger added spice to the event, but the ground seemed to be coming up to meet them in a normal enough fashion. The green turf changed to individual blades of grass and Dicken could see daisies. But Vickery seemed to be still holding off, his head cocked, and Dicken realised he was listening for the blast of Green's whistle.

'Put it down,' he yelled. 'It's all right! We're only two feet up!'

Vickery ignored him, giving the engine short bursts to keep it flying, then, beyond the wing, Dicken saw Green running along, waving his arms and pointing downwards.

'He says to land,' he yelled. 'He hasn't got the whistle! Perhaps he's lost it!'

There were other men running out now, several of them with their fingers between their teeth blowing whistles that were soundless above the engine. The high bank that contained the River Adur was coming closer and in desperation Vickery closed the throttle. The machine settled and the rumble underneath came almost at once. Vickery looked startled, as though he'd thought they had much further to descend; but they were running out of field now and Dicken was just wondering whether it would be wiser to throw himself from his seat and risk being caught like a butterfly in a net against the multitude of bracing wires, or stay where he was and become the first victim from Willys Green of an aeroplane crash, when he realised that they were surrounded by soldiers in uniform, scattering in all directions, and that round the edge of the field were tents he'd never seen before.

The aeroplane ploughed into the nearest. It absorbed its forward motion so that it swung round and came to a stop, and, jumping clear before anything else could happen, Dicken scrambled to his feet, only to be knocked flying again by Green as he galloped up.

'Didn't you hear us shouting?' he yelled.

'Why didn't you blow the whistle?' Vickery yelled back.

'I lost it,' Green said. 'I had a hole in my pocket. But it

17

doesn't matter. You've done it. You've flown further than Blériot. Twice as far. Almost as far as Corbett-Wilson between Wales and Wexford. And he had no passenger.'

An officer in khaki appeared. He wore a peaked cap like a bus conductor and a khaki collar with a woollen tie and a tiepin.

'How dare you?' he spluttered. 'How dare you? I'm going to hold you responsible for that tent!'

Someone opened a bottle of champagne and passed him a glass. It calmed him down remarkably quickly. He blustered a little and blew into his moustache but in the end conceded that little damage had been done.

'Can always indent for another, anyway,' he admitted. 'Can always say the rats had been at it. Some of the damn things have been in store since the South African War.'

'What are you doing here, anyway?' Vickery asked.

'Reservists,' the officer said. 'General mobilisation.'

'Has the war started?'

'No, but it looks like doing any time now.'

Another bottle of champagne was opened and, as they sat in the sun on the bank alongside the river to drink it, someone offered a glass to Dicken. It was the first time he'd drunk champagne and it made him feel lightheaded. Then a photographer arrived and Vickery posed in front of the machine to have his picture taken. No one seemed to think of Dicken. There was a lot of laughter by this time and the officer had been joined by two of his sergeants.

By the time Taggart arrived, with the Ford steaming like a train, to join them, it was obvious they were all beginning to enjoy themselves.

'They said I couldn't do it,' Vickery crowed. 'Have her filled up. I'm going up again to celebrate. A quick flip past my mother's home on the front at Brighton. I promised her I'd fly over the pier if I did it.'

They filled the machine up quickly and turned her round.

'How about you, young 'un?' Vickery suddenly seemed to remember Dicken. 'You coming, too?'

Dicken backed away. He would have given his right arm to go but he was watching the time and it was beginning to hurry past. Flying was flying and he was proud of what they'd done, but dancing with Annys Toshack in his arms was another thing entirely.

'I'll come,' Taggart said quickly.

'How'll you get back?' Dicken asked. 'You'll have to turn.'

Vickery grinned, still elated with excitement and champagne. 'I can always land in a field, swing her round and take off again. I might even have a go at banking. After all, we turned south to the coast road from Wick. A bit, anyway.'

'How about me getting home?' Dicken asked Taggart. 'You promised.'

'I'll be back, kid, never fear.'

Vickery fished in his pocket. 'You can always say you're part of a record,' he pointed out. 'Forty miles with a passenger.' He took out a sovereign and offered it. 'Your fees for your services. Everybody else gets paid. So why not you?'

Dicken eyed the coin for a moment. It was a fortune to him, but his mind was still full of the excitement of the flight, of sitting above the earth watching the fields slide past beneath them and the immense emptiness of the bright blue sky above.

'I'd rather,' he blurted out, 'that you taught me to drive an aeroplane.'

Vickery eyed him for a moment then he smiled and slapped his shoulder. 'Done,' he said. 'We'll start next week-end. That's a promise.'

He climbed into his seat with Taggart beside him and the engine was started up. Taxiing to the other end of the field, Taggart jumped down, swung the tail round and climbed back again. They heard the engine note rise and Green grinned. 'That's not a G,' he said. 'It's a high C. The champagne's talking.'

The machine began to roll forward, moving faster and faster. By this time everybody was laughing and pointing and nobody but Dicken, who by this time was the only sober one among them, noticed the ragged sound that had appeared in the engine.

The machine lurched towards them, the wings quivering, the wheels rattling, the engine buzzing and whining, looking like a mobile clothes line on washing day.

'Get her off,' Green said casually. 'You'll run out of field.'

But the wind had dropped and Vickery was getting no help. Slowly the wheels came off the grass and everybody cheered, but the machine wasn't rising well and the ragged sound was growing more marked.

'Get her up!' Green shouted, suddenly alarmed, and all the soldiers started to shout with him. 'Get her up!'

The machine seemed disinclined to lift and Vickery did what he'd done as they'd left Wick. He dipped the nose to gain extra speed then lifted sharply over the river. The machine soared, the engine screaming as if in terror, but then suddenly there were two loud bangs and a silence that seemed immense.

The machine was just rising into a climbing turn as it ran out of speed and, as the nose dropped, everybody started to scramble up the bank. Dicken was in the lead and reached the top just in time to see the aeroplane flop down at the river's edge. Mud and water flew in all directions and a man who had been fishing started up and began to run.

The white canvas wings crumpled and a great cloud of steam went up as the hot engine vanished below the water, then slowly the machine turned over on to its back and began to sink.

3

'Broke both legs,' Dicken said. 'The pill-roller says he'll be on his back for six months. Taggart got concussion so there was nobody to drive me home and I had to take the train. I cycled as fast as I could.'

Zoë Toshack smiled. 'Well, it wasn't fast enough,' she said. 'She went with Arthur Diplock.'

Dicken scowled. The frantic cycle ride from Willys Green had left his collar like a dishrag round his neck. Even had he arrived in time, he could hardly imagine Annys wanting to dance with him.

'I thought Vickery wanted me specially,' he said bitterly. 'But he sent Taggart for Arthur Diplock and Diplock suggested me. He gave Taggart half a sovereign not to be available to drive me home.'

Zoë smiled. 'Well, it won't matter much now, anyway,' she said. 'There won't be any more dances for a bit. There's going to be a war.'

'We're not involved.'

'Oh, yes, we are. Germany's gone into Belgium and it seems we have a treaty with them that nobody's noticed up to now. The government's sent an ultimatum that they've got to remove their troops or we shall come in against them. It expires at midnight.'

'They'll back down,' Dicken said. 'They're bound to. Nobody would go to war with the British Empire.' He paused, his mind elsewhere. 'I don't see why she couldn't have waited a bit,' he said. 'She couldn't have thought it very important.'

Zoë smiled. 'Tell you what: Take me instead.'

'You're not old enough.'

'I'm sixteen! I can do the turkey trot and the bunny hug and the valeta and the waltz. That ought to be enough for anybody.'

Dicken was tempted. It would give him the chance to get near to Annys and put things right.

'All right,' he said. 'Had we better ask your mother?'

'She'll never know,' Zoë said calmly. 'She's gone to see Grandma to tell her about the war. When she comes home and finds I'm not around, she'll assume I've gone to bed.' She studied Dicken's crimson face and soiled collar. 'You'd better have a bit of a wash, though,' she went on. 'You stink like a polecat after all that sweating. I'll give you some of Annys's scent – it'll take away the smell – and I'll give your collar a run over with the iron.'

He was sitting in the garden when she appeared. She had pinned her hair up and put on make-up and he was startled at the transformation.

'Zoë,' he said. 'You're pretty!'

' 'Course I'm pretty,' she said. 'But nobody ever notices me, because Annys is so beautiful, so I never bother. Besides there are other things more important than sitting in front of a mirror putting stuff on your face.'

'Such as what?'

'Motor cars. I love motor cars.' She grinned at him. 'Dicken, if ever you learn to drive an aeroplane, will you teach me?'

'You? A girl?'

'Why not? Women are driving motors. Soon they'll start driving aeroplanes.' She studied him. 'You know, you're not bad yourself.'

'Not bad at what?'

'Not bad to look at. Got the tickets?'

*

They arrived between dances, with the band silent and everybody standing around talking. There were one or two uniforms, one man embarrassed in the dress jacket of the local Yeomanry, an affair of blue decorated with gold lace.

'He looks like a Hungarian admiral,' Zoë whispered.

22

As the band started again, she grabbed Dicken's hand. 'Come on!' she said.

To his surprise, she was a good dancer, light in his arms and disconcertingly attractive with her face close to his. Her skin, when looked at closely, was as good as her sister's and, he realised now, her hair wasn't mousy as he'd thought, but had reddish tints in it that set off the brilliant cat-like green of her eyes. He felt better and even began to enjoy himself.

As they swept round, he found himself face to face with Annys. She was in the arms of Diplock and was staring furiously. As the dance finished, she came towards them, brushing past the other couples to stand in front of her sister, her eyes blazing. She didn't appear to notice Dicken.

'What are you doing here?' she demanded.

Zoë gestured at Dicken. 'He brought me.'

'You don't dance!'

'That's what you think. The only reason I didn't go to dances was that nobody ever asked me. Well, finally somebody did.'

Annys seemed rendered almost speechless by Zoë's cheek. 'Whatever will Mother say?'

'Oh, fiddlesticks to Mother,' Zoë retorted. 'She doesn't know, and if you don't tell her she never will. I've left the pantry window open.'

Getting nowhere with her sister, Annys turned on Dicken. 'What do you mean by bringing Zoë?'

'I came to see you,' he explained.

'Oh, thanks,' Zoë said sarcastically.

'I wanted to talk,' Dicken went on. 'To explain. It wasn't my fault. I got caught up with Vickery.'

'He's broken both legs,' Zoë put in. 'He tried to turn.'

'It was very nearly me,' Dicken said earnestly, hoping a little sympathy might emerge. 'Only the fact that I wanted to come here to see you stopped me going up again with him.'

'I'm not interested,' Annys said, staring down her nose at him. 'I was waiting for you.'

'Well,' Dicken said angrily, gesturing at Diplock, 'it didn't take you very long to change your mind and come with him. Did he pay *you*, too, like he paid Taggart not to bring me back?'

Diplock opened his mouth and Dicken was just wondering whether he'd be thrown out, arrested, or merely ignored if he hit him, when Annys sniffed, grabbed Diplock's arm, whirled him round and dragged him away.

'And that,' Zoë said cheerfully, 'puts you in your place.'

The band had started again and, green with envy, Dicken saw Diplock put his arm round Annys and lead her on to the floor. Zoë studied them calmly.

'Shall we dance?' she asked blandly. 'It seems to be a waltz this time and waltzes are dreamy.'

*

As they circled together, she deliberately clung tighter to Dicken than he felt was proper for her age. But she didn't seem to care that people were looking and even went so far as to put her cheek against his. It was disconcerting and made him miss his step.

'Ooops,' she said. 'Attack of nerves?'

'People are looking.'

'Who cares?'

She was unexpectedly exciting, he found, and he began to wonder why he'd never noticed her before. Throwing herself heart and soul into enjoying herself, she cavorted around in the two-step in a way that drew startled glances and made him faintly embarrassed. But she was so indifferent to opinion he found it infectious and began to do the same.

It was after eleven-thirty when they began to walk home. Annys had already left in Diplock's father's car.

'That,' Zoë said, 'seems to be that. I suppose any moment now we'll be at war with Germany. Wasn't the ultimatum supposed to expire at midnight?'

'I don't suppose they'll have apologised or withdrawn their troops,' Dicken agreed. 'Vickery thought they'd use aeroplanes. He even thought they'd buy his.'

She put her arm through his and clung to him. 'What was it like?' she asked. 'Flying from Southampton to Shoreham. Forty miles! Nobody's ever flown that far before, have they?'

'Not many.'

'They could use aeroplanes to see where the Germans were, couldn't they? Just imagine. Twenty miles into enemy territory, find out where they are, then back with the information.'

'Providing,' Dicken said, 'that they could turn.'

She giggled and they started laughing. It became infectious and they clung to each other. Then abruptly, his face close to Zoë's, Dicken stopped. She went on for a moment or two longer, then she stopped also. She studied him seriously.

'You can kiss me if you like,' she said. 'I've often thought it might be nice.'

He wasn't very expert and their noses got in the way.

'You're not very good at it, are you?' she said. 'I'll show you.' She put her arms round him. 'Tilt your head that way and I'll tilt mine this. Then you don't bonk conks.'

'Where did you learn all this?' he asked as they came up for air.

'Where does any girl learn things like this? At school. It's all you ever talk about. Let's have another go.'

This time she seemed more expert than ever and Dicken felt his blood beginning to rise. She took his hand from her waist and placed it on her breast, then clutching him fiercely and pressing her body against his, kissed him again.

As she released him, he backed away. 'Steady on,' he said.

'What's the matter?' she asked. 'Surely the intrepid birdman hasn't got the wind up?'

'I'm not an intrepid birdman. I was just a passenger. I might have been, mind. Vickery promised to teach me but I suppose that's gone the same way as his hopes of building for the government.'

She led him through the trees to the end of the garden. The night was warm and they sat in the summer house staring at the stars. She nodded at the house where a light burned.

'Mother's home,' she said. 'I expect she thinks I'm safely in bed. Annys had permission to stay out till midnight so I expect she's clutching Arthur Diplock in the back of his father's motor car to make up for the fact that Dick Quinney didn't come up to scratch.'

'I tried.'

'Who's Annys anyway? There's always me.'

Dicken grinned. 'You're all right.'

'I'm more than all right, Dicky boy. I'm going to be a

25

liberated woman when I'm twenty-one. I'm not going to sit behind the table dispensing cups of tea and cucumber sandwiches. I'm not going to have a horde of kids clinging to my skirt, saying "Yes, sir, no, sir, three bags full, sir," to some man who thinks simply because he can grow a moustache he has the right to be the lord and master. I'm going to run my own life. I'm a bit liberated already, as a matter of fact.'

'So I've noticed.'

They clutched each other again and when Dicken emerged he felt he'd been through a whirlwind.

'I think I ought to go in now,' Zoë said. 'You'll have to give me a bunk-up to the pantry window.'

He allowed her to scramble on his back then took hold of her leg to push her up.

'Steady on,' she giggled. 'Not there!'

'Sorry.'

She giggled again. 'I don't mind really. It's quite enjoyable.'

She sat on the window sill, reaching behind her to move things inside the pantry. Then she turned and looked at him.

'If there *is* a war,' she whispered, 'what will you do?'

Dicken shrugged. 'What can I do? I'm not a soldier. I'm not even old enough to join the army, and I expect it'll all be over by the time I am. They were saying at the dance that it'll be finished by Christmas. Perhaps I could go to sea. I'm a qualified operator.'

'Annys says Arthur Diplock's going to join the cavalry. If you ever get to be a pilot you could fly low and frighten his horse. He might fall off.'

'If I did go to sea, would you write to me?'

She gave a little laugh. 'The poor homesick sailor wanting news of England from his sweetheart?'

He flushed. 'I didn't mean that.'

'Isn't that what every warrior wants? To have the little woman waiting patiently at home while he goes roistering among the maidens in foreign parts.'

'I've never roistered.'

'You will the minute you put on uniform. It goes with the job. Still, I'll write to you, but not just to hold your hand when you're lonely, and not with love and kisses. I told you,

I'm going to be a liberated woman when I'm twenty-one and I've got my eye on more than that.'

He had enjoyed the evening and she seemed to be introducing a sour note. 'I think I'll join up,' he said. 'I could give a false age.'

*

But when he tried, the recruiting sergeant stared at him coldly. 'Run away and play, sonny,' he said. 'It's men we want.'

Furious and disappointed – he'd been so certain they'd accept him he'd even gone to church to pray that his mother would understand – Dicken took a train to Southampton and tried the offices of the Cunard steamship line. At first they seemed interested and sent him along the corridor to see the superintendent of wireless telegraphy. He listened to what Dicken had to say but when he admitted he had only a second class qualification, he seemed to lose interest.

'We need operators all right,' he admitted. 'But we want good ones. Get your first class certificate then we'll think again. Besides, with a first class ticket you'll earn a lot more money.'

It seemed to make sense and the fear that the war would be over before he could get into it seemed to be coming to nothing, anyway. The newspapers were filled with a great new scheme thought up by Lord Kitchener, the Minister of War, in which he proposed to call for a hundred thousand men, and huge pictures of Kitchener himself appeared on the hoardings, complete with bullhorn moustache and pointing finger – 'YOUR KING AND COUNTRY NEED YOU.' It drew a few men from the factories and the fields but nobody else. It certainly didn't seem to concern Dicken because he wasn't of the class that normally became officers yet he also felt he wasn't of the class that normally filled the ranks. Up to that moment soldiers had been regarded without much affection only as a necessary evil who, though they added colour to public occasions, also filled the streets on Saturday nights with drunken brawling.

Suddenly, however, things became different. The newspapers were calling them 'steel-true' and 'true-blue', and

printing the choruses of the songs they sang alongside the
adverts for Wright's Coal Tar soap, which was claimed to be
'a soldier's soap', used by all ranks from private to general.
British troops had come into action and were acquitting
themselves well but, thanks to the over-enthusiasm of journalists who had been nowhere near the fighting and gave the
impression they were half-way to Berlin, the news of a retreat
came as a shock. Round some obscure little town in Belgium
called Mons, British soldiers were dying in hundreds, and
shattered remnants of famous regiments were struggling
among a vast flood of refugees to reach safety. Exhausted
men stumbled behind army waggons pulled by jaded horses
into small Belgian villages, and even the churches were full of
their wounded. The British Expeditionary Force had not
been broken but it had suffered terribly.

Then came the news of the Marne. The French, charging
blindly forward to a prearranged plan, had suffered enormous casualties and the Germans were actually drawing
near to Paris when the situation had been saved by a British
airman who had spotted the German army sweeping round
the British rear. The small British air corps, part of the Royal
Engineers, less than fifty strong and mostly consisting
of elderly French Farmans and Blériots marked by Union
Jacks sewn on the fuselage by their crews, had made their
presence felt.

The war had even forced a change of mind on Dicken's
mother. Knowing inevitably that he would disappear eventually, she had withdrawn her objections to him going to sea
for the simple reason that she couldn't imagine him being in
any danger on a vast Cunarder, and, getting his first class
certificate in November, he applied again at Cunard only to
be told there was no ship available and that he'd be informed
when there was. He could now send and receive messages in
Morse at twenty-two words a minute, and was taking a
course in the building and maintenance of wireless stations.
Christmas came with the battles in France stabilised into a
static front with trenches running all the way from the sea to
Switzerland, and the Toshacks held a party on Boxing Day
to which Dicken was invited – by Zoë, he noticed, not Annys.
There were several young men in stiff board-like khaki

uniforms, because Mons had changed everything and every-body was volunteering now, if only to avoid the white feathers that were being handed out if you didn't. Arthur Diplock wore the Sam Browne belt of a Yeomanry second-lieutenant.

'He couldn't get into the real cavalry,' Zoë whispered.

Annys seemed to have got over her rage at Dicken and Zoë confided that she was thinking of becoming engaged to Diplock.

'Bowed down with a broken heart?' she asked.

'Doesn't worry me now,' Dicken boasted and, to his surprise, he found it didn't.

'You could always get engaged to me,' Zoë said. 'Except that Mother still regards me as a baby.'

She wasn't such a baby that she didn't manage to get Dicken into the summer house for a torrid session in each other's arms.

'I'll wait for you,' she offered. 'Two more years. Then I'll be nearly nineteen. Unfortunately, by then you'll probably be on some wretched ship in the middle of the Atlantic send-ing a message that some rotten submarine's torpedoed you.'

The course in wireless maintenance took Dicken to Lon-don and, since he was still waiting to be called to the Cunard office, he was beginning to wonder if he shouldn't try some other steamship line. He had already passed his first technic-al examination and was almost ready for the final when, as he was walking down Whitehall, he was pulled up by a recruiting sergeant, an enormous man with beery eyes and long waxed moustachios. His vast chest was crossed by a red sash and red, white and blue ribbons fluttered at the side of his cap. He reminded Dicken of a Shire horse at the May Day parade in Willys Green.

'Don't you know there's a war on, young feller?' he said. 'You ought to be in uniform.'

'When I tried in August,' Dicken retorted hotly, 'you lot wouldn't touch me with a barge pole. In any case, I'm waiting to go to sea. I'm a wireless operator.'

'You are?' The sergeant's eyes widened. 'Why didn't you say, lad? We have wireless operators in the army, too, these days, y'know.'

'You do?' It was something that had never occurred to Dicken.

'O' course, we do. Just the type for the artillery, I'd say. Not as big as they like 'em, of course, but wireless operators is different. There's quick promotion for anybody who can do that. You could become an officer.'

Thoughts of appearing on the Toshacks' doorstep in khaki riding breeches and Sam Browne belt ran through Dicken's head. It was an alluring prospect.

'An officer?'

'If you're prepared to wait,' the sergeant said. 'A hell of a long time,' he added under his breath. He looked Dicken up and down and smiled. It looked like the smile of a man-eating tiger.

'I reckon,' he said, 'that you're just the man they're looking for.'

4

Dicken's first nights as a soldier were spent under canvas, fidgeting in frozen fitful dozes until the trembling call of Reveille proclaimed the beginning of a new day.

His service with the Royal Garrison Artillery, which was what he discovered he had joined, started with three weeks pounding the square at Aldershot, boring hours peeling potatoes on cookhouse fatigues, and trying to ignore the agony of feet blistered by new ammunition boots. There was no mention of commissions.

'Part of the horrors of war,' he wrote to Zoë. 'Like bully beef.'

Things improved when he was sent on a wireless course. Compared with what he'd trained on, the army wireless set was crude. It consisted chiefly of a crystal, a cat's whisker and a simple inductance coil, all enclosed in a wooden box. The aerial was a sixty-foot length of wire slung between two masts and the whole apparatus was intended for use with an artillery spotting plane of the Royal Flying Corps.

Eventually he found himself part of a newly-formed Kitchener Army battery, mostly composed of Londoners. There was little glamour attached to the big guns, however. Unlike those of the field artillery, they were not moved to dangerous points in the fighting by horses at the gallop, but were laboriously towed into position well behind the line by lorries or caterpillar tractors, while wireless reports were mere informal messages with little form or pattern.

When the battery was sent to France, Dicken was with the advance party. The officer went ahead with the sergeant searching for billets and left the rest of them to find their own way forward. At midday they stopped at a village called Ruy which had never had British soldiers through it before and the Maire and his officials turned out wearing tricolour sashes, while the villagers greeted them with the *Marseillaise*, to which they replied with a song of their own.

'I don't want to be a soldier
I don't want to go to war
I'd rather hang around
Piccadilly Underground
Living on the earnings of a high-born lady.'

'Are we down-hearted?' somebody at the back yelled. 'No-o-o!'

The French seemed to think it was part of the National Anthem and stood in silence with their heads uncovered.

It took them three days to reach their base near Armentières. As they rumbled in lorries along the interminably straight French roads through lines of poplars in full leaf, the officer turned up again to lead them to a farm where one of the Cockney gunners promptly helped himself to a chicken.

'It's not looting,' Dicken grinned. 'It attacked us and we had to kill it in self-defence.'

They cooked it after dark on a fire built with wood from a nearby copse where nightingales were singing – 'Them bloody sparrers,' someone said disgustedly – and Dicken was just making himself comfortable in a loft above the cow byre when he heard his name called.

'Pack your kit,' the sergeant told him.

'We've only just arrived, Sarge!'

'Well, now you're on your way again. You're going to work with the Flying Corps.'

Dicken's heart leapt. It had never been with the great guns. 'To fly?' he asked.

The sergeant gave him a cold look. 'Who the hell do you think you are?' he said. 'You're going for a course in battery and aircraft communication. They're developing a new system.'

He arrived at the squadron at around midnight and was given a space in a tent. The following morning he was wakened by the dull rumble of an idling engine and, to his astonishment found the wingtip of an aeroplane trembling within three feet of the tent flap. It seemed enormous, power-ful and tremendously strong and he decided he had never seen such a frightening contrivance in his life. He couldn't imagine for a minute that it was tuned with a tuning fork or could be overbalanced by any sudden movement of its crew.

It didn't take him long to discover how different the RFC was from the rest of the army. The artillerymen had been chosen for their ability to lift huge shells and haul guns around, and, despite the fact that the battery was composed almost entirely of Hostilities Only men like Dicken, its officers, mostly ex-Regulars dragged out of retirement, tried hard to fit it into the regulations of the old army. It appeared to be impossible to be efficient without being polished to within an inch of your life, and it was important to stand like a ramrod to salute, to ask permission to speak, even, it seemed to Dicken, to breathe.

The RFC had no traditions at all. Its men were all craftsmen – riggers, fitters, mechanics, wireless operators, even foundrymen, blacksmiths, carpenters and tailors – and were recruited for no other reason than to repair damaged aircraft. They were streets ahead of the rest of the army for intelligence, and spit and polish were considered the least important of their duties. They were there to keep the aeroplanes flying and nothing else, and seemed totally un-concerned that the commandeered vans that had carried their equipment to France still bore on their sides the advertisements of their former owners – Lazenby's Sauce, Peek Frean's Biscuits, Stephens' Ink. It was as if they were openly showing their indifference to the rest of the uniformed world.

The aeroplanes operated from a field full of cows which had to be driven to one side when they wanted to take off, and they were already a vast improvement on the fragile contrap-tions which had landed in France the previous year, many of them put together from parts of differing machines and with top speeds that varied from stalling by no more than a few miles an hour.

One flight consisted of Morane two-seaters, waspish-looking machines, short-tempered and dangerous, with a speed that made them invulnerable to enemy attack. A second flight had Parasols, treacherous, unstable, high-winged monoplanes of bad design, whose diminutive tails made their natural position in the air a vertical nose-dive.

The third flight was equipped with BE2cs, narrow-bodied aircraft whose fuselages were so slender the tails seemed to be detached and following on behind. They were tall and wide-winged, their motors mounted outside, and were not very popular because, with the propeller, the tanks and the motor all in the way, it was impossible to see where you were going. Their maximum altitude was no more than 6000 feet and the only offensive weapons they carried were the revolvers worn by pilots and observers. To Dicken they seemed modern enough to be straight out of Jules Verne or H. G. Wells.

As far as wireless was concerned, the RFC was streets ahead of the army both in equipment and the way they used it. The artillery's happy-go-lucky manner of sending and receiving had been whittled down to the effective clock code, a system that was graphic and flexible and depended on unvarying values that were impossible to misinterpret. The target was considered to be the centre of a clock on which true north was twelve-o'-clock, and imaginary circles drawn round the target represented different ranges and were identified by code letters so that it was possible to state where a shot had landed in a few Morse letters and numbers.

It involved Dicken in short flights to see what battery firing looked like. The calibrated maps were explained to him and, clad in overcoat and borrowed crash helmet, he even sent messages from the air, using a battery-powered transmitter in the observer's cockpit.

As he worked, he began to wonder why he hadn't joined the RFC and all his ideas of going to sea sank without trace with his ambition of a commission in the artillery. All he could think of now was soaring over the enemy trenches amid a storm of anti-aircraft fire to send back the all-important message which would result in winning the war.

For the first time since he had put on khaki he found himself enjoying himself. The RFC men were proud of their skill, and the officers seemed human, happily discussing rigging and engines with their men on easy terms. Even

Morton, the captain in command, was not above getting into a discussion on the merits of an aeroplane, and in his pigheaded tenacity, Dicken started daydreaming of becoming an observer.

The corporal in charge of the wireless section was a genial Regular called Handiside who had arrived in the Flying Corps from the Engineers, and his attitude was benevolent.

'How about wangling me a flight, Corp?' Dicken said.

'You've had a flight.'

'I mean a real flight. I once flew forty miles from Southampton to Shoreham.'

Handiside frowned. 'What the hell are you doing in the artillery then?' He studied Dicken for a moment or two, his eyes almost fatherly. 'I must say you know more about wireless than a lot of the observers. They're mostly just ex-cavalry blokes who've had a quick course in Morse. Hang around tomorrow morning and I'll see what I can do.'

Sleep, breakfast and early morning parade were hard to endure and Dicken was at the hangar the following morning, pretending to adjust wireless sets but all the time watching Handiside's movements. When the pilots began to arrive, he saw him speak to one of them and his heart began to thump. The officer turned and studied him.

He was a tall, lean young second-lieutenant called Hatto, not much older than Dicken. He wore a monocle, dashing leather patches on his sleeves and, as an ex-cavalry man, wore a stock and canvas leggings and carried a riding whip. 'Tell me you fancy a flight?' he said. 'Hear you've been up with Arnold Vickery. I've heard of him.' His face broke into a smile that seemed to light up the hangar with its charm. 'Couldn't turn corners, I heard.'

'That's right, sir. I helped fish him out of the Adur when he crashed. He'd had too much champagne, I think.'

Hatto laughed. 'And why you? Why did he pick you for a passenger?'

'I was the lightest person he could think of. Besides –' Dicken hesitated '– I got to know him through a girl he knew.'

'Cherchez la femme, eh? Right, I'm about to do a test

flight, so report to stores and draw an observer's kit and nip into that machine over there.'

Racing to the stores, Dicken drew a leather coat, helmet and long flying boots and waddled out to the machine. As he climbed into the cockpit among the fumes of petrol and hot oil, a sergeant appeared alongside.

'CO's compliments, sir,' he yelled to Hatto above the throbbing engine. 'If she's all right, you're to do an artillery observation. Number 213 Battery. Same as yesterday.'

Hatto looked at Dicken. 'That's sunk us,' he observed.

'No, sir.' Dicken was in a panic he'd be left behind. 'I know what to do. I've done it more than once.'

Hatto studied him for a moment, then he made up his mind. 'Right,' he said. 'Let's go.'

Sitting under the quivering wings with the tall stacks of the exhausts in front of him, Dicken held his breath as the aircraft rolled across the grass and lifted into the air. His coat was too big and in his haste he had buttoned it wrongly; his scarf was too tight; and his helmet, caught by the blast from the propeller, showed a distressing tendency to take off on its own. But he was breathless with excitement as they circled the aerodrome and, leaning over the side, watched fascinated as the patchwork of fields unrolled beneath. He had never been so high before. On his earlier flights he had not been above a hundred or so feet; now he could see men looking like ants and all round him only the limitless blue space of the sky.

Hatto lifted his goggles. 'All right?' he mouthed.

Dicken stuck up his thumb in the way he'd seen other observers signal their readiness and began to tap out a message to the ground station. 'Are you receiving me?'

Watching with his heart in his mouth, he could see no sign of acknowledgement below and he stared panic-stricken at his equipment, wondering what he'd done wrong. Then, far below, a tiny figure ran out of the wireless hut and laid strips of white on the grass in the form of an L to indicate the message had arrived. Flushed with success, he signalled to Hatto and the machine turned eastwards, the wide wings catching the watery sun.

At 3000 feet Hatto swung on to course for the target, an

36

intersection of trenches near a German fortification known as the Hohenzollern Redoubt. Just to the north Dicken could see a canal running south-east then curving round to head south-west in a dead straight line, overgrown and out of use for a lot of its length, its broken banks marked with shell craters and littered with debris. Then he saw a snake of brown, turned earth running alongside it that he guessed was a trench and realised they had reached the front line. Ahead of them was German territory and everybody below him now was watching him and wondering how to kill him.

It gave him a tremendous feeling of involvement. The land beneath, already battered and soured by the war, looked ancient, every building smashed, every wall that ran north and south broken by shelling. There wasn't a fence for miles and it dawned on him they had all been removed by the chilled troops for fires. Even the trees had been blasted to stark stumps. The land had been scoured clean, its occupants hiding like moles beneath its surface, and it dawned on him that he was one of the reasons why; with aircraft crews able to see beyond the front line, it had suddenly become important to show no sign of what was going on.

Hatto was pointing to the watery sun. 'Keep a look-out up there,' he shouted above the roar of the engine. 'That's where they come from. It's a new dodge they've thought up.'

As Dicken turned his eyes upward, there was a violent crack nearby and the machine lurched sickeningly.

'Archie,' Hatto shouted cheerfully. 'Anti-aircraft fire.'

The aircraft rocked as a puff of black smoke the size of a haystack drifted past beyond the end of the wing. A hole appeared in the fabric but Hatto seemed quite unperturbed. Alarmed, Dicken watched the battery's shells land and signalled back. After ten rounds, Hatto swung the aeroplane towards home.

No longer in danger and with time to look round, Dicken became aware of the immensity of the sky. It was clean and clear and fresh and, swept clean by the breeze every day, was devoid of the detritus of war that covered the earth. And *he* was part of it, a supreme being untouched by dirt, feeling the sun before it reached anyone else.

Descending in a long glide over the trenches, they were

fired on, entirely without success, by everyone in sight, and a few minutes later bumped gently across the turf, everything rattling and creaking as they came to a halt in front of the hangar. Still faraway-eyed, Dicken climbed to the ground, his ears full of the creak and tick of the cooling engine, and that night, wrapped in his blankets, he began to daydream again. Unfortunately, his dreams were cut short the following morning when he was told to report back to the battery with his course finished.

'I suppose I couldn't stay with the RFC, could I, Corp?' he asked Handiside.

' 'T'ain't anything to do with me,' Handiside said. 'You'd have to put in an application for a transfer.'

Half-hoping he'd be sent to another squadron, Dicken returned to the battery to find his job had been changed. Artillery spotting was now being done at ground level from as far out in No Man's Land as they could get.

'What about the aircraft?' he asked.

'Trying to do without them,' he was told. 'We haven't been having much success with wireless.'

'That,' Dicken said coldly, 'is because nobody in the artillery knows anything about it.'

The forward observation officer's job was to sit in a shell hole ahead of the front line, connected by field telephone to the trench where a runner was waiting to carry messages to Dicken who crouched in a dug-out just to the rear with his aerial strung between the remains of two trees. The weather was wet and cheerless and the morning hate the Germans sent over sounded particularly spiteful. Almost at once messages began to come through asking for counter battery fire.

The forward observation officer had never heard of the clock code and his instructions were vague and uncertain. Though the boom of the guns swelled to a jerky roar that was flung from horizon to horizon, to the disgusted Dicken it seemed to have no direction whatsoever and was merely the efforts of a totally ignorant and unco-ordinated organisation. From time to time, also, the set gave trouble as the aerial was loosened by the blast of exploding shells so that he had to slip out of the safety of the dug-out and, with the aid of the two gunners who were with him, re-erect it under a whirring shower of red-hot steel splinters.

It was noisy, smelly and squalid in the extreme, and not at all what he had expected of the war. He'd looked forward to heroism, flags, colour and not too much danger, and he found instead that he lived in constant expectation of the roof of the dug-out, which trickled sand down his collar every time a shell burst, collapsing on top of him. Going outside to re-erect the aerial left his mouth dry and his body moist; and, despite his contempt for the artillery, he was certain the German Kaiser knew exactly where he was and was personally trying to hit him.

After four hours' transmitting, he noticed that the messages had stopped coming back, and he sent one of the gunners forward to find out why. He came back, flinching at the crashes and the shower of stones, to say that the infantrymen in the front line thought something had happened to the observation officer.

Shutting down the set, Dicken headed along the communicating trench. Shells were dropping near the forward positions, showering the cringing occupants with dirt. A sergeant indicated the shellhole where the forward observation officer had been crouching and shook his head. Pulling his cap down, Dicken squirmed over the parapet and began to crawl forward, feeling as big as a house and terrified some German sniper opposite would spot him. But the Germans were also being forced by the shelling to keep their heads down and he wriggled safely towards the shellhole where the forward observation officer was supposed to be until, just as he reached it, a heavy shell landed close by with an iron clang and flung him over the lip to land on his head in a puddle of muddy water in the bottom.

Sitting up, he dragged his cap from his eyes, to see the officer lying with his back against the sloping side of the shell hole, his arms flung out, a red splodge where his right eye had been. The sergeant was twisted into an impossible position near his feet, his head beneath him and one knee up as though he had been about to start running. It didn't take long to realise they were both dead.

Just in front of the shellhole were abandoned packs, rifles

and shovels, and unspeakable bodies from the previous winter, black, damp and decomposing, together with a dead mule, disembowelled by a shell, a man sitting with his back to it, bolt upright but headless.

Nauseated, he turned away to find himself staring into the single dead eye of the forward observation officer, and at that moment he decided he didn't like trench warfare.

*

It seemed to be important to return and report the officer's death but, as he clawed at the charred earth of the side of the shell hole, a new batch of shells came down and he had to cower against the pulverised soil as the shards of steel flew overhead. The shelling seemed to go on for ever and he couldn't take his eyes off the two dead men. Then the barrage seemed to drop a little and he was just preparing to make a dash for it again when the stuttering sound of a motor came to his ears. Swinging round, reminded at once of the sound of Arnold Vickery's aeroplane just before it had cut and plunged him into the Adur, he saw a BE coming towards him, lurching in the sky and obviously in difficulties. Strips of fabric fluttered at the wingtips and grey puffs were coming from the exhaust like the smoke from an overworked cigar.

Fascinated, he watched it drop lower and lower. Just before it reached the shell hole where he sheltered, the under-carriage touched, the nose dug in and it turned over, whacking down on its back with a crunch that shattered the rudder and crumpled the wings.

The pilot was hanging head-down from his straps and before he knew what he was doing, thinking only of the danger of fire, Dicken was out of the shellhole and running towards him. Aware of the whack-whack of bullets close by, he lowered the pilot to the ground. The observer was sprawled beneath the machine, covered with blood and, since he seemed to be the worse of the two, using the training he'd received in the Boy Scouts, Dicken took hold of him in a fireman's lift and hefted him on to his shoulders.

The smell of petrol was stronger as he went back for the pilot and there was a faint hissing sound coming from somewhere in the wreckage with a thin spiral of blue smoke.

Heaving the pilot across his back, Dicken stumbled over the uneven ground until a tremendous 'whoomph' behind him hit him in the back like the punch of a huge soft fist and threw him into the shellhole.

As he sat up, he saw that the aeroplane had finally caught fire and was blazing furiously, sending a long spiral of thick black smoke coiling into the sky. Depressed, he watched it for a while then turned his attention to the two men he'd brought in. The observer was silent and still, his face grey, but the pilot had opened his eyes. For a second he stared at Dicken then reached up, took off his helmet and goggles, fished inside his leather coat and pulled out a monocle. Sticking it in his eye, he studied Dicken carefully.

'Fancy meeting you,' he said.

*

The observer was in a bad way. Dicken opened his coat and, his hands red and gory, struggled with his field dressing to stop the blood that was saturating his uniform. Hatto watched him unhappily, trying to help with an injured shoulder and ankle. The observer died within a quarter of an hour and Dicken lifted his scarf to cover his dead face.

'What happened?' he asked.

'Anti-aircraft fire.' Hatto winced with pain. 'Poor old George never saw what hit him.'

Using Hatto's scarf, Dicken made a sling and fastened his arm to his chest. By the time he'd finished, Hatto was almost fainting.

'Great Ned,' he said as he flopped back against the side of the crater. 'I didn't enjoy that one bit.'

As they cowered and flinched from the bursting shells, they got to know a remarkable amount about each other.

'William Wymarck Wombwell Hatto,' Hatto introduced himself. 'Family calls me Willie. Youngest son of Lord Hooe. Irish title. Don't mean much. Eton and Oxford. All the right things. Got a brother in the Navy, another in the Foreign Office and another in the Church. I was the stupidest so they put me in the army. Cavalry, of course. Unfortunately, you can't argue with a machine gun with a horse and it's difficult to crouch behind a wall. Then I remembered I could fly. I learned before the war because it was the only sport you could enjoy sitting down. So I transferred.'

As he polished his eyeglass one-handed on his scarf and tucked it into his eye, Dicken watched, fascinated.

'Do you wear it all the time?' he asked.

'Helps to hold my eye in.' Hatto managed a smile. 'Without it, it keeps dropping out and rolling on the floor.'

They sat through the rest of the afternoon, listening to the Germans in the trench opposite shouting threats, Hatto by this time with his boot off because his foot was swollen like a balloon. As dusk began to fall, Dicken suggested they should try to make their way back to the British line. There was a little shouting back and forth until they established that nobody would shoot them for a German raiding party then they began to head for the British wire. Half-carrying, half-dragging his companion, Dicken was unhappily aware of the tap-tap of machine guns and several times, their hearts pounding, they had to lie flat as the bullets passed over them. They covered the last fifty yards with Dicken on his hands and knees and Hatto sprawled across his back.

'Just the ticket,' Hatto whispered. 'Perfect target. One up the backside and you get a china vase.'

As they reached the wire, figures appeared in front of them in the dark, grabbed them and rushed them to the trench. As they fell inside it, a burly sergeant dragged Dicken to his feet.

'You fuckin' flyers,' he said. 'You're always 'avin' to be fuckin' rescued.'

'How good it is,' Hatto murmured, 'to hear some nice foul English language.'

Dicken offered to wireless for a tender, but when they reached the dug-out, they found the set, the aerial, the masts, and the two gunners had all disappeared.

'They packed up and cleared off,' an infantryman offered. 'They said you'd been killed.'

Eventually the commanding officer arranged by field telephone for a tender to pick Hatto up and they stumbled rearwards in the dark. As they pushed him into the back of the Crossley, he turned to Dicken.

'No end obliged, old fruit,' he said. 'It might have been

awkward for me if you hadn't come along. If there's anything I can do in return, just ask.'

'Well, there *is* something,' Dicken blurted out.

'Name it. My land? My fortune? The hand of my sister in marriage?'

Awed by his own cheek, Dicken drew a deep breath. 'You could wangle me a transfer to the RFC,' he said.

5

With the death of his forward observation officer, the battery commander seemed to have given up his idea of ground spotting for a while and the following week, the sergeant appeared outside Dicken's billet once more. 'You're for the RFC again,' he said. 'Same squadron as last time. Take your kit with you. It's a long stay.'

His arm still strapped to his chest, Hatto greeted Dicken like an old friend. The work was the same as before but it no longer seemed to have much to do with the artillery and Dicken didn't ask questions. After a week or two, Corporal Handiside appeared.

'Get those artillery brasses off your shoulder,' he said. 'And sew these Flying Corps tabs on. You've been transferred.'

The weather was bitterly cold and wet so that the machines were only vague shapes in the misty greyness. The paths about the aerodrome became puddled with water and the billets were damp and chilly.

Despite the weather, however, flying continued, aeroplanes taking off in the intervals whenever possible. Hatto was still around but Dicken rarely met him and it was Handiside who answered all his demands to be made an observer.

'It doesn't come like that,' he said, snapping his fingers. 'These things have to go through the proper channels. Just hold your water, lad. The war ain't going to end tomorrow.'

It was enough to set Dicken studying the art of artillery observing at every spare moment. He spent hours trying to identify aircraft and, since betting on their ability to see more planes in the air than the next man was a favourite pastime

44

among the ground crews, he had plenty of opportunity. He had excellent eyesight and hoped it would stand him in good stead, because there were rumours around that the war in the air was about to be stepped up. The Germans, it seemed, had a new aircraft with an eighty-horsepower engine and a gun that, unbelievably, fired through the propeller.

Just how this miracle had been achieved no one knew. A Frenchman called Garros had tried it with wedges attached to the propeller blades so that, when the gun fired, the wedges deflected any bullet that was likely to hit them, but unfortunately, it hadn't worked very satisfactorily and, after his first successes, he was said to have shot himself down. The Germans had captured his machine and turned his idea over to a Dutchman called Fokker who was building aeroplanes for them and he'd come up with a much better idea which stopped the gun when the propeller blade was in front of it and fired it when it wasn't. It was worrying the Flying Corps a great deal more than the casual indifference of its pilots suggested.

Suddenly things had changed. For months they'd been flopping about the sky in an assortment of appallingly inflammable aeroplanes which had never been designed for fighting and, in their early twenties or even in their teens – the machines they flew even younger in years – very few of the flying crews understood how their imperfect but obviously potentially lethal weapons should be used. They were as wide-winged as dragonflies and not much more enduring and the thought of fighting in them seemed impossible, because even meeting another aeroplane in the wide expanse of the sky was an event.

Because of this, no rules had ever been evolved, only what they'd discovered as they went along, and most people regarded the job with a mixture of high spirits, mock resignation, a curious belief in the superiority of the RFC and the air of cynical disillusionment and mocking self-deprecation that was the stock-in-trade of all British servicemen. Now, however, it seemed they were going to have to think about it more seriously because the rifles and revolvers which had taken the place of the bricks they'd originally carried to throw at the German machines weren't enough and the

45

BE2c was studied with rather more interest than usual. With the only gun tucked almost underneath the wing, it was unable to fire properly in any direction except backwards, which made things very difficult because you could hardly be hostile while you were flying away from your enemy.

They all knew how the game was played, of course. An aeroplane fixed the artillery on to its target, but as soon as the battery started firing an enemy aeroplane inevitably came across to locate it by its gun-flashes. When that happened, you sent your own aeroplane up to destroy it or drive it away, and so it went on, with the job of actually fighting the Germans given not to men with faster machines, because there weren't any, but to those who were the least skilful at taking photographs or using the wireless.

Now, however, since the Germans were reported to be issuing the new Fokkers to their squadrons in pairs, it was obvious there were going to be more casualties among the observation machines, and they were all getting a little worked up about it because the Fokker was said to be a fast, strongly-structured, highly manoeuvrable aeroplane, which the stately BE2c was not. For the first time Dicken realised there were snags to being in the Flying Corps. You could actually get killed – and not just by anti-aircraft guns either. If Garros could shoot down a German machine in flames with his botched-up device, it seemed more than possible that the new Fokkers could do it even better.

He was a little preoccupied when Handiside appeared and told him he was wanted in the CO's office. His mind full of possibilities, Dicken hurried to the back kitchen of the farm where Morton worked. Hatto was there, his arm still strapped up, and as Dicken entered, Morton pushed back his chair, came round his desk and shook hands.

'Congratulations, Quinney,' he said. 'You're the first non-flyer on the squadron to be awarded a decoration.'

Dicken's jaw dropped. 'What for, sir?'

'Me,' Hatto said. 'And poor old George. You went out twice under fire to bring us in.'

The news staggered Dicken. He'd thought only brave men won medals.

'There's another, too,' Morton said. 'You've been given

the Medal of St. George by the Tsar of Russia.'

'I beg your pardon, sir.'

Morton laughed and gestured at Hatto. 'Better explain, Willie,' he said.

Hatto grinned. 'One of the Tsar's emissaries is touring France inspecting units,' he said. 'Brothers-in-arms and all that. Had a bag full of medals to hand out. Asked if he could give one to the gallant ground staff. Decided it would have to be to you because you're the only one who's actually met the enemy face to face so to speak.'

Dicken looked down at his chest, trying to imagine what it would be like to have two medal ribbons burning a hole there. He had a feeling that the Russian decoration was regarded as a bit of a lark, but it would look good, even so, if he ever went on leave. If nothing else, it ought to impress Annys Toshack. It might even detach her from Arthur Diplock.

He was still in a daze when Morton spoke again. 'Better go and organise a few of your friends,' he advised. 'I suspect there'll be a party in the village bistro tonight. I've posted you from the Wireless Section to C Flight for training as an observer.'

*

The first few days on C Flight were spent on the machine gun range. Dicken was already well above an average shot with a rifle and he proved so skilful with a Lewis gun, Handiside began to call him Dead Shot Dicken.

Like himself, many of the other observers were men transferred from the infantry or the artillery who were skilled in photography, wireless and artillery observation, and it was only as he talked to them that he realised just how much he'd put his life in jeopardy by joining their ranks. Since aeroplanes didn't have dual control, if the pilot were killed there was nothing they could do except sit and calculate how far they had to fall, and nobody took so much notice when a new pilot joined the squadron as the observer who would have to fly with him.

The weather became very stormy and, with the rain pouring in torrents, the wind howling like a demon and all the hangars level with the ground, nobody was very cheerful. To catch the water, deep ditches were dug round the hangars and there were regular splashes and loud curses as someone fell in. With insufficient cover, machines that stood out all night became sodden with rain and, carrying a passenger and a full war load, took some getting off the ground. To combat the sticky conditions, twelve tons of cinders arrived every day to give the take-off area some solidity.

Towards the end of the year they were co-operating with batteries to the north and south of the La Bassée Canal and every morning in favourable weather a tender loaded with petrol, tool boxes, Very lights, a day's rations and white strips to make a landing T went off to an advanced field near the Béthune road.

'Your turn,' Handiside told Dicken as November changed to December. 'There's a machine landing there about mid-day.'

'I'm supposed to be flying, Corp,' Dicken pointed out. 'In the Morane.'

'Well, now you're not. The CO wants one of the new boys to do the job for a bit of experience.'

The Morane was being loaded with melinite bombs outside C Flight hangar, the new observer and one of his friends having the workings explained to them. Dropping bombs from aeroplanes was still virtually a new sport. Few machines were powerful enough to get off the ground with the extra weight of bombs on top of that of the crew and their machine gun, but a few bolder spirits had tried, one of them Hatto, who had found spotting and aerial photography far too unaggressive and, with Handiside's co-operation, had devised a contraption which, screwed to the side of his machine, would hold half a dozen bombs made from stick grenades of the sort you fused by pulling a tape before hurling them at the enemy.

'All you have to do,' Handiside had said, 'is pull this wire here to fuse them, then pull that wire there to drop them.'

Their enthusiasm had been greater than their expertise and Hatto had barely crossed the boundary of the field when there was a tremendous flash beneath the machine which promptly went into a dive and landed three fields away in a cloud of steam and flung debris. The rest of the squadron had arrived panting to find Hatto and his observer staggering about unharmed except for scorched and tattered flying clothes.

'I caught the bloody wire with the button of my coat,' the observer said. 'We'll have to do a sight better than that.'

Since then the bombs and the methods of dropping them had improved; but they were still tricky things to handle and nobody liked them very much, and the tender had just passed when there was a quick double explosion that seemed to strip the flesh from Dicken's bones. As the tender screeched to a stop, he saw the Morane was on fire from wingtip to wingtip.

He began to run. There were several men lying around the wreckage, all badly injured and, with the Morane blazing and still more bombs waiting to explode, they were dragged clear without ceremony. They had just got the last man to a safe distance when the remaining bombs went up, and they were showered with wooden fragments, pieces of metal, bent wheels, scraps of wire and glittering pieces of burning fabric that eddied about in the air like fiery bats.

It seemed that, as in Hatto's case, a safety wire had been pulled accidentally during the loading of the bombs, and as Dicken sat in his tent that evening trying to set his feelings down on paper for the benefit of Zoë Toshack, Corporal Handiside appeared.

'You can shove up your observer's wing,' he said. 'CO's orders. We lost two today so you've been pushed ahead. You fly with Mr. Hudnutt.'

*

Trips to the line began to come regularly. Hudnutt was a sound pilot who made good landings, didn't take foolish risks, and believed in growing old.

This last seemed a very good idea to Dicken, because the BE was far from being a wonder-aeroplane. It was steady, reliable, and easy to handle, but while the dihedral on the main planes made it so stable it was perfect for photography, it was also hard to dodge if you were shot at, while most of the time the observer had to kneel on his seat to keep a sharp look-out over the quivering tail, with little else to do but freeze in the blast from the propeller and contemplate the emptiness beneath him.

Despite the fact that both sides had dozens of machines over the lines, it was some time before Dicken saw his first German aeroplane in the air. It was a day of cream and gold and blue with large masses of cumulus catching the sun, and he caught sight of the German as a mere speck in the sky at the same height, moving backwards and forwards in an easterly and westerly direction, spotting for artillery.

Hudnutt immediately turned towards it but when they were within half a mile of it, the German aeroplane swung away east so they turned back towards their own target area. Identifiable by the shape of its old fortifications, Lille passed under the wing, apparently empty of life, but a shellburst among the ruined houses and a puff of red-brown dust and smoke drifting eastwards made Dicken realise there were troops there.

He was still watching the ground when he noticed Hudnutt shouting at him over the sound of the engine. He had been trying for some time to attract his attention and was beating on the fuselage between the two cockpits with the flat of his hand. As Dicken lifted his head, he jerked a thumb and, looking upwards, over the top wing Dicken saw another minute speck in the sky, glittering in the rays of the sun. It looked like a thin line with a dot in the centre and it dawned on him that it was an aeroplane and that he'd been studying pictures of it for some time.

'Fokker!' he yelled in a panic.

Despite what the newspapers and the staff said, it wasn't bravery and determination that brought success in the air but the simple fact of aircraft performance. The Fokker was good and the BE wasn't.

They were in a shallow dive now and as the speed rose the BE began to shake and rattle ominously. Dicken was trying to make up his mind how to get at his enemy. The arrangements for firing a machine gun from a BE were farcical. He had four fixed mountings to work from, one behind him to protect the rear, one on either side and another in front, with a wire stretched between the centre section struts so that he couldn't shoot away the propeller blades. During a skirmish with the enemy, the weapon had to be changed from one mounting to another and it had been discovered many times that it took so long and aircraft moved so quickly the new one was always the wrong one.

Still trying to make up his mind, he was watching the approaching Fokker when Hudnutt wrenched the BE round so violently, he had to make a convulsive clutch at the side of the cockpit to avoid being thrown over the side. Straightening up, his chest hollow with fear, he set the gun at 'safe' and began to manhandle it from the right position to the left. The straight line with its centre dot was still hovering across their route home and he felt his throat constrict. Immelmann, he thought. Or Oswald Boelcke. He'd heard of both German pilots; they had been taking such a toll of slow British reconnaissance aeroplanes with their new machines, they'd become known in RFC messes as 'the Fokker scourge'.

He had the gun pointing now in the narrow arc between the propeller and the main spar where he could safely fire without removing the wing. The line that was the Fokker grew thicker and the dot seemed to slide forward along it so that he knew the German pilot had turned aside and was preparing to attack from astern. The BE's nose was still down, the wires whining in the wind, the whole machine shuddering with its speed, and he watched dry-mouthed as the German pilot drew closer.

Giving him a couple of bursts to frighten him away, as Hudnutt swung the BE to give the German a difficult deflection shot he got in a further burst as the Fokker flashed beneath. It swung upwards into the first part of a loop, then fell off sideways and came back to take a quick shot at the unprotected belly of the BE.

It was so close, it seemed to Dicken it was impossible for him to miss, but the BE's wing got in the way at the last moment and, in a fury at being unable to fire, he yanked the gun from the rear socket, and, without thinking, rested it on the side of the cockpit and let go with a burst.

He had reckoned without the recoil and the gun jerked out of his grasp at once. Hudnutt's face wore a look of horror that matched the one on Dicken's face as it clattered against the fuselage and went end-over-end to sail downwards in the direction of the Fokker. The German pilot saw it coming and wrenched his machine away as if he thought the gun was going to hit him, standing it on one wingtip, a small neat aeroplane with a cowling that looked like the hand-hammered pewter teapot Dicken's mother used. It was close enough to see that the pilot wasn't wearing a flying coat, helmet or goggles, only a grey tunic with a yellow collar, and that his head was lifted to the BE with an expression on his face of startled amazement. Then his head turned as he watched the Lewis dropping away below them both and, swinging round in a tight turn, he stared again at the BE as if he expected something else even bigger and more dangerous to come sailing in his direction, before abruptly putting the Fokker's nose down and disappearing below them. Dicken watched helplessly, wondering what he could do without a gun to fire, but the German machine kept on going down until it became a mere dot and eventually disappeared against the patchwork greens and browns of the ground. Turning to eye Hudnutt, wondering what was going to happen to him, Dicken could see the observer's wing he had sewn so proudly on his tunic disappearing even before the stiches had grown cold.

Hudnutt's expression was hidden by his goggles and the scarf round his mouth. On the way home, he slipped the machine from side to side in case of another attack and Dicken watched the sky anxiously. The lines passed beneath them and the field came up under the nose. Drifting in to land, the machine rumbled to a stop near the hangars and, red-faced with shame and wondering what sort of ticking off he was about to receive, Dicken waited until Hudnutt had climbed out. As the officer turned by the wingtip, he gestured.

'See me in the office,' he said.

There was no escaping the consequences. Dicken had not only left his machine defenceless in the air but, through his clumsiness, had also lost a perfectly good Lewis gun, and the army's method with lost articles was to charge you the value of what you'd lost and the value of the article that had to replace it. He could see himself not only being court-martialled but in debt for the rest of his life.

Hudnutt was sitting in the office, his leather coat and helmet still on, just finishing his report. He looked up as Dicken entered and held out the sheet. 'You'd better read it, too,' he said.

Dicken read the report carefully, hardly able to concentrate in his nervousness. It was very straightforward.

'. . . We were then attacked by an enemy aircraft over Lille, which was identified as one of the new Fokkers. There was a brief skirmish and Air Mechanic Quinney, having used all his available ammunition, frightened the EA away by throwing the gun at it.'

Dicken looked up, Hudnutt had unwound his scarf and was grinning. Seeing the look on Dicken's face, he burst out laughing.

'You can say you've invented a new form of battle tactics,' he said.

'But I didn't throw the gun, sir, I dropped it.'

Hudnutt guffawed. 'I know that, you ass. Your face was the funniest thing I've ever seen.' He laughed again. 'What a pity you didn't hit him. We could have put you in for another gong.'

6

It was a long time before Dicken was allowed to forget his 'aggressive battle tactics'. Even Morton, the CO, smiled when he saw him and nothing was ever said about the loss of the Lewis gun.

For a while the Fokkers continued to rampage up and down the front, taking a terrible toll of the old British machines, then abruptly things changed. With the Italians now in the war on the Allied side and expected to start a third front against the Austrians north of Venice, a big battle was building up astride the River Somme in France and they set off south, men, aeroplanes, lorries and all the assorted dogs which had attached themselves to the squadron, to the new front in Picardy.

The whole area was alive with men, thousands upon thousands of them, from all corners of the Empire, with thousands of vehicles, thousands of horses, and thousands of guns. The land had not been fought over since 1914 and they were in green, flower-decked fields with thick woods, in direct contrast to the splintered trees and devastated acres of the north.

The battle was to be fought almost entirely by the new Kitchener battalions which had been raised since the beginning of the war. Handiside didn't think much of the idea because he didn't consider the Kitchener men experienced enough, and on July 1st, they learned just how right he was. The newspapers that arrived from home told of immense advances and colossal areas of captured ground, but the men in France knew differently, the RFC best of all because they could actually see how far the advance had carried the army forward. It amounted to little more than a few hundred yards in most places – in some none at all – and the lines of ambulances and hospital trains passing the aerodrome told of casualties greater than all the earlier battles put together.

In their own department there was a measure of relief, because 20 Squadron had arrived in their sector with FE2bs, strong machines with the propeller behind the crew in a structure of wooden booms that supported the tail and the gun firing forward with nothing in the way, and the command of the air had slipped from the Germans' hands just as it had from the British the previous year. Towards the end of the month one of the FEs even got Immelmann, and there were yells of relief because Immelmann had been appearing in quite a few bad dreams, though they were tinged with a certain amount of regret, because Immelmann was a flying man as they were and took the same risks in the same sort of flimsy aircraft, frail and stinking of petrol, that could fall to bits if the slightest thing went wrong.

Despite the best efforts of the generals who, determined to keep the battle going, constantly came up with new ways of killing men, by the end of the year it had petered out in a sea of mud into nothing more than the normal bad temper and Dicken managed to get home on leave, his first since his arrival in France the previous year. The journey to the coast was bitterly cold and the train slower than a donkey cart. The Channel was at its most intransigent, and he was virtually carried ashore at Folkestone by an enormous Guardsman. As he sank down in a railway carriage, it occurred to him that perhaps it was a good job he hadn't gone to sea, after all.

His mother was proud of his medal ribbons and couldn't do enough for him, but she found it hard to understand that the only thing he wished to do was get out his bicycle and visit Deane.

'Mother,' he explained. 'I'm nineteen now and I've begun to notice that girls are different.'

Zoë greeted him with a yelp of excitement and fingered his ribbons enthusiastically.

'Not one,' she said. 'But *two*! Annys will be livid. Arthur Diplock's not got any.'

For once, Dicken was on Diplock's side. 'They don't come

all that easily,' he said. 'He's nothing to be ashamed of.'

When she asked how he'd won them, he explained cautiously, leaving out the truth about the Russian medal and the lost Lewis gun. While they were talking Annys appeared. She seemed to think him mad to go flying.

'People get killed flying,' she said.

'People are getting rather summarily done to death in a variety of ways,' he pointed out.

'Arthur's been transferred to the Service Corps,' she went on stiffly. 'His job's to see the front line troops are supplied with food and ammunition. It's because he's good at languages.'

She seemed more than normally chilly and it was Zoë who explained. 'They're getting engaged when he gets leave,' she said. 'He's a lieutenant now. He has the advantage over you all along the line, hasn't he? Daddy has a motor car. You have a bike. He has two pips on his shoulder and these days sits in an office most of the time. You've got two stripes and risk your neck. He's also taller.'

'And his ears,' Dicken said bitterly, 'stick out like a Parasol's wings. It's an aeroplane,' he explained.

The description seemed to tickle Zoë. 'You could always fall in love with me, Dicky boy,' she said. 'I've always had a soft spot for you. At least you look like a man. Arthur looks like a piece of cold pudding. Besides, I shall be worth something one day. Father says he'll leave the garage to me because Annys wouldn't touch it with a barge pole in case she got her hands dirty. I can already strip an engine.'

'What on earth do you want to do that for?'

'Very useful accomplishment, as a matter of fact. We lost our only decent mechanic to the army and you'd be surprised what a demand for transport there is. There's a new army camp just outside the village and the officers are always telephoning for me to take them into Brighton. I carry a heavy wrench for when they get fresh. I sent one home one night with a lump like an egg on his forehead.'

When his leave came to an end Dicken wasn't sure whether it had been a success or not. Annys had had little time for him and Zoë was never a good substitute, though at least she was enthusiastic and, using her father's car, they went to Eastbourne and London. Her father was proud of her skill as a driver and trusted her anywhere with the machine, which was new, large and roomy and an excellent place for clutching each other in the dark at the end of the day.

He arrived back in France, once more almost at death's door with seasickness after a gale in the Channel, to find that Hudnutt was dead and that the squadron's aircraft had been standardised under a new policy to make maintenance easier. The Moranes had gone and all three flights now had BE2s.

'Pity they can't think of something a bit better,' he commented.

Handiside shrugged. 'Things have changed, kid,' he said. 'We've been hit by a blight. The Germans have got the edge on us again. We'd just got the better of 'em when they came up with a new one. Albatros. Looks like a shark with a tail like a spade and two machine guns firing through the propeller.'

'*Two?*'

'Why not?' Handiside asked. 'If one can fire through the propeller, why not two? One of these days they'll probably have four. Even eight, if they can find room for 'em. We were knocking seven sorts of hell out of 'em when you left but now they've started grouping all their scout machines together in one squadron and one's arrived opposite. They're swatting us down like flies.'

The new Albatroses and Halberstadts the Germans had brought out flew a staggering hundred miles an hour and it wasn't hard to imagine what they'd been doing to the elderly BEs. Their pilots had been hand-picked from both the Western and Eastern Fronts and, flying as a group, were a formidable formation to bump into.

'Intensive course at single-seater scout schools in Germany,' Handiside explained. 'Then more training on the squadron at the front. This chap Boelcke's behind it all. Their morale's sky-high. Ours, I reckon, is at worm-level.'

'What about Hatto?'

'Still around. But the captain's gone home and two others just failed to return. The fellers they're sending out now are only half-trained kids. I hope you're good at jumping.'

The pilot to whom Dicken was assigned, a boy called MacTavish, didn't appear to know much about flying. With only ten hours' experience in England and so far only five in France, he was permanently frustrated by an aggressive spirit that was entirely wasted because he couldn't handle his machine well. It left him in a perpetual state of fuming fury that troubled Dicken a great deal, because he suspected it would lead him into doing something silly.

The BE2e, which was now in use in the squadron, though still no fighter, was a vast improvement on the earlier 2c, but the politicians responsible for providing the machines for France still didn't seem to have grasped what was needed. The Germans had awakened quickly to the possibilities of flying and were developing new aeroplanes and tactics that left the British way behind. In England all that had happened was that somebody had ordered BEs in thousands and seemed unable to stop production, while there was still no means of synchronising the gun to the engine and what British fighters there were, were either pushers or carried the gun on the top wing.

Because of the losses, reconnaissance machines were now only sent out with escorts of scout planes, first three, then, as this proved ineffective, six, and everybody had to start practising formation flying, a highly problematic business in those squadrons equipped with two or three different types of machines all flying at different speeds. They didn't realise it, but the whole concept of aerial warfare was changing and the fact that the prevailing wind blew from the west to carry any unwary pilot beyond reach of his own lines began to make air fighting a dangerous game. Dicken had arrived back in France, he decided, at a decidedly unpleasant time.

*

Christmas passed and the New Year came in a smother of mist and rain that kept them grounded for days at a time, fretting at the thought of the indifference of the authorities at home to the good performance of their machines. Flying became an uncomfortable chore. The oil in the machine guns froze and there was always the risk of frostbite. Covering his

58

face with vaseline and trying to muffle himself up to make sure no part of him was left exposed, Dicken succeeded only in making it virtually impossible to move quickly.

The more he flew, the more he fancied the idea of flying himself. The new pilots were sadly lacking in aerial knowledge and all too often had only the experience of their observers to keep them alive. In the first five days of a new offensive the Flying Corps lost seventy-five machines in fighting and another fifty-six in crashes on their own aerodromes. The Germans, they heard, had lost Boelcke, but in his place they were said to have a new expert who was clawing the old BEs down in dozens with an all-red Albatros. Rumour suggested the pilot was a woman, because only a woman would go in for such a gaudy colour, and another rumour had it that a special squadron had been recruited among the best British pilots in France for the sole purpose of destroying it, even that a reward had been offered.

They got the truth eventually from a German pilot who had been shot down and appeared in the mess for a drink before departing for a prisoner of war camp. The pilot of the red machine was a man called Richthofen and he wasn't the only one either, because there was another called Voss, who was believed to have shot down twenty British machines on his own in a matter of two months or so. The Germans, the prisoner said, were claiming four British machines for every one of their own they lost. Certainly the wreckage of BEs was scattered everywhere, both behind and in front of the enemy lines. Broken tails and torn wings, many of them put there by Richthofen or Voss, seemed to sprout from every curve and hollow of the ground. The year had started with the British operating twenty-eight miles behind the German lines; because of the casualties, the limit was now set at two.

'We don't make it hard for 'em,' Handiside said. 'Not using BEs.'

With flying a deadly serious business again, it was best not to use the imagination too much. The places at table of casualties were deliberately not left empty in case people began to dwell on them, and with everybody pretending they didn't care, hairsbreadth escapes were ignored because they all knew there would be more in the future. If there *was* a future, of course. For the most part, the future didn't exist, because the war stretched in a bloody blur across it, leaving a curious sense of emptiness and want.

Despite this, however, there was a tremendous element of daring among the young pilots, all of whom seemed to wish to emulate Albert Ball, a nineteen-year-old pilot who regarded the war as a crusade and was prepared to tackle any number of Germans at once. Unfortunately, most of them – MacTavish among them – had neither the machine he flew nor his skill, and it was as they were flying over the Scarpe at the end of the month that Dicken finally decided that MacTavish was a danger to the public and to Nicholas Dicken Quinney in particular. More than once he had wiped off his undercarriage, once he had turned the machine over, and once, in an attempt to get over the trees at the end of the aerodrome, had lost so much height he had flown between them, shedding his wings en route, to make what was for him a reasonably good landing.

'A perfect three-point touchdown,' he had said, his young pink face creased into a grin. 'Without wings, too.'

As he watched a German balloon hanging like a fat maggot, obscene and graceless over the river, it suddenly dawned on Dicken that they were approaching it in a particularly determined manner. The morning was cold with a west wind pushing scraps of low cloud before it, the front line marked by smoke streaming eastward like grey wool. High above was a layer of stratus, ice-white so that the sky seemed full of light, and Dicken knew that against it they were silhouetted perfectly and a wonderful target for the ground gunners.

MacTavish was obviously intending to attack the balloon and Dicken began to shake his head and wave his arms frantically to warn him not to. MacTavish merely grinned and pointed, something which made Dicken begin to dance with rage in the observer's cockpit.

The balloon was beginning to descend now and Dicken could see men running to the guns with which it was circled. As they drew nearer, Archie started firing and the first burst exploded within feet of the starboard wing, tearing the fabric and rocking the machine. Making frantic indications to

MacTavish to turn away, Dicken finally decided that, since they were going to attack the balloon, he might as well shoot at it, but MacTavish's skill was not equal to his determination and they hurtled past like a bus out of control on a hill. By this time the machine was being hit repeatedly but, since nothing vital seemed to be touched, MacTavish swung round to have another go.

As they approached for their second run, Dicken spluttering with rage, the air was full of shellbursts, tracer bullets and flaming onions – a particularly unpleasant form of missile in strings of white lights like chain shot and as big as tennis balls – that came up in a maddeningly leisurely way, then whipped past in a manner that made you realise how lethal they were. It was as they swung away a second time, with the only damage inflicted done to their own machine, that Dicken turned round to implore MacTavish not to have another go and spotted a machine turning in beneath them. With alarm he saw it had the sharklike fuselage and spade-shaped tail that Handiside had warned against and it had twice the speed of the old BE and two guns winking deadly orange flashes through the propeller. It was red and evil-looking and was doubtless controlled by one of the Germans' special pilots with their extra training – probably Richthofen himself!

Hammering on the fuselage, Dicken pointed. Appearing to think he was telling him to have another go at the balloon, MacTavish grinned back and nodded. Making frantic signals, Dicken finally got him to understand, and glancing back, MacTavish's expression changed abruptly to one of alarm. As he wrenched the BE violently aside, Dicken almost disappeared over the side and clung for a while, half-out of the cockpit, staring downwards at a thousand feet of nothing until MacTavish righted the machine.

Pushing the nose down, he began to head for the British lines in a shallow dive to increase the speed. The Albatros came round beneath them once more, and the two machine guns seemed to be pointing straight down Dicken's throat.

'Ess!' he screamed, making curving gestures with his hand. 'For Christ's sake, ess!'

It took some time for the idea to sink in but MacTavish finally swung the machine to one side – just in time – and the tracer lines went past the tip of their starboard wing.

'Keep essing!' Dicken yelled, heaving at the gun, and they went down, the tail swinging from right to left as MacTavish kicked at the rudder bar.

Small lines of grey smoke kept appearing beyond their wingtips and Dicken smelled the familiar smell of German tracers, then the Albatros bored in once more, showing its upper wings with their black Maltese crosses. Getting in a quick burst, Dicken managed to make it sheer away, but it came doggedly round again for yet another go.

By this time, they were almost on the ground and, as they crossed the German lines, it seemed that every German in France was shooting at them. Fabric began to flap in long streamers and the engine began to develop a loud knocking noise.

MacTavish was working like a madman to keep the machine in the air, but the rudder was hanging loose by this time and he had little control. The British trenches appeared, with another fusillade of shots, then Dicken saw faces turned upwards as they sailed over, the motor making a noise like a steam traction engine going uphill. The torn brown earth was close beneath the wheels as the engine finally stopped and they continued in a silence that was broken only by the whistle of the wind through the flying wires. There was a twang as the wheels caught a coil of barbed wire and, looking back, Dicken saw they were trailing what appeared to be the whole of the British second line defences, wire, stakes and all. Then abruptly, as the strain became too much, the BE's nose dipped.

The propeller flew to pieces, one of the blades whipping through the wings in a shower of splinters and torn fabric, then the wheels dropped into a shellhole, and the machine turned upside down. Dicken found himself flying through the air to land on his face and almost immediately he became aware of machine gun bullets whack-whacking just above his head. Crawling through the mud, he dived for a shellhole almost on top of MacTavish who was sitting in the slime at the bottom, laughing. All the terror had gone from his expression and he seemed to be thoroughly enjoying himself.

'It's bad enough when the Germans and the French shoot at us,' he said, 'but when the British do it, it's too much. I think I'll complain to the general.'

Dicken stared at him as if he were mad. 'Why in the name of God did you have to attack a bloody balloon?' he snarled.

MacTavish laughed. 'Felt like giving the bastards a fright!'

'In a BE?'

'Got to scrag the Hun.'

'In any scragging between a balloon and a BE, the balloon's bound to come off best. It's much more dangerous.'

Dicken glared, wondering where and how MacTavish had been brought up. At his school – the sort of school which had bred the kind of officer who had fought the Fuzzy-Wuzzies in the last century, facing tremendous odds in front of the flag with blazing eyes and a smile on his lips – no doubt it had been taught that it was bad form not to stand up and face an enemy fair and square. They obviously didn't know much about war, Dicken decided, because a much more sensible maxim was the one about the man who ran away living to fight another day. It even seemed a good idea to hit your opponent below the belt when he wasn't looking.

'I think you're barmy,' he said disgustedly.

MacTavish gurgled with laughter and looked up at the wrecked BE above his head dripping petrol into the ground.

'Don't know what you're going on about,' he said. 'They can't kill me.'

7

But they did.

A week later, as Dicken was working in the hangar installing a wireless set in a new machine, he became aware of the buzz of an engine and everyone moving towards the entrance to stare into the sky. Putting down his screwdriver, he joined them to see a BE just turning over the trees at the far end of the field, its flight growing more erratic with every yard.

'It's MacTavish,' someone said. 'He's in trouble.'

The BE was turning in a wide circle for its final approach, but, as it did so, they heard a flat sound like a paper bag bursting.

'Oh, Christ!' Handiside said.

The upper wing of the BE had lifted and they could see it flapping loose above the centre section.

'Get it down!' Handiside grated.

The wing seemed to be floating away from the struts now, then it finally snapped back and the nose of the machine dropped at once. It fell in a twisting movement round the broken section of wing and they watched, horrified, as it whacked into the next field with the sound of a Jack Johnson shell.

They all started to run and, scrambling through the hedge, the first on the scene, Dicken almost crashed into the observer who was staggering about dazed, with blood across the grey film of grease and gunpowder on his face. A wisp of smoke rising from the motor, the machine lay in a crumpled heap just beyond him, surrounded by a scattering of pulverised earth. MacTavish was trying to push his way clear from the crumpled wreckage of the upper wing that lay half on top of him, and as Dicken began to tug at his leather coat, he lifted his head and two shocked blue eyes stared at Dicken from a ruined face which blew a spray of scarlet mist across his hands. Handiside yanked Dicken away just as the petrol exploded and the two of them were flung backwards.

Only half aware that his clothes were on fire, he was rolled over and over in the wet grass with Handiside beating at the flames. Scrambling to his feet, still shocked, he saw everybody standing in a circle, staring aghast at the furnace and the moving figure in the middle still struggling feebly to free itself, its face scorched to carbon in seconds.

'The silly bugger tried to shoot down that balloon over the Scarpe.' Tense and white-faced, his eyes like a frightened animal's, the observer had recovered his senses now and was standing alongside Dicken, clutching his arm. 'He said he missed it last time and wanted to chalk up a victory.'

*

Standing near the hangar, his hands in his pockets, Dicken stared into the evening sky, his eyes bleak, a lost expression on his face, wondering what idiot he would be assigned to next.

MacTavish's death was just one more of the persistent chilly reminders that he belonged to a lost generation that dared not look too far ahead. Even death seemed sharper, more abrupt and less dignified than it had the previous year and there was something vaguely nauseating about the way the German machines could knock them out of the sky.

'What's up, young 'un? Breeze up a bit?'

Dicken turned. Standing with his hands thrust into the front pockets of his breeches, his tunic flaps pushed back behind his wrists, Hatto looked like some French aristocrat going defiantly to the guillotine.

'No, sir,' Dicken said. 'Not really. Just thinking.'

'Don't pay to do that too much. What about?'

Dicken tried to explain. Before 1914 only a few rash spirits had dared to contemplate using aeroplanes at all, let alone fighting with them in wartime; now, every energy was being bent to devise new ways and means of killing each other in the air.

'But the aeroplanes we've got are so unsuitable, sir.' A

spasm of anger crossed his face. 'We're like boxers with their hands tied.'

Hatto shrugged. 'Well, don't let it get you down too much,' he said. '*We*'ve produced some new machines, too, I hear. Arriving any day now. Better recce machines and fighters as good as the Hun's. Unfortunately, *we* don't seem to be getting many of them. They're all going to the RNAS because Churchill happened to be at the Admiralty and he was sharp enough to bag most of 'em.' He paused then went on briskly. 'Know anything about bomb sights?'

'Not a thing, sir,' Dicken admitted. 'I've never seen one. Do we have any?'

Hatto smiled. 'We have now,' he said. 'They've just arrived. So you'd better find out what you can about 'em. The mechanics are fitting one to my machine.'

Dicken's heart leapt. 'Does that mean I'm flying with you?'

'Well, we get along as merrily as a matched pair, don't we? Mind?'

'Gosh, no!' Hatto had been flying a long time now and it had long since become clear that the longer a man flew the greater were his chances of surviving.

'Right,' Hatto was saying. 'Go and see what you can do about it. We're going to practise with 'em over the aerodrome. Tomorrow we're going bombing. Railway station near Bapaume. You know what Sir Andrew Agnew said at Dettingen: "Ye see yon loons on yon brae face. If ye dinnae kill them, they'll kill you." It's the same here. If we don't drop *our* bombs on them they'll doubtless drop theirs on *us*. Pity we have to do it with BEs. They fly like bedpans with wings.'

*

There were to be two squadrons on the operation and the tactics seemed to be fairly straightforward. As the last squadron over the target, all they had to do was drop their bombs where the other squadron dropped theirs. However, it didn't take long to realise that it was impossible to become proficient with the bomb sight in twenty-four hours because it required two flights over the target, one to get the wind's

speed and direction and make calculations with a stop
watch, and the second to drop the bombs. Since arithmetic
was not Dicken's strongpoint, he couldn't see himself ever
becoming very good at it.

'Don't matter all that much,' Hatto said. 'We can always
go down low and slip the bombs into somebody's pocket.
Meet's at eleven over Béthune. Might not draw a fox, but we
might pick up a Fokker or two.'

'Are we flying in formation?'

'No, thank God. We have enough perils to face without
that.'

The sky was full of slab-sided cumulus reflecting the light,
and, arriving punctually over Béthune, they found the other
squadron had arrived early and hadn't bothered to wait but
were already on their way, strung across the sky like hounds
after a scent, their aeroplanes following each other hap-
hazardly at different distances and heights that suited the
individual pilots. Even the enemy anti-aircraft guns didn't
seem to know what to do about them. Since they were all at
different altitudes and scattered all over the sky, the baffled
gunners couldn't decide which one to fire at and merely
filled the sky with black smoke.

Near the target they became bunched again as they waited
their turn to drop their bombs, and the anti-aircraft guns at
last found the range and began to put the wind up them all.
As far as Dicken could see, the bombs were falling in the
fields at the side of the railway track, and Hatto began
signalling and pointing downwards. As the nose of the
machine dropped it was clear he was intending to do just as
he'd said and place his bombs in someone's pocket.

There seemed to be a lot of uneven rifle fire but the station
they were aiming at appeared to be deserted. Then he saw
Hatto gesturing and, staring in the direction of the pointing
finger, he saw that on a curve a short distance away a train
was standing, the engine blowing off steam. Alongside it was
a swarm of agitated black dots and he realised it was a troop
train and that it was from its occupants that all the rifle fire
was coming.

As they sailed overhead, he watched the bombs fall away.
It seemed impossible to miss by so much. One fell in a field

and the other behind a house, but then he saw a cloud of smoke rising from where the second bomb had fallen and as they circled to see what damage they'd done he saw lorries burning. Hatto stuck up his thumb and grinned. Almost immediately, snow began to fall.

*

They slogged home through the blinding murk, the snow whirling away in front of the machine, huge flakes slapping painfully into Dicken's face, and as the sky grew darker, he began to wonder if they were lost. After a while, as though looking through a frosty window, he spotted a field, and then a corner of Lille fortifications. He pointed and Hatto nodded, his teeth bared in a fixed grin. As they crossed the lines, Dicken breathed a sigh of relief.

They were the last to land and everybody was standing by the machines, noisy with excitement as they discussed what had happened. Most of them were loudly claiming direct hits and the CO, trying to find out exactly what had happened, could hardly be heard above the hubbub. Hatto's opinion didn't coincide with the rest. He was realistic enough to refuse to believe they had done much damage.

'To me,' he said disgustedly, 'it looked a proper old donnybrook. I reckon we can do better than that.'

'What's Corporal Quinney think?'

Hatto slapped Dicken on the shoulder. 'He thinks the world of me. That's what he thinks. A good officer commands affection while communicating energy, and nobody can do that like your Uncle Willie. Corporal Quinney agrees with me entirely.'

The news that they had to have another go the following day set them wondering. Was it because they'd been successful or was it because they'd done so badly they had to do it all over again? A major arrived from Wing to give them a pep talk as they were waiting to take off. He wasn't offering rebukes but he wasn't offering much in the way of congratulations either.

'We have to be prepared to make sacrifices,' he said.

'I dare bet *he* won't be making sacrifices,' Hatto said as they waddled in their heavy clothing to their machine. 'All this laying down your life's so much journalistic twaddle. I've spent the whole war so far fighting like mad to preserve mine.'

This time the bombing was more successful. A barge in the canal alongside the station was sunk – though there was nothing to indicate whether it was being used by the Germans or by some unlucky Frenchman – and the station was partly demolished. It also meant the end of things for one unlucky crew, because the pilot was hit over Carvin and the observer was unable to do a thing about it but watch the ground coming up until they struck. Hatto and Dicken had watched them every inch of the way down, and as they walked away from the machine, feeling depressed and emotionally spent, Hatto spoke slowly.

'No wonder they give us flying pay,' he said. 'That sort of thing makes you feel bloody old at times. We all tend to think it'll never happen to us. Probably *they* did. But when you *see* it happen, it leaves you with the unexpected feeling that *you*'re vulnerable after all.'

Dicken said nothing and he went on in the same tight voice, his expression bleak. 'Has it ever occurred to you, old fruit,' he asked, 'that if anything happened to me, there wouldn't be much you could do to save yourself?'

'It's often occurred to me,' Dicken admitted. 'I don't like it much.'

'Neither do I,' Hatto admitted. 'Because if there's nothing you can do to save yourself if I get wounded, there's also nothing you can do to save *me* either. And to me I'm important because I've already lost two of my nine lives. Once when you fished me out in front of the wire and once in 1914 when we charged a machine gun position on horses. We ended up with all the nags down and my sergeant's spur up my nostril. I take rather a shine to the idea of surviving. How about seeing what we can do to remedy the situation?'

Quite unofficially, the next time they went out, on the way home Dicken climbed on to the wing, and clutching a strut, leaned over Hatto's office to see what went on. The lower wing was cut away at the root to give a view downwards and most of the time, he was hanging over empty air.

'You've got to keep the nose down,' Hatto explained. 'It's

the only way to keep flying speed. If you go for a slow safe glide, at least we ought to hit right side up and under some control.'

They were still waiting for congratulations from headquarters for the bombing raid. It had been cautiously mentioned in the newspapers but no one else seemed interested except the Germans who became more active as a result. Eventually reaction came. Because of their skill, they were informed, they were to start making long reconnaissances behind the German lines to see what the enemy was up to.

'Douai, Orchies, Denain, Anzin and Valenciennes,' Hatto said. 'We circle each place, making notes and count the rolling stock. Then we can come home. *If we're lucky.* Because the Germans have scouts at Douai and we'll be forty miles the wrong side of the lines.'

It was a bright morning when their turn came and they set off with wisps of cloud and mist along the valleys. The towns over which they passed seemed to have been etched against the land and there was no movement anywhere. It was bitterly cold and Dicken hung over the side of the fuselage, peering down at the network of railway lines, trying to count the wagons and make awkward notes with his gloved hands on crumpled and fluttering sheets of paper. As they turned for home, he was slapping his hands and shuffling his feet on the floor of the cockpit to restore some life to them, but it was a losing battle and Hatto managed to make it clear that the compass had frosted over and they were flying largely by guesswork. Fortunately the sun gave them some direction, though, with a strong westerly wind in their faces, they seemed to be barely moving over the ground and, half-frozen, trying to calculate the drift, Dicken decided they were lost. They had been in the air now for well over three hours and their fuel was getting low. His fingers numb with cold, he peered over the side, looking for something which would give them their course, and eventually he spotted Jigsaw Wood which was only a mile or two from the line.

Fortunately, Archie was inaccurate and only a few spent fragments tore holes in the wing fabric. Relieved that they now knew where they were, bored with the absence of anything exciting in the whole trip, and to give himself something to think about other than the cold, he began to count the bursts and came to the conclusion that around a hundred and fifty shells had been fired at them without effect. It was one way of winning the war, he decided cheerfully. If you couldn't beat the Germans in the field, you could always encourage them to bring about their own bankruptcy.

As they approached the lines, they spotted two German aircraft. Hatto pointed and they climbed towards them. One promptly bolted for home but the other continued to fly backwards and forwards and they managed to climb beneath it so that Dicken could fire over the propeller. The German turned and dived away but, almost immediately, Hatto started to hammer on the fuselage and point towards the lines. Another big white-winged two-seater Albatros was sitting above them, the light showing through the fabric of the wings, to outline every rib, spar and painted Maltese cross. It looked like a huge gaudy butterfly catching the sun.

Hatto was gesturing wildly and, as Dicken heaved his gun into position, they clawed their way upwards and drew level, then, keeping well to the eastward so he couldn't escape, they sailed in to engage him.

Because the sun was behind them now and hiding them from view, the German probably didn't see them until Hatto turned away. He had just throttled back to glide for home when Dicken pressed the trigger and immediately the Albatros swung abruptly across their bows, blocked from his view by the propeller. For a moment, they were helpless and in a perfect position for the German observer to fire back at them, but there was no reply and as the machines swung apart, wingtips almost touching, Dicken could see the expression on the faces of the two Germans. Instinctively he raised his arm to wave and just as instinctively the Germans waved back. Then, as the German observer started shooting, Dicken knelt on his seat and fired, and the Albatros sank below them in a shallow gliding turn. Watching as the glide grew steeper, it dawned on Dicken that it was becoming a dive and as the German machine turned westwards Hatto pushed the BE's nose down to follow. But the German's turn seemed unnatural now and Dicken swung round to look at Hatto, who was staring back at him with the same amazed expression on his face. The German was going down out of control. They had shot down an enemy. In a BE, too!

They were just gleefully slapping the fuselage between them when the sudden crack of bullets made them swing round. As Dicken jumped for the gun again – so violently the machine rocked – another Albatros sailed over their heads, the observer firing away for all he was worth and, as they banked away from the danger, he saw there were two more enemy machines heading towards them.

The cold had been forgotten as he hoisted the weapon from one mounting to the other. Hatto banked, but even as he did so yet another German machine arrived on the scene. This time it was an Albatros fighter and its first burst lifted fabric from the wings and sent splinters flying from the centre section struts.

Dicken was busy with the gun when the BE's nose dipped unexpectedly and he had to clutch for a hold as the machine began to descend in an abrupt turn that jerked him from his feet. Dragging himself upright, he saw that Hatto's head was down inside the cockpit, and seeing blood on his cheek, he realised he'd been hit.

'Oh, Christ,' he said.

Hatto's teaching hadn't come a moment too soon. He knew exactly what to do. The question was, could he do it before it was too late? The inherent stability of the BE had brought it into a wide flat turn but he knew that at any moment it could fall into a stall and when it did there would be no chance of escape.

Scrambling with difficulty to the wing, he pulled himself to Hatto's cockpit, while the German machines, considering their task done, drew away and sat high in the sky, watching the descent. It was impossible to push Hatto back and he began to yell.

'Sir!' he screamed. 'Wake up! Where are you hit?'

Below him the earth swung, turning like a flat plate, racing up to them as they fell. Dry-mouthed with fear, as he fought to rouse Hatto his mind was full of that other BE they had seen going down over Carvin after the bombing raid, the observer struggling to stir his pilot and unable to do a thing to save himself. The lower wing and fuselage of the BE were slippery with oil leaked from the engine and, his mouth ballooned by the rushing wind from the whirling propeller, he could feel the slipstream snatching him from his dubious foothold. Reaching for a centre section strut, as he almost disappeared from the wing he felt the hot flush of fear cover his body with sweat.

'Sir, you silly bugger –' almost in tears, his words torn from him by terror, he was shouting at Hatto, hoping that by the very strength of his voice he could bring him back to life '– for Christ's sake, wake up before you kill us both!'

Clinging with clawing fingers to the padded edge of the cockpit, he was almost inclined to climb back to his position and take a chance in the crash but they were still too high and, feeling the machine hovering uncertainly on the edge of a stall, he knew it was a case of doing what he was trying to do or ending up dead.

Bracing both legs and clinging on with all his strength against the wind that threatened to throw him into the empty air, he scrambled half into Hatto's cockpit. His feet kicking wildly, he found he couldn't reach the throttle lever because Hatto was in the way, so he found a tap and hopefully turned it. Nothing happened so he tried another and this time the howl of the engine ceased as the fuel was cut off.

The blast of the wind decreased as the engine died and he was able to lean further into the cockpit. Hatto was still clutching the joystick and, sobbing with frustration, he knocked his hands aside and, reaching down, yanked the machine out of its turn. In his anxiety, he was too eager and, as the machine straightened abruptly, he almost lost his grip and his feet flailed wildly.

The machine was flying straight now and, hanging on to Hatto, half-in and half-out of the cockpit, he was trying to hold it in a shallow glide. But Hatto's bent head was in the way of the air-speed indicator and it was largely guesswork.

'Wake up, sir, wake up!' The ground was coming up fast and from the corner of his eye he could see the white faces of men on the ground staring up at his kicking figure lying across the fuselage. 'Sir! For Christ's sake!'

In a fury that came from panic, he began to shake Hatto

73

and to his joy he finally stirred and opened his eyes. He looked drunk and stupid and stared at Dicken through a veil of blood. Trying to control the machine, he reached for the joystick and pushed on the rudder with his feet so that the glide once more became a flat turn.

'Right, sir! For the love of Christ, turn right!'

'I can't! I can't see! I'm blind!'

'No, you're not,' Dicken snarled. 'Do as I tell you, you silly bugger! You're taking us back where we came from!'

Mechanically, Hatto obeyed and they swung round once more until they were facing west again.

'Straighten her out! Straighten her out! Stick central!'

The flat turn once more became a straight shallow glide and, as the wind pressure lessened further, Dicken was no longer having to cling on with all his strength. In front of them was a plantation of young trees.

'Up with her, sir! Not too much! Steady! Back a bit more!'

Hatto's hands were following the flow of instructions more surely now and the BE cleared all the trees but the last few. As it ploughed through them, leaves, twigs and fragments of wood shot in all directions, then the machine flopped to the earth with a crash that sent Dicken flying through the air to land in a hawthorn hedge that bounced him like a spring on to the ground. Aware of scratches on his face and blood running from a cut lip, he scrambled to his feet and rushed back to the aeroplane to drag Hatto clear.

Flinging him to the ground at a safe distance from the machine, he waited for the explosion of the petrol. But the long flight had used almost every drop of it and nothing happened. Bending over Hatto, he wrenched his helmet off, expecting to find a hole in his head. What he saw was a groove running along it that had raised two long bruises. He picked up the helmet and, staring at the tear in it, realised the bullet had only grazed Hatto's scalp.

'You rotten sod, sir!' he yelled, almost in tears as the realisation of what had happened swept over him and left him shivering with shock. 'You're not properly wounded!'

8

Hatto's wound was enough to take him to hospital and Dicken found himself flying with yet another new pilot.

He felt neglected and unwanted. Because they knew each other's methods, he and Hatto had felt safe together. But Hatto was gone now and the BE was not growing less obsolete. Staring at himself in the mirror, he saw he had grown old in the last two years as he had seen most of his companions disappear. His face had changed. It was no longer the round-cheeked image of a boy, and lurking behind it somewhere there were nerves stretched to bowstrings that showed in dark circles under his eyes and a half-hidden suggestion that he still hadn't got used to the death or mutilation of his friends. It looked like the death mask of a whole generation.

By this time, he was coming more and more to the conclusion that if he were going to fly he might as well fly himself. He loved flying, he loved the freedom and the sense of power it gave him, but it seemed that if he were going to put his life in someone's hands, they might as well be his own and he began to wonder what his chances would be if he put in for a pilot's course.

As it happened, the opportunity didn't arise because a new push started in the north and as he flew with different pilots, he decided that the strain was beginning to tell on him. Again and again he woke up in the night dry-mouthed and reliving his last flight with Hatto.

For some time, he was far too busy to do more than flop into bed at the end of the day, his store of courage drained, and pray that the next day it would be raining, and he hadn't the energy to think of anything but flying. Inevitably, the

75

new push achieved nothing but casualties because, as usual, it was allowed to go on far too long and the Germans brought up reserves so that the line that ran all the way from Switzerland to the coast simply grew thicker and stronger. A French push followed but the Frenchmen managed only six hundred yards instead of the six miles which had been promised, and the casualties were so terrible rumours began to drift northwards that the French troops were mutinying. Thousands were deserting and others marched to the front bleating like sheep. Handiside, who had been sent to a French squadron with a blacksmith's forge, returned with a shocked look. 'The bloody war's over,' he said. 'And we've lost it!'

It certainly began to look like it because it was no secret that ships were being sunk in dozens by submarines, and the Russians had risen in revolution and kicked out the Tsar. Whichever way you regarded it, the future didn't look very promising.

Dicken's flights these days were with a young South African by the name of Friedmann. Quiet and gently-spoken, he looked like a choirboy but he was very nearly as aggressive as MacTavish, and only a little more skilful. Like many of the young men arriving in France, his training had been quite inadequate and he was having to learn as he went along. But aeroplanes had a habit of arriving out of an empty sky with surprising speed and he still hadn't overcome the newcomer's fatal inability to see them in time so that several times it was only Dicken's experienced eyes that saved them.

A period of bad weather kept them grounded but, as it began to clear, flying started again and, heading across the lines, Dicken was leaning over the side reporting the fall of shot for a battery near Pilchem when he spotted white anti-aircraft smoke below them. Since it was British, he could only assume the battery below was warning them and, leaning further out of the machine, he saw three Albatros fighters climbing up under their tail, swarming in like sharks round an injured swimmer.

'Ess,' he yelled at once. 'Ess!'

Unable to fire downwards, he had to wait for Friedmann to take evading action but, though he was better than

MacTavish, Friedmann was still not very good and a cluster of bullet holes appeared in the wing.

'Keep on essing,' Dicken yelled. 'Don't fly straight!'

But the BE was no match for the Albatroses and no matter how much Friedmann hurled it about he was unable to throw them off. At one moment, squinting over the top of the machine gun, Dicken found himself staring one of the German pilots straight in the face. As his machine swung away in a tight bank, he seemed only yards away and Dicken felt that he could have tossed a drum of ammunition into his cockpit.

By this time the machine seemed to be hanging together only by its wires and was barely flopping about in the air.

'Do something!' he yelled at Friedmann, but the pilot could only give him a sickly grin because, with the controls gone, there wasn't much he could do.

There was a terrific jolt as they hit the ground and a tremendous crash as if the sky had fallen in. For a moment, Dicken's ears were filled with ripping, rending noises, then everything was silent.

'You all right?' Friedmann's voice, fainty dazed, came from under the wreckage.

As they scrambled clear, they heard machine guns start and, giving Friedmann a shove, Dicken began to run.

Stumbling across the shell-torn ground, feeling like frightened rabbits surrounded by beaters, they flung themselves over the British parapet to be picked up by kilted soldiers. Cigarettes were stuck in their mouths and an officer gave them both a large mug of rum. Dicken downed his without thinking and, red-eyed and speechless, he sat down abruptly on the firestep.

They were given a guide through the reserve trenches and a squadron tender met them on the road to Béthune. As he made himself comfortable in the back, Dicken studied Friedmann with a frown. With the best will in the world, he decided, he wasn't ever going to survive flying with someone else, and when they reached the squadron he put in his application immediately.

'No reason why not,' the major said. 'I'm surprised you haven't applied before.'

To Dicken's surprise, he was accepted with remarkable speed and he could only put it down to the fact that the RFC had been losing pilots at such a rate they needed to replace a few quickly. He was glad to be going. The aerodrome contained too many ghosts and they had begun to chill him with a nagging fear that he would be joining them before too long.

'Tender will pick you up tomorrow morning, kid,' Handiside said. 'Make sure you're ready.'

That afternoon, Dicken flew for the last time as an observer. Wing had ordered a bombing attack on a gun park near Courtrai and every machine that could fly was to go, with a newly-arrived FE squadron acting as escort. Dicken walked to the aeroplane faintly resentful at having to fly. It would be just his luck, he thought bitterly, to be caught by Richthofen's lot on his last trip. They had been reported in the area again and everyone was having nightmares about them.

Nine BEs set off, lumbering down the field like ungainly birds to struggle into the sky and climb slowly eastwards. The countryside seemed empty, with just an occasional drifting spiral of smoke but, as they lifted upwards, the afternoon sun was tinting the blue earth below to bronze and picking out roofs and walls and streams in gold.

Dicken was flying with a pilot called Lewis who knew how to get the utmost from his machine and slowly they forced their way upwards until their reached their ceiling, though they were still terrifyingly vulnerable to attack. The FEs were waiting for them over Armentières and as they arrived the whole group began to head along the railway line for Courtrai.

The FEs, which were flying just above them, didn't seem terribly skilful and kept wandering off to the south. Finding the target, the BEs circled to the east to approach into wind and, as the gun park drew closer, they began to go down one after the other to drop their bombs. Dicken saw flashes and smoke but not a great deal of damage. A motor lorry was burning fiercely and men were running, then a horse galloped madly away, its saddle empty, a toy animal below the wing.

Though the sky seemed to be full of smoke, the anti-aircraft fire didn't seem to be doing much harm and he was just wondering why the Germans bothered with it when there was the crack and flash of a shell and one of the FEs just above seemed to collapse in mid-air. The nacelle and engine hovered like a wounded bird then lunged forward, the wooden booms that held the tail flapping about like useless sticks. One of the crew fell out, his legs and arms going as if he were running, his leather coat catching the sunlight until his falling body fouled the wing of the machine beneath, which swung sideways under the wreckage of the broken machine, so that it flopped on top of it and lay heaped up on the upper wing.

Lewis yanked the BE clear of the fluttering tangle of wood, metal and fabric and, stiff with horror as they slipped past, Dicken saw one of the broken tail booms slide back into the propeller which immediately flew to pieces to shatter its own tail. For a second the whole clutter seemed to hang in the sky, engineless, then the observer of the lower machine began to climb on to the top wing as if to shove away the wreckage. But as he did so the whole mess collapsed and, his eyes glistening with tears, Dicken saw his despairing expression as the wreckage thundered past, only yards away, the landing wheels seeming to slam past within inches of his face, to leave a trail of yellow struts, smoke, and strips of fabric.

*

As they turned for home, they were dispersed all over the sky, and over Comines they saw a flash in the distance and a rapidly descending column of smoke that told them the German fighters were among the scattered machines.

As they touched down and taxied towards the hangars, another BE glided in behind them, the pilot wounded, the observer shuddering with shock. As they waited, another machine landed, and then another – and then no more.

There was an air of gloom about the squadron that night and Dicken found he wasn't sorry to be leaving.

The following morning he was waiting with his kit as the tender arrived. It stopped near one of the empty hangars where Corporal Handiside was waiting with a group of mechanics. As Dicken began to walk towards it, he saw them lifting out two bodies. They were burned beyond recognition, the blackened remains of what had recently been two high-spirited young men.

'Who is it?' he asked.

Handiside directed a glare at him. 'How the hell do I know?' he snapped. 'Could *you* tell by looking at 'em?'

Dicken backed away, aware that the normally unmoved Handiside was suffering the same sort of shaken misery he was feeling himself.

'Well, go on –' Handiside turned from where he was helping to cover the two bodies with a tarpaulin and gave him a shove '– get in and go! You're away from it for a bit. For Christ's sake, make the most of it!'

Part Two

I

'They're very pretty,' Zoë said, fingering the wings on Dicken's tunic. 'And I see you've got another medal, too. What's that for?'

'Saving Willie Hatto's life.'

She touched the ribbons. 'I thought *that* was for saving Willie Hatto's life.'

'This one's for saving it again.'

'It sounds like a put-up job to me. What does he do? Go around getting himself into trouble so that you can drag him out? Were you very brave?'

Dicken shrugged. He was young and resilient and, away from the fighting and the constant narrow escapes that like small deadly cuts had drained away his courage like blood, was recovered enough to be blasé.

'You don't go out winning medals because you think they'll look nice on your coat,' he said. 'It's usually a case of do something or end up dead.'

She said nothing for a moment, only barely aware of the fading tensions inside him. 'It'll make Annys jealous as hell. Parasol Percy hasn't got any medals at all. Did you know he'd joined the Flying Corps? He didn't like the mud.'

'He's not the only one. Neither did I.'

'They took him out of his office. I think he thought a pilot's course would take a nice long time and would be safer than the job he'd been given. What's it like, learning to fly?'

Dicken grinned. 'Chiefly, they seemed to want to know if I knew anything about internal-combustion engines. I said I had a four-horse Bradbury single-geared, single-cylinder motor bike.'

'But you haven't.'

'No. But I knew they wouldn't go out and check.'

She backed away to get a better look. 'Vickery's in the RFC, too, now,' she said. 'Did you know?'

'I hope they've found him a job where he doesn't have to turn corners. It's a useful asset when a German's coming.'

She giggled. 'Actually, he's testing. They decided he was too old and too short-sighted to fight.'

'Who blows the whistle?'

'Nobody. They allow him to wear glasses.'

'What about Annys?'

'Thinking of wedding bells.'

'With Parasol Percy?'

'Who else? After all, he's got himself up to captain. I think he joined the RFC because he didn't like being shot at.'

'What makes him think you don't get shot at in the RFC? What about you?'

'Running Pa's business. Pa was asked to organise a re-mount depot near Winchester, so Mother and an old man run the stables and Annys and I run the garage. Annys does the books and looks beautiful for customers. I do all the work. She thought you were mad to go flying but when Parasol Percy went in for it, she changed her tune. You're heroes of the air nowadays. What's your next move?'

'Fighter training. We have to learn to throw aircraft about the sky.'

'And then you go to France and come home with medals jangling all over you and get your picture in the news-papers?'

'That's the idea.'

'I hope you manage it, Dicky boy.'

As it happened, so did Dicken, because he wasn't half so confident as he pretended. He'd been surprised how difficult it was to fly an aeroplane and had clutched the controls in a deathlike grip until the instructor had screeched at him to let go and hold them gently; then he'd held them as if they were made of eggshells and been told to get a grip on the bloody thing before he lost it.

His first solo had come as a surprise because he'd not thought himself at all ready for it, but he'd got the Rumpety off the ground and enjoyed the climb until at 1000 feet it had

84

suddenly dawned on him that he was lost. Flying round in circles, staring in every direction and asking himself where on earth the aerodrome had gone to, it suddenly occurred to him it might be directly beneath him and, peering anxiously over the side, he found that it was.

His first landing had been eighty feet in the air, so he had put the nose down and finally managed it after two more tries, one at forty feet and the third at eight feet. The crash as the wheels finally slammed down had almost jarred his spine loose. The instructor had appeared alongside him, smiling but shaken. 'I think, son,' he said, 'that you ought to have a few more lessons before you go solo again.'

The following week, with five hours' solo behind him on the Farman Shorthorn, he was posted to Brooklands for training on service type machines. Almost the first person he saw was Diplock. He still wore his captain's pips and was entitled to a salute but he hadn't changed much, his pale face a little plumper, his ears more protruding than ever. He was full of jealousy for the medal ribbons Dicken wore and Dicken was careful not to tell him their history.

Other officers were entering the mess now and among them Dicken recognised Hatto.

'The one with the monocle's Lord Hooe's son,' Diplock said smugly. 'No side at all. Often speaks to me.'

As Hatto bore down on them, he drew himself up, the smile fixed on his face, but Hatto merely nodded and threw an arm round Dicken's shoulder.

'Delighted to see you, old fruit,' he said.

'How's the head?'

'The quacks boarded it up safely and pronounced me fit.' Hatto tapped Dicken's chest. 'Glad to see you got something for it. They grow on you like wassail balls on a Christmas tree. You'll have so much metal on your chest soon you'll walk lopsided. Let's wet its head.' He turned to the startled Diplock. 'Have to excuse us, old fruit. Just for a minute. Things to talk about. Old friend of mine. Saved my life. Twice. Get remarkably attached to people who save your life.' He jabbed a finger at the ribbons on Dicken's chest. 'He wants to be the most decorated man in the Flying Corps and I keep trying to oblige.'

Aware of Diplock's flushed angry face, Dicken pushed to the bar.

'Who's that gadget?' Hatto asked quietly. 'He's always trying to get me into conversation. Calls me "sir". Bags of unction and dropping on one knee sort of thing.'

Dicken grinned. 'Instinct. Father's a parson.'

Hatto smiled. 'Flies a bit like a parson,' he said. 'Crash-landed in the sewage works. Nobody would speak to him for a fortnight. You'll like it here. CO's Morton.'

'What buses are you hoping for?'

'SEs or Camels. Brand new types. Good as anything the Germans have got.'

Dicken eyed him curiously. 'I'd have thought that a chap with your connections would prefer a job on the staff. After all, the staff's full of people like you.'

Hatto's face was suddenly solemn, all his humour gone. 'Not Hattos, old son,' he said. 'None of 'em are Hattos. We were blessed with privileges to start with and we always considered that was a good reason for not asking for any more.'

It said all there was to say about Hatto, why he never shirked a job and why he remained an unimportant member of a squadron when many of his contemporaries were living comfortably in safe jobs behind the line.

'All the same,' he smiled, 'you don't get born with a silver spoon in your mouth without learning to make use of it. We'll go to a squadron together.'

It was exciting to be in a mess full of men who were totally dedicated to flying. There was every kind of uniform imaginable, tartan trews, khaki slacks, the blue of the Royal Naval Air Service and the buttons of county regiments and the Guards. The men who wore them had given up their loyalties to their regiments – sometimes even their professional careers – because they felt they had to fly, and it indicated the free and easy atmosphere of a new young service, totally devoid of the stuffiness of the army or the navy.

They were all young, mostly boys fresh from school because maturity wasn't wanted in fighters, only good eyesight and quick reflexes, and for the most part they were flying not because they wanted to win the war but because they'd been caught up by the new fangled art and it set them apart. To a man, they were convinced of the future of aviation – even, Dicken supposed, Diplock, who must have felt something for it or he wouldn't have applied for a pilot's course.

The talk was all of take-offs and landings and in every corner men were making movements with their hands to indicate what they'd done with aeroplanes. Like sailors, they had a special quality and a special presence, and the newspapers had not been slow to notice it. Though they jeered at the articles they read, they enjoyed the references to 'death dives' and 'loops' and 'Immelmann rolls', which could always be guaranteed to get the girls.

The RFC was suddenly news. Aviation was still virtually a mystical cult restricted to those who took part in it and journalists had discovered there were stories in these young men who flew. Though Ball was dead, there were new heroes for the public to enjoy – McCudden, Mannock and a Canadian called Bishop – and the references to 'intrepid airmen' and 'gallant fliers', which grew with the talk of dog-fighting and aerial battles above the clouds, tended to make the men who flew take advantage of the lack of knowledge of the men who questioned them.

Flying an Avro with an instructor, Dicken found himself forced down by an unexpected fog and, though the instructor took over the landing, they managed to crumple a wing tip against an unseen stake. Immediately a man with a notebook appeared on the scene.

'Why did it crash?' he demanded.

'That damned observer,' the instructor said, indicating Dicken. 'Overstoking. I told him to stop but he just went on shovelling it on and the fire went out and the water went off the boil.'

To everybody's delight, the story appeared word for word in the local newspaper.

There was a certain amount of truth in the statement, however, because overstoking *could* be said to be one of the hazards of flying an Avro. Since the motor was either shut off or at full throttle, the pilot had no control over the speed, and it was sometimes necessary to ease the fuel lever back to stop the mixture becoming too rich. If it were, the machine trailed black smoke, which the pilot couldn't see, then frightened him to death by giving a despairing cough and cutting out. The corrective action was to close the fuel lever and wait ten seconds but most beginners were too nervous to wait that long and opened after five, which merely accentuated the problem, resulting in a forced landing with the student in such a fret he hadn't selected a suitable field and found himself at 400 feet in no position to land and with no idea which way the wind was blowing.

Dicken still had a long way to go. His landings were enough to make everyone shudder and more than once the ambulance was turned out as he came in. Though he managed to survive without smashing any aeroplanes, nobody could have called him the world's best pilot close to the ground.

'I think some swine winds the bloody field up or down as I come in,' he complained.

'Shouldn't worry, old son,' Hatto said. 'On my first go on an Avro, I flew through a greenhouse. Pickin' bits of glass out of my face for days after.'

On the day he was due to go solo on the Avro, he screwed up his courage, determined to make no mistake, only to find at the last minute as he was reaching for his flying clothing that all training flights had been cancelled for an unexpected visit by a member of the royal family who, accompanied by assorted senior officers dazzling in red tabs, was to be treated to a display by what was considered to be a specialised and highly skilled flight.

Nowadays, not only were they being taught to fly, they were also being taught to fly in that highly dangerous fashion known as 'in formation'. The Germans had discovered that by flying in large numbers, layer on layer, they could overwhelm the opposition so that the British were being forced to adopt the same tactics, and the formation flew across the field, closely tucked in one behind each other to show their skill, wings overlapping in a way that seemed to Dicken to be totally useless because there wasn't an inch of room to manoeuvre.

'Rather a ragged formation, sir,' one of the bigwigs said modestly.

'Oh, it's meant to be a formation, is it?' Dicken heard the royal personage reply, a little blankly. 'I thought they were having a race.'

The flight leader was showing off a little and as they passed the spot where the visiting bigwigs stood, surrounded by privileged civilians and the lesser mortals of the RFC, he threw into the performance an unannounced turn of his own. As he swung to the right the man behind him flew into his tail and, even from the ground, they could hear the crunch of the propeller chewing away at wood and fabric, then both aeroplanes dropped out of the sky in uneven jerky swoops to slam to the earth just in front of the royal presence. As everybody started running and the ambulance and fire engine howled across the field, the visitors were hurriedly stuffed into staff cars and driven away. The flight leader stepped from the debris unhurt but the man who'd flown into him was carted off in the ambulance spraying blood in all directions.

Training started again even as the wreckage was being cleared and Dicken was ordered to take up the Avro at once. With the ambulance barely out of sight it was an unnerving prospect.

Diplock was standing in the hangar entrance. He had finished his course as a steady if unimaginative pilot and was enjoying the fact that Dicken appeared to be anything but.

'Don't break anything,' he called out.

His face set and grim, Dicken didn't reply. New Avros had a cruising speed of around seventy miles an hour but new ones rarely reached the hands of a learner and an old one with soggy fabric on the wings, oil-soaked fabric on the fuselage, dents in the cowlings and a near-time-expired engine would be lucky to do much over sixty. However, it was a forgiving aeroplane and, despite the fact that the rotary engine seemed to vomit flames from the open exhaust ports and spray fuel in all directions, it seldom caught fire after a crash and men had been known to step unharmed from the debris of what had appeared to be an appalling crash.

Hatto was standing by the machine to see him off. 'Take your time and go steady,' he advised, 'But let us know if anything terrible's about to happen. It's considered very anti-social not to call your friends from the hangar in time to view the spectacle.'

Taking off in an unsteady fashion, Dicken climbed to 9000 feet. The sun was sinking and to the east night was approaching like a shadow lifting over the edge of the earth. The ground below was a dim blueish patchwork of fields with here and there the ribbons of roads, dark patches of woodland and the glint of water. The last of the sun was touching the edges of the wings and the curve of the fuselage with a red glow so that they seemed on fire.

For the first time, listening to the beat of the big brass-bound propeller, Dicken became really aware of the magic of what he was doing. He was sitting on a wickerwork seat two miles above the ground, so high in the cold purity of the air that he could see the curve of the earth. Nothing held him there but the throbbing motor and the slender wood and fabric wings that stretched away on either side of him. Startled at his discovery, he studied the machine, wondering what sorcery enabled it to remain suspended in the air. The fabric of the wings was rippling and drumming in the slipstream, the machine was nosing up and down, and all around him there was a smell of petrol, hot oil and dope, and he was nothing but a speck in the sky, separate yet totally alive. He was so high he felt he was touching the face of Heaven, and suddenly, exhilarated beyond belief, he laughed and yelled at the top of his voice, full of exaltation and delight. 'Oh, God,' he shouted. 'Let me do this for the rest of my life!'

In sheer joy, he pushed the stick forward until the wires screamed then, shutting his eyes and gently pulling the stick back until it rested against his belly, he held it in that position until the wires screamed once more. Opening his eyes, he found he had done a loop and out of sheer joy promptly did three more and began to fling the machine about the sky as if he were mad, chasing his own shadow across the clouds. Tight turns, rolls, dives and zooms followed until he was down to four thousand feet and could see tiny figures outside the hangar watching him. Though he knew he was almost too low, he tried another loop, but this time the engine failed on the climb and on the top he found the forces which held him in weren't working so that he was hanging in his straps with air between his trousers and the seat.

As his feet left the rudder bar, he clutched frantically at the joystick, all his elation gone. Out loud, he shouted, 'My God, I'm falling out!' but, while he was still yelling with fear, his clutch on the joystick wrenched the machine over so that he dropped neatly back into the seat and the nose of the machine was pointing earthwards once more. Without realising he was in a spin, he automatically put the controls in the opposite direction to stop it and the earth stopped whirling as the machine steadied.

Frightened silly, he put as much distance between himself and the earth as he could, then, levelling off, looked nervously round again. The circle of fire that was the sun had gone and a cluster of rays lifted to the heavens like a fan, turning a scrap of cirrus into gold dust against a jade sky. But it was suddenly colder, below him the aerodrome was fading into a mauve light, and he could see mist creeping across the fields. Christ, he thought, I must hurry.

In his haste he did a vertical bank over the sheds and scuttled earthwards in a tight spiral. At a thousand feet he pulled out, gave the engine a nervous burst to check that it was still functioning and made his way back over the sewage farm, his mind full of the warnings of his instructor. Assuming that the engine failure had been caused by a too-rich mixture, he eased the fuel lever back, but the exact position depended on speed, height, pressure, the aeroplane's attitude in the sky and a host of other things and, worried sick, he decided he wasn't experienced enough to be a very good judge and merely made a blind stab at it.

Positioning himself carefully, making sure he hadn't done anything wrong because it was fatally easy to close the fuel lever and then forget it, at the last moment he opened it again. Immediately and quite unexpectedly, there were two loud bangs which frightened the life out of him and the engine came on again at full throttle so that, instead of being in danger of landing in the sewage farm, he was in danger of being carried to the far end of the field and through the hedge. Imagining the embarrassment and the amount of repairs that would ensue, in a panic he closed the lever once more and to his horror found he was now undershooting again. Instead of crashing through the far hedge, he crashed through the near hedge –fortunately at a point where it was thin – bounced on to the thick grass on the perimeter of the field and ran to a stop just on the take off and landing area. As he looked at the torn fabric of the wings, he decided he could say goodbye to flying.

*

As he waited outside Morton's office, Diplock appeared from the orderly room.

'Hard lines,' he said, smiling. 'They don't go much on people breaking aeroplanes.'

Dicken wondered what it would be like flying BEs. He'd had enough of BEs and wanted no more of them. But people who bent aircraft or landed them eighty feet up or outside the aerodrome perimeter – and he'd done all three – couldn't expect to go to a fighter squadron. He couldn't make out why, since it required just as much skill to land a two-seater, probably more because they were bigger and heavier and less manoeuvrable.

The Recording Officer put his head round the door and beckoned him in. In front of the commanding officer's desk, he listened to the report he'd written being read out aloud. Not only did it seem to condemn him utterly, it didn't even seem to be well written. As the Recording Officer finished, Morton sat with his fingers together in the form of a steeple, and standing stiffly at attention, Dicken waited for sentence to be passed. For a long time, Morton said nothing, then he looked up, an amused glint in his eye.

'Do you always land like that?' he asked.

'I try not to, sir,' Dicken stammered.

'I should hope not. It was less of a landing than an arrival, and it's always better to run into the far hedge rather than the near one if you have to run into a hedge at all. By the time you've crossed the field your speed's rather less and you do less damage. Try to remember that.'

'Yes, sir.' Dicken waited, wondering when the chopper was going to fall.

'That was quite a remarkable bit of flying you did up there,' Morton went on conversationally. 'Do you think you could do it all the time?'

'When I'm up I'm fine, sir,' Dicken said miserably. 'It's getting down that bothers me.'

Morton scratched his nose. 'Well, I think that will come in time and, after all, it's one of Bishop's little problems, too. Despite the suggestion that you should go to a two-seater squadron, I'm putting you in for single-seaters with the rest. It seems much fairer to let you take a chance on killing yourself on your own than make an innocent observer share your fate.'

*

Hatto decided they should go up to London to celebrate.

'How about it?' he said to Dicken. 'Set the place alight a bit. Might even see a Gotha or two. The old Hun sends 'em over regularly these days. Can't think why. They never seem to hit much.'

He had a large open tourer with a square snout and headlamps like searchlights and they rolled towards London together, Dicken in a seventh heaven of delight. He'd avoided BEs, he liked Hatto and Hatto seemed to like him, and it was flattering to be liked by a nobleman's son, especially as he knew it filled Diplock's mind with worms of jealousy.

They picked up two girls Hatto knew, gorgeous creatures Dicken considered way out of his class because they wore dresses which would have startled even Zoë Toshack, and had accents from the best schools and titles that belonged to great families.

'Good sports,' Hatto whispered. 'Do a lot for charity. Hired 'em out the Avro when they had a garden party during the summer. Landed in the field next door on a cross-country and charged a bob a nob to sit in the cockpit. Even took a few up at five bob a go. RFC never noticed and it raised a quid or two for the widows and orphans.'

They ate at the Café Royal, feeling luxurious and faintly

93

lecherous in the fin de siècle atmosphere of red plush, mirrors and gilt, and after *The Maid of the Mountains* at Daly's, scrambled into the tourer, Dicken swamped beneath the two girls while Hatto drove towards the Ritz.

Everybody there seemed to be thoroughly enjoying the war and a few Americans who had crossed into Canada and sworn they were Canadians were giving an extra impetus to the drinking. To Dicken's surprise, Diplock was there with Annys, who, he had to admit, was looking more beautiful even than usual. As Hatto offered introductions all round, he saw her eyebrows lift a little at the names of the two girls. She'd obviously seen their pictures in one of the society papers.

While they were talking, the air raid buzzers went and the laughing crowd dissolved into a shrieking mob. A woman with a high-class accent and a bust like a frigate under full sail turned to Hatto, red with indignation, a fat finger pecking at his wings.

'Why aren't you up there?' she yelled. 'Driving those swine away!'

Hatto gave her a little bow. 'Sorry, Madame,' he said. 'My mother warned me not to talk to strange women in the street.'

As the mob poured into the foyer, Dicken and the two girls headed for the Underground. The platforms were crowded with people, some of them already equipped with mattresses and rugs. When the air raid stopped, Hatto said he knew where a party was being held and they all scrambled back into the tourer and headed for a flat in Baker Street. A gramophone was playing for dancing, but nobody seemed to be taking any notice and there was a great deal of noise as everybody tried to shout everybody else down.

Champagne seemed to be flowing in bucketfuls and Dicken remembered nothing of what happened next until he woke up in a bed that wasn't his own and smelled faintly of perfume. Sitting up, startled, he saw one of the girls alongside him, fast asleep with her head on the next pillow. He'd been warned many times by his mother not 'to bring trouble home,' and this, he decided, was trouble with a capital T.

He was just knotting his tie when the girl turned over, opened her eyes and beamed at him. 'Hello, Dicky darling,' she said. 'You were so sweet.'

Dicken didn't enquire what at but he had a pretty shrewd idea. 'Where are the other two?' he asked.

'Willie took Caroline home. After that I don't know. Do you think you could make me some black coffee? I think I had too much to drink.'

Making his escape as fast as he could, Dicken headed for the Ritz bar. Hatto was leaning against the counter, looking pale.

'What happened to you?' Dicken asked accusingly.

'Kissed Caroline good night on the doorstep and went to the old family home to sleep. What about you?'

'I took Maud home.'

'And stayed?' Hatto's wan expression cheered up. 'I ought to have warned you. She's rather hot stuff.' He looked at Dicken's alarmed visage. 'Is it the first time?'

'Yes.'

'No need to blush. Comes to us all in the end. I think we ought to be getting back.'

They drove slowly to Brooklands, Hatto with his jaw clenched and his eyes narrow as though his head hurt. Diplock met them in the mess.

'Postings are through,' he said.

Hatto and Dicken eyed each other, then they made a dash for the notice board. 'France,' Hatto said. 'Ste. Marie-le-Petit.' He slapped Dicken on the shoulder. 'What are they flying there?'

After the names of the squadrons there was a code of symbols with the answers to it below.

'Says Sopwiths. Must be Camels.'

'No, they're not,' Diplock said. 'They're One-and-a-half Strutters. Two-seaters. I'm going there, too.'

Dicken and Hatto stared at each other.

'Two-seaters?' Dicken said. 'You said we were going on to fighters.'

Hatto frowned. 'Something must have gone wrong. Hang on, I'll find out what happened.'

He disappeared into one of the offices where he bribed the

clerk with half-a-crown to let him use the telephone. He returned looking shaken.

'It's true,' he said. 'We were *all* to have gone to single-seaters, but it seems they've been losing two-seater crews so fast in France, they had to change their minds.'

2

The aerodrome was close to the cluster of one storey houses that formed the village of Ste. Marie-le-Petit. There was a church, a mairie, two farms and a public washplace, whose approach was a sea of mud tinted grey with the curdled suds that escaped from a huge stone sink.

Almost the first person Dicken saw as the tender stopped was Handiside, now a sergeant.

'Hello,' Dicken said. 'I see you've got your third.'

'And I see they've made you into a gentleman at last, sir.' They grinned together. 'They can give a man a pip any time, sir, but it takes time to become a sergeant.'

The landing area was a square field surrounded by every imaginable obstacle to getting in safely, though the hedges had been cut away at the ends so that if an aeroplane overshot it could run through into the next field. Bessoneau hangars ballooned in a strong wind from the east alongside a road to the front, which was being strengthened and widened by a regiment of pioneers who dug and hacked along its length, accompanied by rumbling lorries and puffing steam-rollers. The grass was scored by wheels and the marks of tail skids, and outside the hangars a line of graceful machines stood, quivering in the wind. A hammer clanked on metal, drowned occasionally by the hissing crackle of a radial engine being tested at the other side of the end hangar.

The squadron offices and buildings consisted entirely of Nissen huts, tents and square wooden boxes that looked like chicken houses, and the mess was an ugly shed like a portable stable with a stove that rattled every time the guns near the lines fired. As they took their places for their first meal, Dicken was conscious of the gloomy silence. A firm believer in evading boredom, Hatto made a few attempts at conversation, but they were not sustained by anyone else.

'Petrifaction's set in,' he whispered.

The dish was some sort of stew and he peered at it suspiciously, poking at the lumps of meat with his fork.

'Wonder if it was dead before it got in,' he murmured. 'Or whether the stew killed it.'

Halfway through the meal, the squadron commander, a major called Rivers, arrived. He wore the DSO and had been badly injured in a crash in 1915. He limped heavily and had a stiff arm, so that Dicken wondered if, when the war was over, there'd be anything left but wreckage – wreckage of buildings, wreckage of machinery, and wreckage of human beings. As he made for the empty chair at the head of the table everybody rose but he waved without a word to them to be seated. The Recording Officer introduced Hatto and Dicken.

'You one of the Northamptonshire Hattos?' the Major asked.

'Yes, sir.'

'Knew your father. Senior to me in the Lancers.'

That was all. He barely looked at Dicken.

'Hardly the type to halt moral disintegration after a disaster,' Hatto murmured as they returned to their seats. 'As inspiring, in fact, as if he'd said it was a wet day.'

An observer called Almonde explained. 'Doesn't like sending people up to get killed,' he said. 'Especially as he's been grounded.'

Diplock had not arrived with them. He had slipped climbing from the Avro on the last day of their stay at the flying school and sprained his ankle, and it meant that Hatto and Dicken moved into a small room in one of the Nissen huts with a man called Walter Calthrop Foote. Over his bed Dicken hung a picture of that Lady Maud he'd taken to bed in London when he'd been too much under the influence of drink to appreciate the fact. It was a studio portrait she'd sent him and she looked serene with a tranquillity he hadn't noticed when he'd been with her.

Foote was a tall man with crisp curling blond hair, a transatlantic accent, and a wide friendly smile.

'You Canadian?' Hatto asked.

Foote grinned. 'Officially. Actually I'm from Boston. I crossed the border, told 'em I was born in Toronto, and I was in before you could say "Jack Robinson".'

'Why don't you join your own air force?' Dicken asked. 'America's in the war now.'

Foote grinned. 'Not likely,' he said. 'There are guys back home who talk of making the skies of Europe black with American planes. They haven't got a one yet. For once, we're years behind Europe.'

'They'd probably make you a colonel.'

Foote laughed. 'The guys they're making colonels back home have been sitting behind desks so long the ass of their pants is shiny.'

It seemed that Foote had a younger brother who also wanted to join the RFC.

'How many Feete are there in your family?' Hatto asked.

Foote grinned. 'Three kids. I've got an older sister, May, who married a newspaper proprietor. We call her Foote Print. Then there's me and my brother Albert. He's left-handed and I'm right-handed, so May calls us Right Foote and Left Foote. I think he's crazy. I've told him to stay out of the war where it's safe but he won't listen. Rats, I keep telling him there's already one of the family laying his neck on the line; it doesn't need two. Strutters are hardly God's gift to an airman.' He shrugged. 'They're supposed to be fighters and have the same engines as Camels but they're bigger and carry two men and don't have the same performance. Be careful of the brakes.'

'Brakes? They've got *brakes?*'

Foote smiled again. 'To slow you down as you come in to land. There's a wheel on the left of the cockpit and if you turn it, it lifts a set of surfaces on the lower wing. They're supposed to make landing safer but actually they cause so much turbulence over the tail it's safer to forget 'em. So you either approach very slowly, or arrive at normal speed and swish your tail about. But you've got to be pretty expert, because the undercarriage's been specially designed to collapse at the earliest opportunity.'

'You seem to know all about 'em,' Hatto said. 'How long have you been flying 'em?'

'Just long enough to tell *you* about 'em. I came out last week.'

*

The mess was no more cheerful when the evening meal came round.

'Is it always like this?' Hatto asked.

'I guess so,' Foote murmured. 'The major fractured his skull badly, and had to be trepanned. Mebbe the pan's rusty.'

Dicken was looking about him. 'I think they're all tired,' he said.

'Mebbe they are,' Foote agreed. 'Tired of each other. Tired of the war. Tired of flying Strutters.'

After the meal the mess settled into the same gloom as before, but eventually Foote produced a gramophone, new, up-to-date and with all the latest gadgets. It was his own and he guarded it jealously. He had a whole pile of records which included all the sickly-sweet nostalgic songs they played over and over again to remind them of home and, though they were a little scratched through being around too long, at least they drowned the silence.

There was also an impromptu band consisting of three men who could play a fiddle, a trombone and a piano, and they actually managed to lift the mood a little with *Chu Chin Chow* and *Maid of The Mountains* and a few of the dolefully humorous songs like 'The Dying Airman's Lament' and 'The Ballad of R. Suppards'.

Finally Hatto found his way to the piano and got everybody yelling 'If You Were the Only Girl in The World', 'They Wouldn't Believe Me' and songs from the London shows.

'Well brought up,' he explained. 'Paint, play an instrument, and ride a horse.'

Towards the end of the evening, Dicken was informed by a pale-faced captain called Dunne that he was in A Flight and was taken out to the hangar where the mechanics were still working on the machines by the light of hurricane lamps. His experience as an observer made Dunne wary of him. He didn't have to be shown the ropes, had learned a few of the tricks of the trade, and couldn't be fobbed off with untruths.

'Better get some practice,' Dunne advised. 'Strutters need careful handling. They're out of date and underpowered and we haven't a chance against the new German fighters.'

During the next few days, in a sky busy with aeroplanes, Dicken went up several times to familiarise himself with the area. When he was turned loose on his own, the observers came out to watch, but his landings didn't seem to impress them very much, especially when he broke a few wires and bent an axle. Told to land more slowly, he floated over the squadron office and a Strutter parked in front and was just congratulating himself that he'd done it right for a change when he was called to the CO's office.

'I don't mind you risking your own machine,' he was told sharply. 'But it's too much when you're likely to damage not only other machines but my office as well.'

The squadron didn't seem a particularly resilient one. Under the regulations which prohibited squadron commanders flying over the line, Rivers, who was a reserved type at best, was thoroughly unhappy, and his unhappiness found its way down through the other ranks.

Handiside added to the gloom. 'They've got a new fighter over there,' he pointed out, cocking a thumb towards the east. 'Albatros.'

'That's not new,' Dicken said.

'This one is. It's an improved version with V-struts. If you see one, watch out for yourself. We've been having a lot of casualties.'

The first of these occurred a week after Dicken arrived. The 110-horsepower Clerget engines in the 1½-Strutters could produce a top speed of no more than 95 miles an hour and at 10,000 feet no more than 80 miles an hour. In addition, they'd been heavily overworked and were in the habit of developing minor troubles during flight, which left the crews without the comforting thought that they could rely on them in an emergency. Valve springs, valve rockers and ignition wires broke regularly; oil pumps were often defective and there had even been a rash of blown cylinders. When a man called Hanover failed with his observer to return after a patrol, with Hatto as his companion, Hatto let it be known quite clearly that he hadn't been shot down but had been forced to land behind the German lines because he'd been let down by the people in England who had given him a 1½-Strutter to fly.

'Rivers seemed to think I was uttering a blasphemy,' he told Dicken as he appeared in the hut with a flea in his ear.

There was another casualty three days later. One of the machines came in with flying and aileron balance wires shot away, both tyres punctured, a longeron cut almost in half, wings and fuselage badly holed, the pilot's flying cap ripped by a bullet and a dead observer in the rear cockpit. His eyes stricken and shuddering with shock, the pilot said he'd been attacked by Siemens-Schuckerts.

'They looked like bloody Nieuports,' he said, almost weeping with rage. 'I didn't bother to take evasive action. It was only when the bastards swung away that I saw they had crosses on the wings. By that time, the bloody machine was like a colander and poor old –' he stopped, choking '– he was dead.'

The following week yet another aeroplane failed to return and as the new pilots appeared Dicken found himself accepted as an old hand. But, looking around him at the grave wisdom in the young-old faces, he already found it hard to distinguish the old hands from the recent new-comers.

Patrols were divided into offensive, defensive and line patrols. Offensive patrols operated ten miles beyond the German lines, defensive patrols four miles beyond, and line patrols directly above. As they became absorbed into the squadron, he and Hatto were allocated regular observers. Dicken's was an ex-cavalryman called Slattery, who was like a stage Irishman with his wildness, his uproarious be-haviour, his strong accent, and the strangled Irish tenor he liked to use in the mess. On only the third trip they flew together, Dicken was aware of a feeling of foreboding even before they set off. During the previous day, he had broken his mirror and, though he tried hard to convince himself he didn't believe in omens, nothing could alter the fact that it was 1917 and he was still alive when a lot of his friends were dead.

They crossed the lines near Lille at 6000 feet beneath high cirro-cumulus that looked like a fan, and flew through the normal anti-aircraft barrage over Quesnoy until they reached 10,000 feet. In the east there was a pyramid of cumulus, clear and creamy-white as an iceberg in the sun, and, deafened by the hissing crackle of the engine, Dicken slipped between the clefts and gorges, caught by the beauty about him. The sky seemed empty, without a German aircraft to be seen, and after two hours they turned towards the British lines. As they swung back they saw the white puffs of British anti-aircraft shells in the sky which indicated that somewhere in the vicinity there were German machines.

Underpowered and obsolescent, the 1½-Strutter laboured upwards until near Messines Slattery pointed and Dicken saw a German two-seater approaching above the shell bursts. Because the Strutter was already at the limit of its power, it was impossible to lift the nose and the only alternative was to fly beneath the German so that Slattery could use the rear Lewis.

Expecting the anti-aircraft gunners to stop firing as usual when a British machine moved to the attack, they ignored the shell bursts, but the gunners obviously considered they could do better than a man in an aeroplane and, even as Slattery lined up his gun and fired a long burst, Dicken felt the machine shudder and saw the white smoke of a British shell drifting away alongside.

He was glaring over the side of the fuselage at the ground as if he could indicate his annoyance to the gunners when it dawned on him that the machine was no longer completely under control. It was swooping down in a long curving dive and he heard Slattery yelling with fright. Swinging round, wondering what had happened, he saw the German machine they had attacked falling away, trailing fragments of broken wing, and Slattery, his jaw hanging open, pointing towards their tail.

Glancing over his shoulder, he saw that one of the elevators was hanging off and fluttering behind on a length of control wire. The shell which had just burst above them had torn it off, leaving him with little control. As he struggled to pull the machine out of its dive, a second shell removed what was left.

As he fought to bring the machine's nose up, it slowly began to turn, then fell over into another dive. Slattery had stopped shouting and, wondering what had happened to him, Dicken saw him clinging on with both hands, his eyes wide, his mouth hanging open, his cheeks ballooned by the wind. Shot down by their own bloody artillery! Great bloody Ned, what a fine way to go to war!

They were still falling, neither of them hurt but both hanging on like grim death to avoid falling out.

'Do something,' Slattery was shrieking above the wailing of the wind through the wires.

The machine steered its erratic course downwards towards the clouds and they found themselves surrounded by grey mist that fled past them like smoke. The string that Dicken had tied on the centre section struts to indicate the plane's attitude when he couldn't see the horizon for mist, was standing out at right angles to the fuselage so that he knew the machine was in a side-slip. As she levelled off on her own there was a bang near the tail that jerked his head round.

'Ammunition drums,' Slattery shrieked. 'They've rolled down inside the fuselage.'

With the engine silent it was possible to shout to each other over the whine of the wires and the one thing that stood out in Dicken's mind was the fact that for the first time they could hold a conversation but that the only thing it concerned was their approaching end. Slattery's burst of profanity reached lyrical proportions.

How long they had been falling, Dicken had no idea, but as they burst out of the cloud the gunners opened up again immediately.

'The stupid bastards must think we're a Hun,' Slattery yelled.

His heart in his mouth, still wrestling with the controls in the hope that somehow they would knit together and they could creep home, Dicken found himself calmly wondering how much longer they could expect to survive.

Then, at two hundred feet the Strutter's nose lifted without any effort from Dicken. She stalled, then swooped into another dive and, as the earth rushed up, Dicken braced himself. But, just as they were about to hit the ground, the nose lifted again entirely of its own accord and she was almost level when the wheels struck a hedge. There was a crash as the machine stood on its nose then it flopped back to a horizontal position, the wings crumpled around it.

Crawling slowly out, dazed, shocked and emotionally spent, Dicken saw Slattery lying in the grass, his face covered with blood.

'You all right, Paddy?'

'Just a dose bleed. Bashed it od the bloody gud.'

Dicken sat up. 'I'm going to find that blasted gunner and get an explanation,' he said.

Slattery's face darkened. '*I'b* going to putch hib id the bloody dose so *he* cad see what it feels like.'

*

They actually tried very hard, and in their rage and the excitement of shooting down a German aeroplane – from a 1½-Strutter too! – they forgot their fright.

Rivers gave them several days off to recover and, instead of dwelling on their descent, they toured up and down the front on a motor cycle in a black fury to find the culprit. Nobody was admitting anything, however, and either through guilt or sympathy, responded to their enquiries by regaling them with whisky. When Slattery ran the motor cycle into a ditch it no longer seemed to matter and they concentrated instead on finding the German aircraft they'd shot down. It had fallen near Ploegsteert and they drove as near as they were permitted, left the motor cycle with a field gun battery and went forward on foot.

It was lying on its side, one wing starkly in the air. The Maltese crosses and the machine's number had already been cut from the fabric for souvenirs and there was little left but the skeleton, a broken mass of splintered spars and struts covered with fabric that was torn into small flags flapping in the cold wind.

The day was sunless and Dicken looked upwards at the ice-white sky. This mass of wreckage had fallen from up there, a victim of Slattery's gun and his own small skill as a pilot. There had been two men in it and all that remained of them was under the soil nearby, two graves marked only with the broken blades of the propeller. Someone had hung a notice on them. 'Unknown German aviator.' That was all.

Looking round at Slattery, Dicken saw his face was white and bleak and touched with pity. For the first time it had dawned on them what they had so narrowly missed.

3

Summer trudged its way onwards in a bloody swathe of dead men and wrecked machines. There was plenty of courage but none of it the sort that produced medals. The 1½-Strutters were long past their prime and every day seemed to bring a disaster of some sort. As men came and went, the character of the squadron changed and, because casualties were heavy, the change came at times with heartbreaking abruptness. Slattery vanished, then the piano-player, then the violinist.

Finally the trombonist disappeared. That night there was a binge in the mess, chiefly to hide the barely hidden fear that lay behind the façade of noise. Hatto's piano playing was twice as noisy as usual and the song twice as lively. The trombonist's observer returned in the middle of it, his arm in a sling, his face pale and strained.

'Poor bastard looks like a ghost,' Foote commented.

'We've all been ghosts for a long time,' Hatto said quietly.

They had been shot down in No Man's Land and the observer had managed, despite a shoulder broken in the crash, to escape.

'Did you bring the watch back?' Rivers asked and the observer gave him a sullen shrug, incensed that all he could think of was to complain that he hadn't.

Rivers could have done a lot to help but he was past his best and the flight commanders were all privately praying they could last long enough to go home, all of them when they thought no one was looking wearing an expression that told of a mixture of strain and outrage that had come from seeing too many of their friends disappear.

If they had arrived at a bad time, Diplock arrived at a worse one. As he entered the mess, he looked nervous and ill at ease.

'Your parson friend,' Hatto observed. Then, seeing Diplock's uncertainty and Rivers' indifference, he deliberately left the table, rose and approached with his hand out.

'Hello, old man,' he said warmly. 'Nice to see you again. Dick Quinney's here, too. It's almost home from home.'

Diplock began to smile and Hatto took him round the table, introducing him, so that even the major had to acknowledge his arrival. For the first time, Dicken realised how much he liked Hatto, and just how much store he set by duty and decency.

Shamed by his efforts, Dicken also went out of his way and, calling in Diplock's room, he made sure he had everything he needed. Diplock was grateful but as he started unpacking he took out a photograph of Annys and placed it on the locker alongside his bed with what appeared to be a deliberate attempt to show off.

'How is she?' Dicken asked.

'Oh, fine,' Diplock said. 'Fine. Zoë's working on the aerodrome at Shoreham now. There are quite a lot of women mechanics there these days. They got a man who's been invalided out of the Service Corps for the garage. She was getting bored with it, of course. She's not got Annys's staying power, you know. She's going round with a Canadian at the moment.'

It fell to Dicken to show him the lines. The experience seemed to depress him.

'You'd better get in as much practice as you can,' Dicken advised. 'They'll not let you go into action until you do.'

Diplock seemed in no hurry and, as Hatto had said, though he was a safe pilot he seemed to fly as if he were driving a bus. There was no flair to his handling of a machine; it was almost as if he were remembering the rule book all the time, instead of having an instinct for it. He made no effort to practise and in the end Dicken was told to tell him that he'd better get on with it because he was needed. By this time, Dicken had a suspicion that his lack of haste was because he'd suddenly decided wartime flying wasn't all it was cracked up to be.

A fortnight after his arrival, one of the machines returning from a photographic reconnaissance was seen to be coming in too fast and the old hands appeared in front of the hangar, aware already that something was wrong. As it drew nearer, they saw wires loose and flaps of fabric fluttering in the wing and the rudder at an odd angle.

It struck the ground in too steep a descent, bounced into the air, came down again, bounced once more, then slewed round in a ground loop that wrenched off the undercarriage. Immediately everybody set off running.

The pilot had been badly hit and was barely conscious, and Almonde, the observer, stumbled from the wreckage, white-faced and shaking. As the ambulance came tearing up, the pilot was lifted from the cockpit and placed inside. As it roared away, Almonde dragged his flying cap from his flattened hair and wiped the oil from his face.

'He was hit over Dickebusch,' he said. 'Three Albatroses attacked us. But he flew her all the way back because we'd got our photographs. I don't suppose anybody'll thank him.'

Hatto refused to allow them to sink into gloom and, sitting himself at the piano, began to pound the keys. When they were all feeling better, he nodded towards Diplock sitting in a corner of the mess, brooding and glum.

'I think our friend Parasol Percy's having doubts,' he murmured. 'Think he's suddenly not all that keen on flying.'

It was not entirely unexpected that the following day Diplock reported sick with pains in his head.

'Crack on the skull I got with the Service Corps at Ypres,' he explained.

He managed to get away with another fortnight on the ground while the doctor from Wing examined him, then he was reported fit again and almost at once, as though he were determined not to let him escape again, Dunne put his name down for a photographic line patrol with him.

Half an hour after they had taken off, Diplock was back complaining about loss of pressure.

'Couldn't get her up,' he complained.

That night, as he prepared his machine for the next day, Dicken found Handiside alongside him.

'There wasn't anything wrong, you know, sir,' he murmured. 'The fitter told me so. He worked like mad on it and he couldn't find anything at all.'

Two days later, Diplock flew a line patrol with Dicken, both machines taking photographs.

'Watch him,' Foote murmured as Dicken dragged on his flying cap.

Climbing into the cockpit, Dicken wriggled himself into his seat, checked the controls and looked at his instruments. The waiting air mechanic called out.

'Switch off. Petrol on. Suck in.'

The propeller was turned to dribble away excess petrol, then the mechanic wiped his hands, scraped his boots on the ground to make sure of his foothold and, leaning forward, his hands resting on the propeller, tried his balance.

'Contact!'

The magneto switches clicked.

'Contact.'

The engine coughed to life, seemed in some doubt, then caught and began to roar. Inside the cockpit, his head down to listen for vibration, Dicken watched the revolution indicator and the fuel-tank air pressure dial. He glanced at Diplock then, with a wave, the chocks were dragged away. Taxiing across the field, blipping the engine, everything on the machine rattling, he turned into wind. As he began to gather speed, he pushed the stick forward to bring the tail up to a flying attitude, lifted her into the air, keeping close to the earth until the speed built up, then began to soar upwards, climbing quickly.

The sky was clear and immensely blue, a long cloudscape away in the west like the edge of a polar ice barrier, white, blue, purple, pink, yellow and green. To the north it was possible to see England, the comforting ditch of green sea separating it from France. The white cliffs were easily visible and it was clear enough to see the Isle of Wight. In the Channel a convoy of tiny ships moved.

The ground was ashen-looking, the lines to the south-east like the trail of a giant slug in an erratic course across France, the smoke of an artillery barrage hanging in the air, dirty-brown as if it were diseased. As it disappeared behind them, the German anti-aircraft fire started. The shells were wide of the mark, but glancing sideways, Dicken saw that Diplock had swerved wildly in a wide half-circle.

As he regained his position, more shells arrived, and Dicken smelled the smoke as he passed through it. Diplock had again swung in a wide circle.

'Come back, you ass!' Dicken yelled furiously. 'They're nowhere near you!'

As it happened, the anti-aircraft guns were particularly good that day and the next crack forced the tail up, sent the nose down and caused the Strutter to swerve and sideslip. When Dicken looked up, Diplock was again moving away in a wide circle. In a fury, Dicken climbed up to him and, gesturing angrily, signalled him to stay close.

Reaching the lines, they separated and as Dicken began to circle to the north, Almonde, his observer, bent over the camera, Diplock began to circle to the south, so that the strips of photographs would overlap. As they turned, Dicken kept his eyes moving about the sky. Photo-reconnaissances brought most of their casualties because the Strutters had been designed as two-seater fighters, and it was considered unnecessary to give them an escort.

The sky seemed empty, however. Below, the country was clear in the sunshine, roads, canals, lakes and woods standing out distinctly against the patchwork. It was almost too quiet to be true and, with the experience of weeks at the work, Dicken was nervous.

'How about the photos?' he yelled to Almonde.

'Two to go!'

Turning the machine in a quiet circle, Dicken noticed that Diplock was already haring for home, his nose down, then he realised that the sporadic anti-aircraft fire had stopped and he studied the sky warily, guessing that something was wrong.

'Finished! Home sweet home!'

As Almonde's voice came, he banked and immediately saw why the firing had stopped. An Albatros was climbing up under their tail and, intent on the photography, neither Dicken nor Almonde had seen him. Sticking the nose down, he turned, diving fast, and opened fire with the forward gun. The German banked away steeply, but as he did so, he swung into Almonde's line of fire and the roar of the Lewis rose above the thunder of the engine. As the Albatros swung away, it passed within yards of them, the pilot looking up, a stare of amazement on his face, then he slowly sagged forward in the cockpit and the machine rolled over and began to fall, nose down, like a spent rocket. A wing folded back with a bang they could hear above the engine, fragments of wood and canvas breaking off and floating away. It checked the machine's descent and it began to fall more slowly, spinning round and round the broken wing like a leaf in autumn.

Almonde was hammering on the fuselage and pointing. Turning, Dicken saw two more Germans climbing to intercept him, and, pushing the nose down again, headed for home in a dive. The trenches came up under the nose and he realised he was doing almost a hundred and twenty miles an hour. Though they were in danger of tearing the wings off, at least Archie couldn't catch them and they far outdistanced the German fighters.

Diplock was outside the flight office with his observer when Dicken landed.

'Why did you shove off like that?' Dicken demanded. 'We're supposed to give each other support. I nearly got jumped.'

Diplock was suitably contrite and Dicken even began to wonder if he'd been unnecessarily harsh, but the following day he learned from Almonde that Diplock's observer had complained that he hadn't been given the time to do the job properly.

'You know,' Hatto said slowly, 'it's my view that the old Parasol's a teeny bit saffron-coloured.'

*

The summer was at its height now and there were rumours of another big push.

'I'm sick of big pushes,' Hatto said. 'They're always having big pushes. When they don't know what to do next they have a big push. All they do is cause casualties, get the general a new medal for his best suit and cause verbal diarrhoea among the war correspondents.'

The signs of a push increased until finally nine machines

from two flights were allocated to photograph the railway station at Valenciennes.

They all knew what Valenciennes meant. It lay well beyond the German aerodromes and they were going to have to fight, if not all the way there, then certainly all the way back because the new Albatros DV was beginning to appear in numbers opposite them, easily recognisable because of a distinctive rake to the tips of the upper wing and a Mercedes engine that gave an extra ten miles an hour and a better rate of climb.

The night was warm and full of stars but Dicken found he was unable to sleep. As he lay awake he could hear the minute sounds from the hangars where the mechanics were still working to make sure there were no engine failures.

'You awake?' he whispered to Hatto.

'Yes.'

'What are you thinking?'

'That here goes the last of the Hattos.'

'I'm trying *not* to think about that.'

'Me, too.' There was a long silence. 'Didn't tell you, did I? My older brother disappeared at Jutland.'

Dicken didn't know what to say.

'In *Invincible*. Staff of Admiral Hood. The Hoods were friends of ours, and the Old Man fixed it for him. Doesn't seem to have done him a lot of good. Just hope he doesn't have to mourn another tomorrow.'

*

The morning was tremendously hot with the mechanics stretched out under the wings of the machines to keep cool.

Standing by the door of the hut, holding his flying clothing, Hatto stared at the blue sky. 'Rather be in a deck chair at Slapton,' he observed.

The aeroplanes stood in line, their beauty belying their lack of power. In the east a line of captive balloons seemed to dance in a heat haze. Mail had just arrived and they stood in a group, reading their letters. There was one for Dicken from Zoë, telling him of her work at Shoreham. She seemed delighted with her luck but her letter was totally clinical. There was also a letter from the Hon. Maud, that seemed remarkably affectionate. Why she'd written out of the blue Dicken couldn't imagine and he began to wonder if he'd been missing something.

Foote was scowling at his letter. 'My kid brother's joined the Flying Corps,' he said. 'He says he's asked to be posted here. He must be crazy.'

As Rivers appeared, they gathered round him in a circle.

'You know what to do,' he said. 'Dunne and Snell will take the pictures and the rest are escort. It's your job to make sure the photographs get home. The staff think the Germans are moving up reserves and we've got to find out. I'm sorry we couldn't get an escort. I'll see the drinks are waiting.'

Nobody smiled. They pulled on their flying caps and coats and walked awkwardly to their machines. Nine crews. Nine pilots – Dunne, Foote, Hatto, Dicken, Diplock, Scarati, Roode, Johnson, Snell. Each with his observer.

'Notice the old Parasol's slap in the middle,' Foote murmured as they adjusted buckles and scarves and gloves. 'Dunne's on to that guy.'

One after the other the engines roared into life, the machines quivering and throbbing as they thrust against the chocks. As Rivers raised his hand, they moved forward one behind the other, the engines burping.

Fifty-two minutes later they had reached their height and were crossing the lines in formation, nine drab, blunt-nosed machines rising and falling alongside each other as if suspended on wires, Dicken nervously watching Roode, his next-door neighbour, who wasn't very good at formation flying and looked likely to slither into his wingtip. The sky was a vast blue bowl above their heads, cloudless and bare, but he wasn't deluded by the emptiness and his eyes roved into every corner, watching for movement. For a while, he thought they were going to get away with it, then below him he saw something move against the patterned carpet of the earth. At first it was almost indiscernible and he had to look again to make sure. This time he caught the flash of sun on varnish and knew he'd made no mistake. A small cluster of tiny specks was moving like a formation of ants and he knew it was a group of German fighters climbing to intercept them.

They were still short of their objective and he found

himself glancing ahead and then below, trying to judge whether they could do it or whether the Germans would arrive first. Dunne had clearly made up his mind, and when the anti-aircraft fire began he ignored it and drove on in a dead straight course. There was no other way and the machines clustered more closely together, because only the concentrated fire of the observers' guns could hope to hold the Germans off.

They were approaching the railway station at twelve thousand feet in tight formation when the first German reached their level three miles away, a heavy-shouldered DV screwing its way in a curve up into the sky ahead of them. It was still some distance away when a movement in the formation made Dicken's head flick to the right. One of the Strutters had fallen out of formation, leaving a gap, and he saw puffs of smoke from its exhausts as it fell below them and swung west in a long swift curve. He recognised it instantly as Diplock's.

The two photographic observers were exposing their plates now, trying to do the job quickly but carefully, bending over their cameras, the pilots flying in a dead straight line and counting the seconds so that there would be a lap-over for each exposure. By the time they'd finished the sky seemed full of Germans and, as they fell on the Strutters, the firing started.

Grim-faced, his eyes all over the sky, Dicken tried to hold his position, relying on Almonde to protect his rear. Almost immediately, Snell's machine began to drop below the formation as the engine was hit and at once two Albatroses fastened on its tail. Two seconds later it was spiralling downwards in tight curves until it began to break up in the air under the hammering it was receiving. Still trying to hold his place, Dicken saw the wings fold back and the fuselage begin to drop straight down, looking like a coffin, the tail slowly coming over beyond the vertical. The observer fell clear and began to follow it down, a sprawl of arms and legs, his coat open as though he were trying to use it as a brake to slow his descent, surrounded by all the photographic plates he had so laboriously exposed.

There were too many Germans for the observers' fire to be

effective. One of them went down, turning and twisting like a falling leaf, but three more took its place. His nose down, Dunne was bolting for home, with all the rest protecting his tail so that the photographs would arrive safely. Three DVs swept down on him and failed to head him off, but two Strutters were already falling out of control, one of them pouring smoke. A moment later the smoke became a flame and the machine curved down, a blazing crucifix that seemed a blasphemy, trailing a black coil behind it. The second simply disappeared. Dicken was watching as one of the DVs swooped on it, then there was a flash and a puff of smoke and the machine vanished in a growing black cloud, while glittering fragments of blazing wing fluttered down, and two black objects fell like stones after the bulky shape of the engine that trailed a length of fuselage, fabric and spars behind it like streamers.

It was impossible to tell who had gone because the machines were scattered all over the sky now in a running fight as they struggled for home. An Albatros headed for Dicken, trying to cut him off but, leaving his observer to protect his tail, he put his nose down and charged. As the Strutter came thundering down on him, the German pilot wrenched in alarm at the stick and his machine jerked sideways just as a second Albatros came tearing in from above. For a second all three machines were close enough for the crews to see each other's expressions.

As Dicken slipped clear, the two Germans – one swerving to avoid the diving Strutter, the other swerving in the opposite direction to avoid the observer's fire – swung together. One moment they were attractive, brightly-coloured machines moving gracefully in tight curves, the next second they were hanging in the air, their wings crumpled as if they were locked in each other's arms. The crash could be heard over the roar of the Strutter's motor and, glancing upwards, Dicken saw the two aeroplanes clutch each other for a second before sweeping earthwards in slow spins, a tangle of wreckage trailing a thin stream of dark smoke.

A new group of Albatroses came swarming in, swinging sideways to avoid the debris and, as he watched, he saw one of them fly into the fire of the machine in front of him and writhe away, streaming petrol. As it burst into flames, the pilot climbed out of the cockpit to try to wrestle it into a sideslip that would carry the blaze away from him but, seconds later, Dicken saw it again, one wing almost burned away, as it stalled just ahead of him, clawing at nothing, with the pilot no longer clinging to the wing root.

As he watched, it exploded and the Strutter hit a fluttering red rudder with one of its struts. The impact sounded like the explosion of a shell and for a moment he thought his machine had broken up under the hammering it had been receiving. He managed to wriggle clear as the twisted fuselage hurtled past his tail, but they were taking a terrible beating and German aircraft were charging in from all angles, their tracers drawing a patchwork pattern against a sky which seemed to be littered with broken wings and struts that flashed and glinted as they twisted and fell, and with bundles of wreckage that scrawled crayon marks of smoke down the azure backcloth.

Tired and angry, he swung away and drove headlong at a new group of attackers, his front gun going. The Germans turned away, too, and he followed them for a while, trying long range shots at them. When he recovered from his fury, the sky was empty except for a solitary Strutter dropping slowly towards the west, trailing wires and flags of fabric.

Trembling with reaction, he realised that the characteristic buzz of the Clerget engine had become like the clattering of a can full of stones, while the smell of castor oil had changed to one of hot metal. He knew it couldn't last, and finally, as they approached the field, with a tremendous crash something tore through the starboard cowling into space and there was a terrific gout of blue flame from the air intakes. The aircraft shuddered violently and he thought the engine would tear itself from its bearings, then the propeller jerked to an upright halt and they were surrounded by silence except for the wailing of the flying wires.

An inlet valve had broken and smashed the piston and the damage had affected the stability so that he was unable to fly the machine properly. It seemed to drift sideways in to land and there was a crash as the wings clipped the trees at the end of the field. A wingtip touched the ground as the machine levelled off and it banged down and began to slide sideways across the grass, shedding undercarriage, wings and tail in flying fragments. Gouging a great wound in the turf, it finally slithered to a stop, the fuselage practically denuded, and decanted Dicken and Almonde on to the grass.

As he stumbled dizzily out of the wreckage, a car drew up and a tall man with a shaggy moustache asked him in a voice like a foghorn if he'd hurt his leg.

Still dazed and limping, his eyes wild, Dicken glared at him. 'No, I always go around like this,' he snarled. 'I've got one leg shorter than the other.'

It was a grim day for the squadron. Dunne's machine was canted over at an angle, one wing crumpled, and they were still trying to lift his observer out. Roode arrived shortly afterwards, his machine full of holes, the engine poppling and burping as he blipped the cut-out button.

'Where are all the rest?' he asked.

'There aren't any more,' Dicken growled.

'I had to turn back.' As he turned away, he heard Diplock apologising. 'An inlet valve broke.'

Dunne stared at him but said nothing. 'The bloody staff must be mad,' he growled. 'Sending Strutters on a job like that without an escort. Well, they've got their bloody pictures. I hope the bastards enjoy them.'

As Dicken turned away, Diplock began to explain again to Roode, but Roode wasn't listening and was lighting a cigarette with shaking hands.

Stalking back to the hut, Dicken flung down his flying clothing and sat on his mattress, scowling at the two empty beds at the other side of the hut. They looked like tombs already. No messages had come in from anybody and all they knew was that out of the nine machines that had taken off, Diplock's had returned early, and five others were missing, two of which had been seen to burn. Roode thought the machine which had exploded was Hatto's but as Dicken sat on the bed, smoking, Almonde put his head round the door. Scarati and his observer had been found, he said, but no aeroplane, and it had been concluded that theirs had been the machine which had exploded.

The tall man who had asked Dicken if he were hurt turned out to be General Trenchard, the Chief of Air Staff, the man who ran the Flying Corps, and he had come to give them a pep talk. He said he was offering no easy way out and, despite the losses, they had to continue. 'Reconnaissance is of no use whatsoever on our own side of the lines,' he said. 'And it's reconnaissance that will win the war, not duelling one aircraft against another to run up a score.'

The mess was silent that night, nobody speaking, Diplock sitting on his own at the end of the table. He had tried once or twice to make noisy explanations but nobody was interested and he had lapsed into silence. Later in the evening, the telephone went to inform them that Foote had landed unhurt at Izel, but that his observer, a man called Burgin, had died of wounds. For Dicken it was hard to decide whether it was good or bad news, and soon afterwards the telephone went again to inform them that two more bodies, too badly burned to be identified, had been discovered alongside the burned-out wreckage of another Strutter. Certain it was Hatto, he drank more than was good for him.

By eleven o'clock, with Foote, tense and white-faced, back in the mess, they decided they had the full butcher's bill. Six machines had been destroyed, and it seemed that four pilots, Snell, Scarati, Johnson and Hatto, had been killed with their observers. Two other observers had been mortally wounded.

At midnight, Dicken was in the middle of a nightmare in which he was surrounded by flame when the crash of the door opening brought him bolt upright in his bed. Framed in the opening was Hatto, his monocle screwed into his eye, holding a bottle half-filled with rum. He was singing at the top of his voice.

'Oh, Willie, you've come home, lad,
Drunk, drunk again!'

'Willie!'
'Hello, darlings! The last of the Hattos is back.'
Jumping from bed, Dicken and Foote grabbed him and they all started to waltz round the room together, Dicken and Foote trying to yell above Hatto's discordant singing.

Clutching each other, they lost their balance and, as they fell across Hatto's bed, one of the legs collapsed and they all rolled to the floor. Almost weeping with laughter and relief, Dicken pawed drunkenly at Hatto's face to make sure he really was alive.

'What happened? What happened?'

'Miracle, old boy. Pipped us in the clockwork. Sort of slithered down and splashed into a shellhole full of water just behind the front line. Carthew was hit. Bunch of infantry-men dragged him out and carried him away. Thought I was dead but I was only unconscious. Arrived a few minutes later, mad as hell at them for leaving me. Apologised suit-ably.' He held up the bottle. 'Have a go?'

Dicken shook his head. 'No thanks,' he said. 'We thought you were dead and we've had too much already.'

'Because you thought I was dead? Dear old fruits, what a jolly decent thing to do. I'll do the same for you if the occasion arises.'

'How about Carthew?'

'A few splinters in the bum which left it looking like a cross between a night watchman's fire bucket and my aunt's string bag. But he's not complaining. When they shoved him face-down in the ambulance he was laughing his socks off because he'd got the best kind of Blighty – the sort you recover from.'

Hatto suddenly calmed down, his face grim. 'What hap-pened to the Parasol?' he demanded.

'Full of apologies,' Foote said. 'Claimed an inlet valve went.'

'It's probably thanks to that gadget that they got Scarati, Johnson and Snell. He broke the formation. I saw them both go down.'

'*And* Burgin,' Foote pointed out. 'He didn't make it either.'

'Three pilots, five observers, and six machines either destroyed or crashed.' Hatto laid his bottle down and lit a cigarette slowly. 'I just hope the old Parasol manages to live with it.'

4

By the following morning, Diplock had disappeared. Dunne had refused to have him in his flight and they assumed he'd been sent home, but a fortnight later they heard he'd turned up at Wing headquarters as the personal pilot of the Wing colonel.

'I guess he knew somebody who could pull strings,' Foote said.

'The major,' Dicken growled, 'should have given him a good kick up the arse.'

'Listen to Old Testament Quinney talking,' Hatto said. 'I suppose everybody gets the breeze up from time to time and there's nobody more sympathetic than another chap who's been through it. Unfortunately, the way *he* bolts means the death of someone and it was very nearly *me*.' He sat at the piano and tinkled a few bars of *If You Were The Only Girl In The World*. 'The story's different, actually, and I have it from Sergeant Cecil, the managing director of the orderly room. The Wing colonel was originally an Engineer and, when the RFC was formed, in the clever way they have on the staff he was given command of one of the very first squadrons. Now that he was considered to be an aviator, it was thought he should learn to aviate, and he was given a quick pilot's course. Unfortunately he wasn't very good at it and I don't think he's ever flown since, and now that the fronts are bigger he needs someone to tote him around so he can do his thinking on the way. Needs looking after, y'see.'

'Well, Percy's the right guy for that job,' Foote growled. 'He'll *never* take risks.'

'If you're like Little Dave and try to be brave,' Hatto said, 'all you get for your trouble is a bullet in the gizzard, a grave on the lone prairie and no thanks from anyone. If you're like little Seth and get frightened to death, you get a nice cushy job at headquarters, flying the Wing colonel about. And, as everybody knows, Wing colonels never take risks, only think up risks for other people to take. Parasol Percy'll end up with a putty medal and his name in the VC column of the *Daily Mail.* I'll bet he never comes back here.'

He turned out to be dead right. The next they heard of Diplock was that his RASC rank of captain had been confirmed.

Because of the casualties they had suffered, the squadron was given no work to do until they could recover a little. They were half-hoping they might be given RE8s, newer reconnaissance machines which were stronger, faster and safer and a great deal better than Strutters, but instead the replacements were more Strutters, dangerously uncertain after standing all summer in the aircraft park and even more vulnerable than the ones they'd lost.

'The goddam things are born victims,' Foote growled.

Soon afterwards another battle started near Ypres and developed into a series of engagements which proved to be the Somme all over again, with the same lack of success and thousands of lives sacrificed for a few miles of blood-soaked ground. As usual, the press made it sound like a walk-over.

'I suppose it depends how you look at it,' Hatto observed. 'When we got licked at Colenso in the Boer War, my old man said, they claimed it wasn't a defeat – we just failed to take the place, that's all.'

Despite the disasters on the ground, the new British fighters – the SE5, the Camel and the Bristol – had wrenched the command of the air from the Germans once more, pushing them far back behind their trench lines again, reaping the glory while the 1½-Strutters continued to trudge over the German lines in the menial task of taking photographs.

By this time, with casualties and home postings, Foote, Dicken and Hatto were senior pilots. It was noticeable that the casualties, at least, seemed to avoid the experienced men and simply took away the newcomers. If you survived the first month, the chances were that, barring accidents and ill luck, you had a good chance of eventually going to Home Establishment. Then, as they struggled with the hated Strutters, Hatto suddenly started shooting down German machines. He seemed startled by his success, but by the end of the month he had accounted for nine, including two in one day, and was awarded the Military Cross.

'Very gallant,' he said. 'But I don't think they could have been very good. Probably articled apprentices to Richthofen's mob.'

The following week, attacked by a whole skyful of Albatroses, his observer's Lewis jammed and his engine stopped by the very first burst of fire, he was shot at all the way down to the ground, but one of the Germans, who was stupid enough to get in front of the drifting Strutter, was hit by Hatto with the front gun which also shot off his own windmilling propeller. His tank holed and soaked with petrol, expecting every minute either to blow up or catch fire, as they struggled across the trenches a bullet from the ground smashed his rudder bar and entered his foot, and the Sopwith subsided gracefully on top of the second line trench and fell apart. Hatto and his observer dropped neatly into the trench.

When the tender arrived from the hospital, Hatto was sitting in the back with his plastered foot resting on a sandbag. Dicken pushed his kit in alongside him, almost in tears.

'You stupid bugger,' he said. 'Getting shot about like that, just when we were getting used to your snoring.'

'Sorry, old fruit,' Hatto smiled. 'Don't want to leave you but I know I have to go. Hold your end up. I'll be back when they've cobbled me up. I'll give your love to the Hon. Maud – if she hasn't married a general in the meantime.'

He was still smiling as the tender drew away and, feeling he would never see him again, aware of an unbelievable longing to be going with him, back to the peace of England, Dicken was still staring after it as the tender disappeared from sight.

*

On the last day of the month, the Strutters were called on to do low reconnaissance work over the German trenches. It consisted largely of diving to fire the front gun then zooming upwards so that the observer could use his Lewis. It was a job for which the slow Strutters were quite unsuited and two disappeared in two days.

'This war,' Foote announced portentously, 'is growing goddam dangerous.'

The next day, Dicken flew with five others on a distant offensive patrol, crawling across the lines at 8000 feet. Archie plastered the sky on either side of them, but Dunne led them on, disregarding the fire until the lane of bursting shells through which they flew grew narrow enough to be dangerous. One of the Strutters began to lag behind with engine trouble and an Albatros appeared from nowhere towards its tail. Swinging round, Dicken fired a burst at it to drive it away and, as it swung off-course, held the Strutter steady so that the observer could have a steady aim. The Albatros appeared to go down out of control.

Soon afterwards, a second Strutter had to leave the formation but the rest flew steadily on below a layer of cloud. Despite the fact that they must have shown up clearly against the whiteness, the anti-aircraft guns had become silent and the silence put Dicken on the alert because silence usually meant danger. Staring about him, his eyes narrowed, some instinct told him Germans were about, despite the empty heavens. But nothing happened, and they were just about to turn towards home when a Camel fell out of the cloud directly in front of them, followed by a red and grey Albatros, the pilot swinging it from side to side and pumping bullets into the Camel whenever he could.

Suspecting there might be other Germans about, the Strutters began to circle, each machine covered from front and rear by the guns of the rest. The Camel pilot dived beneath them, the German still on his tail, then tried to climb back towards them, still followed by the Albatros. As they passed, Dicken tried a snap shot and the German flew right through the stream of bullets which raked it from nose to tail. Fragments broke from the fuselage as it disappeared beneath them. Swinging round, Dicken saw it going down almost vertically in a curious uneven flicking turn, but the Camel was also going down a mile away in the same sort of uneven spiral. Close to the ground, a tiny spot of flame came from the Albatros and it began to trail smoke, then it seemed to level out and pass beneath them until finally it vanished into a patch of woodland.

Confirmation on the crashed German came through within minutes of landing. With halves and odd portions he had shared with other pilots, Dicken's score now amounted to three and a half. It wasn't much and didn't match Hatto's score of nine but at least he was paying his way.

He had achieved some skill and some success, but there had been no fiery meteor across the sky. He had started in the lowliest of jobs and it had taken a long, long time, much of it saddened by the deaths of friends. While the old men sat safely at home making the machines of war, finding the money – and making it, too! – and formulating the plans, it was the young who were being destroyed. He supposed it was always so. In the beginning it had worried him but now, older, tougher, wiser, more fatalistic, he had come to terms with it, so that only occasionally, as when Hatto had vanished, did he feel a sense of hopelessness and anguish.

They were just celebrating the crashed Albatros when news came in that leave was on again and, as Dicken's name was top of the list, he was told he could go with Foote the following morning.

'My kid brother's arrived in England,' Foote said. 'I'll get to see him, I guess. They're training in Norfolk somewhere.'

The London papers were full of a big defeat in Italy where the Austrians, who had been facing the Italians in the Trentino, had been reinforced by the Germans and what had been a quiet area had suddenly flared up into a disastrous battle on the Isonzo which had forced the Italians to start a retreat from Caporetto. The entire Italian front appeared to have collapsed and for the first time in three years the war had become one of movement again. It seemed to have taken even the Germans by surprise and there was a great danger of Italy being knocked out of the war.

It didn't seem to have affected London much, however. It was full of strange uniforms and it was hard to celebrate being home because there seemed to be nothing to drink, and only the reserves of an American captain they met saved them from dying of thirst. Dicken's mother seemed pleased to see him but she couldn't understand why he wanted to spend part of his leave with Foote in London, and it was hard to explain that England felt like a foreign country and Foote was part of the real life he lived in France.

Together, they looked up Hatto. He was still limping a little but was in high spirits because he'd pulled strings to get himself put on Bristols.

'You've got to get us on to Bristols, too, Willie,' Dicken said. 'People get killed in Strutters.'

A group of Americans led by Foote's brother were holding a party at a house they'd rented near the West End and Foote dragged Dicken along. His brother was a junior edition of himself, tall, shambling, always smiling, with the same good looks and crisp curling blond hair, but he seemed centuries younger and Dicken put it down to the fact that Walt Foote had seen too much of the war.

The party was a wild affair and Dicken woke the following morning on the settee, with a girl's silk stocking round his neck. Low mutterings were coming from the bedroom as he dressed.

The rest of the leave followed much the same pattern. His mother was called to look after a sick relative in the Midlands, so he took her north and spent two days with her before heading back to London to rejoin Foote. Growing bored with parties, he decided he'd better return home for the last day or two. Annys Toshack no longer meant much to him but he decided Zoë might be willing to spend an evening with him and might be fun.

There was an official-looking letter awaiting him when he arrived. To his surprise it instructed him not to return to France at the end of his leave but to report to Upavon in Wiltshire. He had no idea what it meant but he regarded it as offering him a little more life to live. Nothing could be worse than 1½-Strutters, and Upavon was a long way from Richthofen and his circus.

A few enquiries by telephone revealed that virtually every kind of aeroplane made was available at Upavon, even a few captured German ones which had been flown to England for evaluation, and he automatically connected the good news with the battle going on in Italy and assumed that he was part of a big move-around of units and personnel brought about by the disaster. Whichever way he looked at it, it remained good news and he decided to celebrate by asking Zoë out to dinner, though he guiltily wondered if it was because he wished to see her or because she had access to her father's motor. To his surprise he found her sewing and in no mood to go anywhere.

'No time,' she said sharply. 'I've got to finish this.'

'I expected to see you in the garage under a motor,' he said. 'What's going on?'

She glared at him. 'Wedding,' she said shortly.

'Yours?'

'No, you ass! Annys's. She's getting married to Arthur Diplock.'

'Is he home?'

'Shouldn't he be?'

'My God, he works fast!' He explained how little operational flying Diplock had done.

'He must have done more than that,' Zoë said. 'He's got a DSO.'

'He's got *what?*' Dicken was furious. 'My God, what it is to be at the seat of power. They tell me that at headquarters they play snakes and ladders for 'em.'

Gradually she wormed out of him what had happened. 'Well,' she said. 'You'd better get over it because you'll be invited to the wedding.'

'To hell with the wedding!'

'I'd like to say the same. With the war, you can't get anyone to do anything for you because everybody's making fortunes in factories, so we've got to do it all ourselves, and I can't touch a car in case I get grease on my fingers and it gets on the dress.' She looked at Dicken. 'For God's sake, Dicky boy, if you're asked, come. Arthur Diplock's family's claimed all the seats in the church because we're a bit short of relatives and we shall need a little support.' She jabbed her finger and swore. 'These bloody needles and cottons!' she said bitterly. 'Why the hell can't Annys get married in something I can fasten on with nuts and bolts? Women always get themselves up like Christmas puddings so their males can look on them as sacrificial offerings – all soft and clinging and virginal.'

Dicken laughed. 'Wouldn't you get dressed up like that if you were getting married?'

'Not on your life! I'm not having the Rector mooing over me about eternal love and till death us do part, for ever and ever, amen. Statistics show that only about ten per cent of all marriages are happy, ten per cent are murderous, and the other eighty per cent are just boredom. Marriage's just something invented by human beings to make sure of a cosy old age. I'm a liberated woman, and the liberated woman's coming, Dicky boy. I told you she would.'

'What *is* a liberated woman, anyway?'

'One of them works at the aerodrome at Shoreham. They gave her a fortnight off to help with the wedding.'

'What are you doing there? Typing?'

'Typing?' She gave him a disgusted look. 'Engines. I'm an inspector. The foreman was having a hard time with the girls so someone had the bright idea of placing a woman in charge. As there aren't many who know anything about engines, I got the job.'

'Doesn't it involve some odd hours?'

'I've taken a flat in Worthing, and I've got a runabout to get to and fro.'

'Don't you share it with anybody?'

'Why should I? Mother doesn't think much of it but Father's with the army at Brighton now and he's supposed to keep an eye on me. As a matter of fact, I think he's got a girl friend and I've never seen him since the first week or so. Mother doesn't know, of course. She thinks he comes round regularly.'

It seemed to suggest all sorts of dangers and reminded Dicken of something Diplock had said.

'Who's this Canadian I hear you're going about with?' he asked.

She gave him a quick look. 'Who told you that? Arthur Diplock?'

'Yes. Is it true?'

'It's Casey Harman. He came over here to learn to fly and got a job with Sopwiths. He's got more money than he knows what to do with and after the war he's going in for building aeroplanes himself.'

She didn't volunteer any further information and he wondered what there was between them, and if the Canadian were liberated too.

5

When Dicken arrived at Pewsey, the station for Upavon, Foote was also there, standing on the platform waiting for a tender to pick him up and take him to the aerodrome.

'Willie, I guess,' he grinned. 'Pulling strings. I must get him to pull a few for the kid brother.'

Their duties turned out to be very vague. Upavon was a bleak, windswept, inhospitable place and their attachment seemed to be very uncertain and very temporary. They were given a job checking machines for design and appearance, the way they handled, their suitability, comfort, and areas of vision, but it occupied very little of their time and they slipped in and out of the camp as they pleased. It wasn't far to Sussex and, buying from a local doctor going into the army a small wheezy two-seater known as One-Lung, Dicken was able to get home easily, putting Foote en route on the train for London, where his brother was learning to fly.

Most of the pilots at Upavon had seen hard service in France and many of them were itching to get back. They didn't like the atmosphere in England where the civilians tended to regard the war as if it were a rather rougher type of football match, and they didn't like the way men who had never heard a shot fired in anger were picking up rewards. However, the disaster in Italy had started a panic round the home stations where comfortably-established officers began to reflect the politicians' alarm by imagining, not for the first time since 1914, that the war was about to be decided in Germany's favour. To their great alarm, some were even snatched from what they had considered secure jobs and sent to France to replace those hurriedly despatched to help the Italians, and it came as no surprise to Dicken and Foote to learn they were not going back on 1½-Strutters.

'Experienced men are being kept at home,' they were told, 'to give their knowledge to new squadrons which are being formed. Some of you will be given flights. Some will be given squadrons. You're to do all the flying you can. On Bristols.'

There was a saying that an aeroplane that was good to look at was also good to fly, and the Bristol looked good. Fitted with a Rolls Royce engine, because of its size it looked like a fighter and Dicken studied it like a man buying a horse. It had a businesslike air about it and, while the pilot, boxed in between the upper and lower wings, was virtually blind above, the observer had a good arc of fire.

Hatto turned up at Upavon soon afterwards and, deciding it would be pleasant if they could all go to the same squadron, they began to play poker to decide who should have command of the squadron and who should have command of the flights.

'I guess we should give Willie the squadron,' Foote decided. 'After all, the guy's been in this goddam war since the beginning but he doesn't seem to progress much.'

'Lieutenant to lieutenant in three years,' Hatto smiled. 'What a career.'

'Comes of getting wounded so much,' Dicken said.

'And making so many enemies. Careless all round.'

There was still no sign of them moving and the war didn't change much. Hatto appeared to have a direct line to the War Office and came up every day with the name of someone else they knew who had been killed – Dunne had flown into a house and Friedmann had been killed by a student pilot he was instructing – but, despite the casualties, despite Italy, in England there remained a strange offhand attitude to the war. The politicians seemed to be giving more of their time to their party squabbles than to beating the Germans and there was a lack of realism among the people who provided the new aeroplanes. Even the SE5, a well-built fighter sturdy enough to stand up to the rough and tumble of air fighting, appeared to be badly undergunned.

'Why in God's name stick one gun on the upper wing?' Dicken asked. 'If you tried to reload it, the slipstream would slap the ammunition drum into your face like a soup plate in a gale. I bet no pilot thought of *that*.'

'Some chap like Parasol Percy, shouldn't wonder,' Hatto said. 'Hear he's no longer the colonel's pilot, by the way. Aide now. His languages, y'see. Sits in an office and tells people what to do and where they're posted. Getting married they tell me.'

'I've got an invitation to the wedding,' Dicken said. 'He's marrying my girl friend's sister.'

Diplock himself turned up later that week. The Wing colonel had been posted home and brought him with him. They arrived by car.

'At least a car's safe to fly,' Foote said as they watched them climb out. 'Never leaves the ground.'

Diplock was at the bar when they arrived in the mess and, finding himself face-to-face with them, he seemed at a loss. They were an anarchical trio and he was unsure how to deal with them. 'Have a drink?' he suggested nervously.

Dicken was on the point of refusing when Hatto nodded.

'Jolly decent of you,' he said. 'After all, when a chap's getting married, he has to push the old boat out a bit, doesn't he?'

'What the hell did you do that for?' Dicken demanded later. 'I didn't want to drink with the bastard.'

'Peace, child,' Hatto said calmly. 'Leave it all to your Uncle Willie, who's a devious, conniving, calculating sort of cove always known to have something up his sleeve for gadgets such as Diplock.'

It almost started a quarrel between them but that afternoon a Camel flew in and everybody wanted to try it.

'Shouldn't be difficult,' Hatto said. 'Same engine as a Strutter so you don't have to learn any new tricks.'

In fact, there were a lot of new tricks to learn because, after the Strutter, flying a Camel was like flying a wild animal. All the other Sopwiths Dicken had flown had been stable, well-behaved and smooth to handle, but the Camel had to be held back all the time because it seemed eager to wrench itself free. Handled with confidence and intelligence, it was a superlative machine but it was always quick to take advantage of stupidity or nervousness. Because of its short fuselage and stubby wings, the big rotary engine tended to force the nose down in a right-hand turn and it didn't take Dicken long to discover that to avoid losing height he had to apply left rudder the minute the manoeuvre began and hold it on hard. Then the Camel would turn on a sixpence.

'She'll never catch anything by surprise, though,' he admitted. 'She's not fast enough. So all you can do is sit up high and go down like a stone. Still, when you've gone down, all you do is pull the stick back and she goes straight up again like a lift.'

'I like nice comfortable aeroplanes,' Foote said.

'Nice comfortable aeroplanes get shot down,' Dicken insisted. 'I reckon I could enjoy flying Camels. I'd be hard to hit, and that counts more for me than being nice and steady. Besides, you can recognise 'em a mile away and the Huns'll probably think twice before going for 'em. *They* know Camels waltz their way out of anything.'

*

At the week-end Hatto announced he was going to Diplock's wedding.

'Not as a guest, of course,' he pointed out hastily. 'Not invited. Just to the reception. Drink the bride's health.'

'You won't catch *me* drinking his health,' Dicken said.

'Didn't say we were going to,' Hatto said mysteriously. 'Just the bride's.'

Shaved, brushed and combed to within an inch of their lives, they climbed into Hatto's car and headed for Deane. When they arrived the guests were all parading before the bride, the groom and the parents. Diplock's father, tall, plump and smiling, had no idea who they were but Hatto's title carried weight.

'Come in, dear boy,' he said. 'You'll be one of the Norfolk Hattos. I was at Oxford with Rudolf Hatto.'

'Actually,' Hatto said, 'we're from Northamptonshire and we don't have anything to do with the Norfolk lot. Especially Rudolf. He ran off with the curate's wife.'

'Do you know this bloody Rudolf, you glass-eyed bastard?' Foote whispered as they made their way into the marquee.

'Never met the chap in my life.'

Looking surprisingly beautiful, Zoë appeared at Dicken's

elbow. 'What are you doing here?' she murmured. 'I thought you weren't coming.'

'When Willie Hatto gets an idea in his head,' Dicken admitted, 'you tend to go along with it. He probably fancied the free champagne.'

A man who looked well-stomached and prosperous started discussing the war with them. 'Next time we make a push,' he insisted, 'it's got to take us to Berlin. No half-measures. We've just got to disregard the casualties.'

'You in the army?' Hatto asked silkily.

'Not me. I'm reserved.'

'Thought you might be,' Foote commented.

The sarcasm passed unnoticed, and the well-stomached man went on enthusiastically. 'It must be very exciting flying over the lines as you do,' he said.

'Not always,' Dicken snapped. 'Sometimes you don't come back.'

It seemed to startle the stout man, and they were just about to set about him when Diplock's father started banging on a table with a spoon. 'Ladies and gentlemen, I think we've come to cake-cutting time.'

An uncle droned on about Annys and the bridegroom, going on so long Diplock's father had to nudge his elbow, then the best man, who turned out to be the Wing colonel, a man with narrow lips and cold eyes, proposed the toast.

'Making sure his future's secure,' Hatto observed dryly. 'If you want to get ahead, get a high rank to your wedding.'

The Wing colonel's speech was short and witty and the congratulatory telegrams, they noticed, were mostly from members of his staff. Diplock was just on the point of replying when Hatto raised his hand.

'Permission to speak, sir?' he asked. 'Old comrades and all that.'

Diplock's father beamed. 'Just one more word then,' he conceded. 'The Honourable William Hatto would like to add his mite. You'll all know his father, Lord Hooe, of course.'

There was a spatter of applause and Hatto screwed his monocle into his eye.

'Bit out of order really,' he apologised. 'Normally, at these affairs, it's always the bride who gets the attention. This time, I think the bridegroom ought to be noticed.' He gestured at Diplock who was watching him suspiciously. 'Captain, you'll notice. Very important. Until recently, personal pilot to the colonel at Wing. Very dangerous job.'

Annys smiled proudly and there was a ripple of applause because nobody had the slightest idea what the Wing colonel's pilot did.

'Still,' Hatto went on, 'we're not here today to draw attention to his flying skills. Just to the fact that he's a lucky bridegroom with a bride as beautiful as ever appeared in the society magazines.' Annys looked coy and Diplock tried a nervous smile. 'The only advice we can give him today is on his future.' Hatto paused. 'I'm not going in for all that nonsense about "May all his troubles be little ones" and so on. That's old stuff and marriage is serious. Like war. And in that our good friend has already brought himself very much to the attention of his comrades.'

Dicken exchanged a glance with Foote and he saw Diplock going pink.

'Doubtless,' Hatto went on, a dangerous look in his eye, 'he's feeling nervous, faced with all his relations and the friends who know him. Marriage, y'see, like many things in life, is sometimes enough to make a man break out in a cold sweat.' There was a low murmur of laughter and a rumble of approval from the men. 'But courage is a splendid virtue and our good friend, Arthur, knows all about courage. He's been called on to show it.'

Dicken was unable to hold his head up because he knew exactly what Hatto was getting at and so did Foote.

So did Diplock. He was frowning deeply, his face red, his fingers twitching at his side. The guests were smiling and nodding approval. It was a serious speech, they were thinking, not the flippant trivialities of most weddings, because the times were serious, with men dying in France and almost everybody suffering loss.

Diplock's father, plump, smooth and smug, was nodding approval. Nobility, his manner said, gave tone to a wedding.

'The way Arthur demonstrated his courage –' Hatto was well into his stride now '– became known to everybody who flew with him. Every man on the squadron knew its quality because they watched him in action against the enemy and saw how he behaved. And, as you can see, he wears a medal on his breast, and we all know how these medals are won.' This time, not only Diplock but the Wing colonel frowned, because he, too, wore a DSO that had been won for organisation rather than action.

'Marriage needs courage, too,' Hatto smiled. 'As he'll surely discover. It requires the same trust that *we* needed in him when we were with him in the air. So let him make sure he screws up his courage and makes a success of his marriage. Like war, marriage's dangerous.'

There was a burst of laughter and Hatto lifted his glass. 'Let me ask you then to drink to Arthur, our Paladin, our Hector, our Hotspur, our Achilles.'

'To Arthur!'

As the glasses rose, Dicken noticed that Hatto very pointedly placed his on the table untouched. With the babble of conversation starting again, he faced him. 'That was bloody cruel, Willie,' he said.

'It didn't harm the bride.' Hatto studied the guests crowding round Diplock and Annys. 'Come to that, I doubt if it's hurt the bridegroom. With the Wing colonel on his side, his friends are more powerful than his enemies and his performance in Strutters will be forgotten so quickly it won't be worth reminding anybody of it.' He paused, watching Diplock, his eyes suddenly contemplative and strangely cold. 'I've always been prepared to forgive a man for running away, because I've often wanted to myself. But this one's different. A man who can get himself a cushy job, promotion and a medal out of it has more to him than meets the eye. This one's crafty, ambitious and dangerous, and what I said probably makes up a bit for Snell, Scarati and Johnson. I don't like our friend. I never shall. He's the sort of shabby type we haven't seen the last of. I think we'd better go now. This place stinks of moral turpitude and stale piety. Some of the bastards, in fact, look as though they're doing very well out of the war.'

As they collected their hats, he spoke to the maid. 'Tell Captain Diplock,' he said, 'that we had to leave, but that we shall be watching his future progress with great interest. Make sure you get the message right.'

As he went off with Foote to find his car, Zoë appeared.

'Your glass-eyed friend managed to muck up the wedding beautifully for Arthur,' she observed. 'He looks as though he's turned up an amputated hand in the fruit salad.'

'I think,' Dicken said, 'that was the idea.'

She gestured. 'You don't think he'll take it lying down, do you?' she asked. 'He was boasting the other night that he has the power to send a man anywhere in France. He'll probably send you lot to the penal battalion.'

6

Just how right she was, was proved less than a week later when Hatto was informed he was to fly Bristols from St. Sylvestre.

'I'm not getting the flight I was promised,' he said ruefully. 'I expect Parasol Percy fixed it. His ju-ju seems to be stronger than mine.'

Before lunch, news came through that Foote and Dicken were to proceed to Ste. Bernardine Cappel. They were to fly Camels but were also not getting flights.

'We're going to end this goddam war right where we started it,' Foote decided.

On the last evening, Dicken drove Zoë to Brighton for a meal. The place had changed a lot and the hotels seemed to be full of women and girls who had found a new freedom with the war.

'They go into pubs, too, these days,' Zoë said. 'On their own. A lot of them are earning more than men and they feel they've a right to. Casey's all for having women in his factories. He's going to the top, you know. And when he does, I'm going with him.'

'What about marriage?'

'It won't make any difference. After the war, women will be working alongside men and even taking their jobs. You see.'

'What about when children come?'

'Who wants children?'

'I'd want 'em for one.'

She seemed in a bad temper and he got it out of her that Vickery had killed himself that day at Shoreham.

'He never could turn corners,' Dicken said.

On the way home, she suggested he stopped at her flat for

a coffee and a last drink. It was a tiny place on the top floor of an old house, and instead of making coffee, she simply offered him a drink.

'You can stay the night if you like,' she offered.

'How many bedrooms have you got?'

'One.'

There was a long silence.

'Where's the settee?'

'I haven't got one.'

'You inviting me to share?'

She shrugged. 'We might all be dead tomorrow. Some German might fly over here tonight and drop a bomb on us.'

A nagging worry entered his head. 'Has Casey Harman ever stayed here?' he asked.

'He's married and I don't go in for other people's left-overs.' The words were brisk but he wasn't convinced.

She leaned towards him and kissed him. It was slow and experienced but, as he felt his pulses quicken, she pushed him away.

'My, aren't we excitable?' She seemed to be laughing at him. 'I'm going to change. This dress is hell.'

He recognised the ploy. 'Not the thing for romping on the sofa,' he said.

'I haven't a sofa,' she said coolly. 'And I wouldn't romp on it if I had. When I do things, I do them properly.' She indicated a door. 'The bedroom's through there.'

*

The following morning, Dicken woke warily, wondering what was in store for him. Zoë's half of the bed was empty.

He lay for a moment, deep in thought. It was always the young soldier's fear, he had discovered, that he would go to his death without ever having made love to a woman. Well, what with Zoë and the Hon. Maud, at least he'd done that. But he had a feeling that this time something was missing.

Half-expecting her to arrive with coffee and toast, he lay silent until, finally deciding there was to be no coffee and toast, he rose and dressed. He found her in the yard at the back of the house. She had the bonnet of her car open and her head inside.

139

'Damn' thing goes like a run-down bit of clockwork,' she said. 'It ought to have its points cleaned. But if *I* do it, I expect there'll be trouble. Annys is due home today and I'll be expected to turn up with clean hands. She's staying with Mother while Arthur's in uniform. Why do people have to get married? It seems to be in the air these days.'

'It's something I've thought about myself.'

She lifted her head and studied him. 'You asking me to marry you?'

He hadn't been but, as she'd said, marriage seemed to be in the air.

'It's an idea,' he said.

'All right,' she agreed. 'When? Tomorrow?'

'Good God, no!' He backed off at once. 'Not as fast as that.'

Suddenly, what he'd done alarmed him but she didn't seem to have noticed. 'No, perhaps not tomorrow,' she said thoughtfully. 'Too soon.' She poked delicately with one finger at the engine as if it were of far more moment. 'Father would have a fit. Especially with the cost of Annys's wedding and his girl friend in Brighton.'

'We could get engaged.'

She gave him a long slow smile. 'I'd say,' she observed drily, 'that we *got* engaged. Last night.'

*

Meeting in London before catching the boat train, Dicken, Hatto and Foote celebrated their return to France with a night out in the West End. Foote's brother seemed to know every girl in London and where all the parties were and they took in three before making their way to Victoria Station. They slept all the way across the Channel, managed to miss the train south and had another night out in Calais before heading for St. Omer.

No 1 Aircraft Depot sent aeroplanes and men to the squadrons to replace their casualties. It was an ugly sprawling place, with scores of canvas hangars and workshops, and rows of Nissen huts for living quarters. The pilots' pool was situated there.

'Sort of livestock depot,' Hatto observed.

The base staff – and it didn't take them twenty-four hours to discover that Diplock was part of it – had the boxes and the stalls, while the pilots waiting to sell their lives over the lines had the cheap seats at the back. It was a little like being in prison. There was a plethora of notices – 'No Admittance' and 'Keep Out' – and even sentries to make sure you did as you were told. The place was full to overflowing and there was a waiting list a mile long.

'Oh, well,' Foote said. 'Perhaps the war will be over before they get to us. Let's go and find the town.'

They didn't get the chance. Hatto was whipped off that afternoon, over the heads of men who'd been waiting for weeks, and Foote and Dicken the same evening. 'Parasol Percy,' Dicken decided. 'I think Willie was righter than he knew.'

'They say there's another push due,' Foote pointed out. 'Perhaps Percy's hoping we'll get killed so there'll be nobody to tell the truth and stop him becoming a general.'

They had just packed their equipment and were waiting for the tender when information reached them that their destination had been changed, because the squadron was leaving for Candas on the Picardy front, and they arrived next morning just as sixteen Camels began to appear in groups and ones and twos. As the pilots pulled off their flying caps and smoothed their flattened hair, they began to un-strap what appeared to be personal gear which had been lashed aboard.

'What's going on?' Dicken asked.

'We've ceased operational flying,' he was told. 'We've just been struck off the strength of the wing.'

'Don't tell me,' Foote grinned, 'that the war's over.'

'Not on your life. It's just getting into top gear. We're being sent to another front.'

The commanding officer turned out to be Morton, and he looked up with a smile as he saw Dicken.

'You've just arrived in time,' he said. 'We're on our way to Italy. The Italians have been complaining that it was a condition of their entry into the war in 1915 that we should send troops and guns and aircraft to their front and they blame Caporetto on the fact that we never did. Well, now the powers that be have decided that if we don't, we'll lose them and guns and infantry have gone, 28 and 45 Squadrons are on their way, and we're joining them as soon as possible. You'll be in C Flight.'

It didn't sound too bad. Wine and food were said to be cheap in Italy and the Austrians couldn't possibly be as good as the Germans and certainly never as dangerous as the Richthofen Circus. There seemed a chance not only of enjoying themselves but also of surviving.

'Willie's schemes,' Dicken said, 'always seem to have a twist in the tail. However, occasionally, they also have a bright side.'

Trenarworth, the leader of C Flight, was a Cornishman who'd been flying at the front since 1915. He had a habit of referring to himself always in the third person, and had several victories to his credit, but seemed over-excitable and not quite sane.

'These bloody Austrians are going to get a shock, me dear, when Trenarworth and his boys arrive,' he said. 'So brush up your shooting. With your experience, you ought to be knocking the bastards down in dozens.'

Almost the first person they met in the mess was Foote's brother.

'One Foote was bad enough,' Dicken said. 'Two Feete will be horrible.'

Foote's enthusiasm was not so marked. 'The goddam kid's got no experience,' he pointed out. 'He's only got seventeen hours' flying time – only two on Camels. Rats, I'm going to have to take care of him.'

By the following day half the machines were looking like coffins on wheels without their wings. Packing cases stood everywhere and armourers trudged backwards and forwards carrying guns. Two trains were set aside for their use, the carriages for the officers and senior NCOs small and ancient, the men as usual packed into waggons – 40 hommes, 8 chevaux. Transport and stores were loaded on trucks and the transport drivers and mechanics were to travel in their own tenders and lorries, while camp cookers were installed in a waggon between the men's and the officers' accommodation to provide food for those on the trains.

'Italy,' Foote said, 'here we come.'

Unfortunately, that night the push they'd been expecting in France started. For a change there was no barrage to warn them and the first they learned of it was when their trains were shunted into a siding.

The French stationmaster shrugged. 'Messieurs, you 'ave not heard? There is a great battle. British tanks attack at Cambrai. Nearly four 'undred of them. They cross three German lines and there is a 'ole in the German defences four miles wide. Ten thousand Germans are captured with two 'undred guns. The cavalry go in to exploit the break-through.'

They listened with amazement. After three long years of slaughter, had someone found out at last how to do it?

As they waited, men, munitions and material passed by on the main line, the waggons and carriages crammed to capacity. A French locomotive was waiting near Amiens to haul them to the Italian frontier but on the route between they were dependent on British locomotives and every one of them was in use.

Day after day they waited under a lowering sky full of low clouds and mist. Morton went to Candas to find out what was happening and returned with the news that, as usual, everything had gone wrong. While they'd been ringing church bells in London to celebrate the victory, which everybody had thought was the final breakthrough that was to end the war, the Germans had reacted swiftly. The infantry couldn't keep up with the tanks and the cavalry had been destroyed by machine gun fire, and while the Germans had brought up their reserves, the British had had none available because they'd all been used up in the disastrous offensive at Passchendaele earlier in the year. The German counter-attack was already taking place and everybody expected it to recover every bit of lost ground.

'I volunteered to unpack and join in,' Morton said bitter-ly, 'because they're flying in the duddest of dud weather to hold the Germans back. All it did was remind them we're here, and instead we're being sent to bore ourselves silly on a refresher course at an aerial gunnery school, learning to do what we've already learned to do in action.'

Morton was eventually sent ahead and the rest of them finally left a fortnight before Christmas, moving down the Rhône via Lyons, Avignon, Marseilles and Toulon. The journey took six days and halts were made to stretch legs and eat the food which had been prepared en route. As they passed the Alpes Maritimes they saw orchards, vineyards and water of intense blue. In Nice, Foote came up with a big surprise.

'It's not Italy we're going to,' he said. 'It's Egypt. I've seen the route order. It says Cairo.'

'There can't be much fighting there,' Dicken said. 'Perhaps we're being sent for a rest.'

The train nevertheless continued doggedly in the direction of Italy. In Nice, they decided to spend the day in town and to make sure the train didn't go without them, they took the protesting driver with them. When they reached the border of Italy, they decided they were going to take the ship for Egypt from Genoa or Naples, but the train turned inland and they crossed the border to stop at a small station. Dicken stuck his head out of the window.

'Guess where we are,' he said.

'Where?'

'Cairo.'

Foote grinned. 'There's one in Illinois, too.'

The Italians seemed to have heard of their coming and there was a reception at every station, many of them like gardens with terraces of flowers, all the buildings decorated with red, white and green bunting. Headgear was exchanged and bersaglieri in khaki RFC caps had their photographs taken with pilots wearing Italian patent leather hats with curved feathers. The railway track was lined with people who waved flags and threw apples and oranges through the carriage windows.

The train was garlanded with palm fronds by this time and they arrived in Savona in fine style, pulled by a huge electric engine. Straw-covered bottles of wine were bought in large numbers and the cooks surpassed themselves with a feast to celebrate their arrival, so that they were lethargic with food and drink when the Italian interpreter, who had joined the train at the border, arrived to invite them to meet an Italian colonel in the station buffet.

Already replete on Italian wine and food, half of them had gone to bed and were reluctant to get up. But the Italian insisted that his compatriots would be insulted if they failed to appear, so, since he had been sitting up late writing to his mother, Dicken finally agreed to go as the only officer fully dressed. To his surprise, he found the buffet full of people, with long tables and chairs and a carpet laid out for them. Every available light was on and additional oil lamps had been set up. Piled high with fruit and flowers, the tables were dotted with small Italian flags, and women and girls stood ready to serve.

The Italian colonel who was running the affair seemed to regard Dicken as the commanding officer. He touched his medal ribbons approvingly and announced that the British had sent their best pilots. 'But where are the others?' he asked in English. 'Surely you are not the only one?'

Hurriedly, Dicken whispered to the interpreter to rouse all the other pilots. 'Tell 'em to get dressed quickly,' he said. 'Tell them the King of Italy's here and handing out medals.'

The others arrived in a rush, their hair still tousled from sleep. It raised a cheer and the Italian colonel made a speech in English about British and Italian friendship, and glasses were filled and food passed round.

'My niece married an Englishman,' the colonel said to Dicken. 'His name is Smith. Do you know him?' He seemed surprised that he didn't.

They were still going strong when the stationmaster dashed in to announce that an express was due into the station and he must move the train.

'Go away,' the colonel said.

'*Ma, Colonello mio!* Excellency!' The stationmaster flapped his hands. 'The express will arrive and – paf! –' he slapped his hands together '– there will be no train for the so brave British pilots. The Austrians will then not be thrown back and Italy will be defeated.'

'Go away,' the colonel said again and, as he turned once more to Dicken, the stationmaster began to dance about like a dog wanting to be let out before finally heading for the platform, shouting warnings. '*Dieci minuti!*' he yelled. '*Dieci minuti!*'

There was another speech and Dicken got the impression that, since British and French reinforcements had been passing into Italy for some time, the colonel and his helpers had become expert at conducting welcomes.

'Mazzini, Garibaldi, Cavour,' the colonel said. 'The soul, the sword, the brains of modern Italy. *Viva l'Inghilterra.* Eeep, eeep,' ourrah!'

The stationmaster appeared once more, red in the face. '*Dieci minuti!*' he screeched. '*Ho sei treni chi stanno in agguato. Nelle gallerie.*'

Nobody took the slightest notice and when he next appeared his eyes were bulging with his frustration. '*Il treno parte! Ora! Subito!*'

'What's he saying, me dear?' Trenarworth asked.

'I think –' Dicken had worked it out carefully with the aid of a dictionary '– it's something to do with six trains in tunnels waiting to come in, and that our train's going. Immediately.'

They heard the screech of a whistle and the clanking of couplings and everybody was on the point of rushing outside when the colonel shouted in Italian and pointed to a spot on the carpet immediately in front of the table where he stood. The stationmaster went red and advanced. The colonel shouted at him in Italian and the stationmaster ground his teeth, stamped his feet, slapped his forehead, and departed in a fury.

'The train will be brought back,' the colonel said.

There was a lot of shouting outside and when they finally left, the officers' carriage was directly opposite the strip of red carpet which had been laid on the platform to the waiting room. Their arms full of fruit, posies of flowers and little red, white and green flags, they climbed back into the carriages amid cheers, and the stationmaster hurriedly slammed the doors and waved them away.

7

The following day they passed through Verona and Castel-franco, which was packed with newly-arrived British troops, and pushed on to Treviso, where the weather changed abruptly. The train was unloaded in pouring rain and tenders trailed the Camels to the airfield at San Pelagio to be assembled.

The retreat from Caporetto had ended now but the last of the survivors were still coming back. They had fallen back seventy miles – an unbelievable distance in a war where advances were normally measured in hundreds of yards – leaving behind nearly 200,000 prisoners and 1500 lost guns. They had been forced to withdraw from the Isonzo River front through the mountain passes all the way to the River Piave, and a tremendous amount of territory had been given up, the enemy advance halted only by the flooding of the country between the Piave and Venice.

Broken regiments were still moving south to reform, ex-hausted men devoid of weapons, some of them only half-clothed, wearing ill-fitting grey uniforms and helmets that all seemed too big and came down over eyes and ears. Lorries full of wounded crawled past, the men inside looking like lolling rag dolls, the unwounded in shuffling streams, wet to the skin, their shoulders draped with blankets, their dark eyes hollow and sad, their faces grey with tiredness, their ears still cocked for the distant rumble of Austrian guns. Stumbling horses struggled to keep their feet among the columns of vehicles moving nose-to-tail, in one cart a group of frightened girls who had come from a soldiers' brothel, the whole shambling mass moving like water from a burst dam, edging round obstacles in the road, and when the road became jammed, flooding into the muddy fields to rejoin the stream further along. It was possible to hear mutterings of '*A basso ufficiali!*' – Down with the officers! – and '*Evviva la pace!*' – Long live peace! The Italian soldiers were in a dangerous mood.

They were dirty, torn and unshaven, their transport a miscellaneous collection of unmilitary carts and waggons of all sizes, crammed with bedsteads, bedding, tin baths, chairs, trussed chickens and ducks. Domestic animals were intermingled with the straggling column and soldiers with their toes showing through broken boots led half-starved horses, a calf, a flock of sheep. Ahead, men were still fighting in the rain and mist, firing at enemies who appeared as shadows between the trees, and there was still the fear of another breakthrough.

Among the moving columns were British artillerymen who had arrived in Italy earlier in the year, like everybody else wet through, miserable and cold. The tractors which pulled their guns seemed to be giving them a great deal of trouble and with them were a lot of shellshock cases with staring eyes, jumping at every noise. The medical officer was in despair because there was no food, no medicaments and little transport.

The wretched streams of humanity were still filtering past as the Camels were tested for airworthiness. Since nobody had yet flown them in action, Morton insisted they should all get plenty of practice on them and, since they were always tricky, before any of them were allowed near the Austrians, they all had to take one up and spin it over the aerodrome. The Camel's fierceness suited Dicken, who had always been a heavy-handed pilot, but it was remorseless and there was always an imp of evil in it that allowed no one to take chances. One of the newer pilots held his spin too long, and as he realised his mistake and heaved on the stick there was a ridiculously harmless sound like a balloon bursting as the machine disintegrated. The fuselage, the engine still scream-ing in terror, dived straight into the ground with the crun-ching noise of someone treading on a matchbox, the tattered fragments of wings fluttering slowly to the earth behind in the appalling silence that followed.

The Italian front had claimed its first victim.

'1917 wasn't much cop,' Foote observed grimly. '1918 doesn't look as though it's going to be all that promising either.'

*

Just before Christmas they were due to leave for a new aerodrome being constructed at Issora on the Piave front but, just as they were about to take off, the weather broke and only Dicken and Foote got away before low cloud, fog, mist and rain came down to shut out the airfield. Finding themselves in the air, they had to fly by guesswork until they found the railway line that ran from Verona towards Trieste, and follow it at tree-top height until they came to an airfield which they guessed correctly was the one they wanted. Italy, it seemed, wasn't all it was cracked up to be – especially in winter. The Venetian Plain was a maze of small soggy fields edged with willows and cut by deep drainage ditches which would make forced landings difficult. The weather changes appeared to be sudden, too, the sunshine vanishing abruptly and unexpectedly behind thick fogs which could extend upwards to five hundred feet.

Issora aerodrome took its name from a group of farm buildings black with the damp weather, and lay on a flat plain alongside a wide canal with raised banks edged with poplars. As Dicken and Foote climbed from their machines, an officer of an RE8 squadron also using Issora appeared with a bottle of Strega to welcome them. He was in high spirits because two pilots from 28 Squadron, deciding on an impromptu raid on an Austrian aerodrome at Motta, ten miles over the lines, had dropped a large cardboard Christmas card wishing the Austrian Flying Corps a merry Christmas from the RFC, and had then proceeded to shoot up the hangars and any personnel they could see on the ground.

'Sounds as if we might be winning the war out here,' Foote said.

Since there was little in the way of living quarters at Issora, they found that, like the pilots of an Italian Hanriot squadron which was also flying from the field, they were to live for the time being in Capadolio, a small town that lay

149

just beyond the canal, and to make transportation simpler, a spur line had been constructed from a queer little electric tramway that circled the outer fringes.

Capadolio had arcaded sidewalks full of mediaeval buildings, which made Dicken think of Shakespeare, a moat, a portcullis, and an ossario full of the bones of soldiers of the Risorgimento. Its streets were muddy and filled with refugees, but it contained a galleria where you could buy anything from cigarettes to women and one good restaurant where they celebrated their arrival with dinner. Foote made sure of good service by announcing to the manager that Dicken was a very special individual. 'Take care of him,' he said. 'He's the bastard son of the King of England.'

The restaurant was full of Italian officers wearing jackets so tight they looked like the chorus from an operetta. Their collars were coloured according to the corps, regiment or brigade to which they belonged, and they were quick to introduce themselves, standing stiffly upright at their tables to shake hands. Trying to describe the fighting in the mountains, they said that more Italians were killed by avalanches than by the Austrians.

Dicken's billet was with the family of a junior British consular official called Aubrey, and since Foote was to live with a family who owned a bar, he decided Foote had got the best of the bargain. But Aubrey had a French wife who was as dark-eyed and good-looking as her husband and they had five daughters and two sons ranging from nineteen down to ten, each an exact replica of their parents and their brothers and sisters, and things began to look a little better because the eldest daughter was a beauty in the manner of Annys Toshack.

At breakfast the following morning, Dicken was surprised to find the whole family lined up to meet him.

'We thought,' Aubrey explained, 'that the least we could do was offer a home to one of our soldiers until things are organised.'

'My father was also in the consular service,' Mrs Aubrey explained. 'And I have a brother fighting with the brave French Army. He has a very dangerous job. He is a railway Transport officer at Dieppe.'

She was a full-busted woman, as French as the Eiffel Tower, and her conversation was larded with references to brave, loyal France and her courageous soldiers. The children were solemnly introduced – George, the elder of the two boys, who was due to go to university; Nicola, the eldest girl, pink-faced and beautiful; Bernadette; Marguerite; Mark; and two small ones, Cecilia and Marie-Gabrielle. The youngest, Marie-Gabrielle, pulled at Dicken's hand. 'Take some notice of me,' she said. 'Nobody ever does.'

They shook hands in the French fashion and the children smiled and bobbed their heads, and Dicken wasn't slow to notice that the eldest girl kept her eyes on him longer than she needed to.

'We have come to Capadolio,' Aubrey said, 'because of the arrival of British troops. We're here to look after the diplomatic side of the business. My French opposite number's at Villaveria on the Trentino front.'

As breakfast finished and Aubrey vanished to his office and his wife to the back of the house to attend to her children, Dicken was delighted to find himself alone with the eldest daughter. With her mother she had joined the Red Cross and worked several days a week at the hospital in the town.

'There have been so many wounded since Caporetto,' she said. 'And the men have to lie on the stone floor. They sleep like logs, they are so exhausted, and they're terrified they're going to be abandoned.'

The Italian soldiers, she said, had a dread of fresh air and when the ward sister's back was turned, got out of bed and shut the windows she'd opened. Her own patients were mostly not wound cases but men suffering from trench feet, bronchitis, influenza, and typhoid from drinking water out of shellholes.

'They're such babies,' she said. 'A lot of them are country boys in contact with town diseases for the first time in their lives and they persist in dying of ordinary things like measles and mumps, and then we have to hurry to fetch the priest because they want absolution. We're Catholics, too, of course. We came here from Rome after Caporetto.'

Because the house was in line with the aerodrome, their

conversation was constantly overlaid with the sound of aircraft taking off and landing.

'Sometimes,' she said, 'they look as if they're going to fly in through the window.'

She described the panic which had swept through the country after Caporetto. 'The Italian army was accused of cowardice,' she explained. 'It wasn't true, of course. It was simply that the Germans massed for the attack without being seen, but Father says the Italian command should have known. When the attack came they lost their heads and now General Cadorna's been replaced by General Diaz and a communiqué he issued blaming the Italian soldiers has been suppressed by the government. It's said –' she dropped her voice '– that many soldiers were shot for running away. Officers, too. Many of them senior. Would you like some coffee? People here drink coffee all the time.'

Dicken was just coming to the conclusion that he was going to enjoy Italy when the sound of aircraft over the house grew louder, and he turned to the window with a frown. Outside, people were pointing and beginning to run, and he wondered if some idiot was in trouble. Then he heard the rattle of machine guns and, jamming his face against the glass, saw aeroplanes wheeling in the sky above the airfield outside the town. They were circling at a height of no more than two hundred feet, and he was just peering upwards trying to identify them when he heard the crash of a bomb and felt the glass quiver against his cheek. Almost immediately, Nicola burst into the room again with the coffee, a look of alarm on her face. He pushed her against the wall at once.

'The glass might fall in,' he said. 'Some fathead's fooling about with bombs.'

Crossing to the window again, he saw now that there were at least a dozen machines over the airfield and, as he stared, one of them lifted away through a long column of brown smoke, and he saw Maltese crosses in the centre of yellow-painted wings decorated with red and white stripes.

'They're Austrians!' he yelled. 'It's a raid on the aerodrome!'

Running into the street, he stared towards the north and

this time he identified the machines as Aviatiks, German bombers powered with Mercedes engines. Escorting them were a whole host of Albatros DIIIs, with one or two square-bodied small-tailed machines with a curious lattice-work strut formation that he recognised from the photographs and drawings they'd been studying on the way south as Hansa-Brandenburgs.

Aviatiks normally operated at a height of over 5000 feet but these were floating about close to the ground, milling around in every direction as though trying to commit suicide. As the air shuddered to another crash, the windows rattled and Dicken saw debris fly and a cloud of smoke lift up beyond the houses. Outside, the cries of surprise had changed to cries of alarm, and the people in the streets began to run for shelter. A car driven by an Italian soldier hurtled round a corner opposite to run into the rear end of a cart drawn by a panic-stricken mule lashed on by its peasant driver. The cart vanished to matchwood and the mule went galloping on, dragging the front pair of wheels, while the driver clung to the reins and was towed on his face through the mud behind.

The bombs were exploding one after the other now but the ground defences were beginning to answer with machine guns and anti-aircraft guns, which were filling the sky with puffballs of smoke, white from the British, red from the Italian. From the town he could hear the wails of women, and from the back of the house Mrs Aubrey screaming at the children to go to the cellar. Nicola was watching from the steps.

He jerked a hand towards the north where snow-capped mountains showed above the orchards outside the town. 'I'd better get out there,' he shouted above the din.

'God go with you!'

'He can go in my place if He likes,' Dicken said with a grin, then wished he hadn't because she looked so startled he realised he had probably offended her.

Grabbing his coat, he ran from the house. There was no other means of getting to the field except by tram, but one was just rounding the corner, its sign reading *Campo d'Aviazione*. Just as he jumped on it, it clattered to a stop.

'Get it going!' he shrieked at the driver, but the Italian shrugged and pointed to the trolley bar.

'*Elettricità*,' he shrieked back. '*È chiusa la corrente*. The electricity's cut off!'

The tram was emptying rapidly and Dicken was just wondering what to do when an Italian Air Force tender filled with officers shot past. Among them was Foote and as he saw Dicken he pounded on the driver's shoulder and the vehicle slid to a stop with locked wheels.

By the time they reached the field, one of the hangars was on fire together with two of the machines inside. Ammunition was exploding and bullets were spitting in all directions, but the Italians were manhandling the rest of the machines out, and more were being started up by mechanics ducking at the fusillades of exploding cartridges.

Every one of the British RE8s had been hit by splinters but the Austrian machines were lifting away now and bolting for the north, while Italian Hanriots, French-built single-seaters like Camels, were beginning to streak off the ground in all directions. Dicken's Camel had been refuelled and, climbing into the cockpit, dressed just as he was, he gestured wildly at the Italian mechanics.

The engine started with a crackling roar, filling the air with blue smoke and the smell of castor oil, and as the chocks were dragged away he shot off, his tail up immediately. Lifting in a climbing turn, he was horrified to realise that every gun on the ground was shooting at him. In the excitement, no one was bothering to check the nationality of their target and as machine guns, rifles and even field guns joined in, he saw little flags of canvas start to flutter above the centre-section. Then, in the distance above him, he saw a patrol of Camels, their wings translucent against the sun, which he recognised as from 28 Squadron. They were heading south after a patrol, and as they spotted the Austrian machines, they dropped out of the sky one after the other.

Almost at once several of the two-seaters began to fall to earth. The DIIIs and the Brandenburgs seemed powerless to help and merely milled about the sky in a hamhanded fashion as if they didn't know what to do. As Dicken bore down on the machine at the rear of the formation like an enraged farmer after an apple-stealer, he saw the Austrian observer trying to warn the pilot. As his guns rattled and jumped, a cloud of smoke burst from the Aviatik's exhaust as the pilot opened the throttle, but he saw the wings had started to move as the outer struts broke loose and a cloud of steam had escaped from the engine. Then the port wing drifted free and the machine began to spin round what was left in a slow descent like a falling leaf. It hit the earth in a lopsided glide and, as its wheels touched, the tail lifted and the machine cartwheeled across the field, scattering wreckage until it came to rest in a clump of trees.

Circling over it, Dicken was startled at the speed and suddenness of the victory, then, since he was safely behind the Italian lines, he decided to go down and land alongside. To his surprise, the two Austrians were staggering about the field, one of them with a broken arm, the other with a badly cut face. At first he thought they were dazed and shocked, then it dawned on him they were befuddled with drink.

'*Wein*,' one of them said cheerfully. '*Wein und Schnapps. Das Fest. Weinachten. Das Christfest. Nur zu vertraut.* Too much. Too good.'

Gradually he made out that their squadron had been having a Christmas celebration when they had been unexpectedly ordered to avenge the shooting up of Motta airfield the previous day by 28 Squadron, and they hadn't had time to sober up.

'*Nun sehr nuchtern*,' the Austrian said. '*Vollkommen nuchtern.* Very sober. Like a judge.'

The Italian pilots were excited by their success and invited Dicken and Foote to their mess to celebrate. They were a high-spirited lot, proud of the fact that it had been an Italian, Giulio Douhet, who had prophesied before the war that the air was about to become a battlefield. Their country had entered hostilities with only seventy-two pilots but, with a boundless enthusiasm and a hard conviction about the potentiality of the air, had poured money into aircraft production.

They had covered a long table with bottles and swept the RFC men inside with a yell of welcome. The two Austrians arrived soon afterwards, bandaged and pale, for a few drinks before disappearing to a prisoner of war camp, and the Italians taught them all to sing *La Campana di San Giusta*, the song of the Italian Irredentists, and in return were taught the song of the dying airman by Foote.

> 'Take the cylinders out of my kidneys,
> The connecting rod out of my brain.
> From the small of my back take the camshaft,
> And assemble the engine again.'

They were still singing when the shell case hanging outside as an air raid warning started to clatter. As they ran to the door, they saw another wave of machines approaching from the north, four large bombers escorted by five fighters.

'Gothas, by God,' Foote said in amazement. 'The bastards sure are determined!'

Once again the Austrians were unlucky. An Italian patrol was just returning and the Austrian fighters bolted. As the Hanriots fell on the Gothas, one of them burst into flames and began to spiral downwards.

'You know,' Foote said. 'One way or another it looks like being quite a Christmas.'

8

When Dicken reached his billet that night he found the whole Aubrey family bustling round laying the dining table.

'What's this?' he asked. 'A celebration?'

Mrs Aubrey's hands flew. 'Have we not a hero in our midst?'

'Who?'

Mrs Aubrey looked at him, startled. 'But you, Monsieur! Did you not destroy the enemies of France this morning? My daughter tells me how you leap into a car and drive at full speed to the airfield where you destroy the Austrian formation single-handed.'

As she clapped her hands, the children began to take their places at the table. There was a lot of whispering and scuffling alongside Dicken between the two boys and Nicola before Nicola emerged triumphant to take the next-door chair. Grace was said, then chicken appeared, cooked with tomato and pepperoni, and the wine began to move round the table.

'This is a good wine, my boy,' Aubrey said. 'Orvieto. Golden-yellow and very dry.'

'Not as good as a French wine, of course,' Mrs Aubrey explained. 'But good. Afterwards we have Barbaresco, an aristocrat among wines.' She kissed her fingertips. 'It will remind you of violets.'

When the meal was finished, the kitchen staff appeared in their best clothes, the cook and maids in green skirts with white blouses. An elderly footman, in green trousers and a red waistcoat, sang folk songs with them and played an accordion for dancing. Aubrey danced with his second eldest daughter, the eldest boy with his mother, and the rest of the children paired off, leaving Nicola very noticeably free to dance with Dicken. It was an Italian dance Dicken didn't know but, with everybody pushing him, he found himself circling with Nicola, their hands on their hips.

'I am very happy, Mr Quinney,' she said.

'Dick. Please call me Dick. You're very pretty, Nicola. Do you know?'

She blushed.

'Nicola's a pretty name, too.'

She looked up at him, her eyes meeting his for the first time. 'Do you know many girls?' she asked.

The question startled him. 'Everybody knows one or two.'

'Particularly soldiers. I know England very well,' she went on. 'One day I hope we shall go back there. I'd like to live in London and be English like my father. Are you married, Dick?'

He hastened to reassure her.

'You are engaged?'

He wondered about that. He'd been to bed with Zoë Toshack and had even suggested marriage, but he had a feeling she'd been much more interested in the car engine she was looking at. He played for safety.

'No,' he said firmly. 'I'm not engaged.'

*

The rest of the squadron arrived four days later, flying in, in ones and twos. Huts had been erected by this time and Dicken was well aware that his stay with the Aubreys was already short. Occillotti, the Italian interpreter, said that, because of the retreat, riots had been taking place in Treviso as they had left, but that there would be no more fighting now that the winter was on them.

Since the enemy line ran roughly along the northern bank of the Piave, their patrols would carry them up and down the river, where the Austrian observation machines would range to spot for the artillery shelling the southern slopes of the Montello, a hogsback that ran along the front near Montebelluno. To the north the mountains rose like the backcloth for a stage setting and at night they could see pinpricks of light which were shells bursting on the slopes where the Italian trenches ran.

Near the aerodrome was a river, the water as clear as gin, the pebbles and the boulders that lined the banks white as old bones in the sun. All around the aerodrome the plain was full of troops. The backward movement had finally stopped and reserves were moving north again, and all the tree-trunks were plastered on one side by the mud flung up by wheels. The traffic seemed to go on constantly, even through the night, big guns pulled by tractors, their long barrels camouflaged with branches, mules carrying ammunition, grey trucks filled with men.

The country was dark with the winter rains and the valleys held mists, while on several days there was a wreath of cloud round the mountains. The troops, splashing past, their dark Italian eyes haggard in the grey light, seemed to be wet through to a man and mud-spattered by the lorries and the grey staff cars that roared indifferently past.

The countryside they were to fly over was very different from the squalid wasteland of Flanders. It was thickly populated and the steep round-topped hill of the Montello was clearly going to be a problem in low cloud.

The Austrians were known as the Kameraden Schnürs-chuh – the laced boot comrades – which was what the Germans called them because of their distinctive laced boots that were said to allow them to run away faster. Despite their recent victory at Caporetto, nobody seemed frightened of them. 'Everybody beats the Austrians,' Foote said. 'Even the Italians.'

C Flight were first to be ready and, flying a practice formation over the Montello, found themselves looking down on the Piave, a river of many streams, some mere rivulets, others broad and thrusting, running through rib-bon-like channels of shingle and between stony banks and innumerable pebbled islands. As they turned north-west with the shining river the stones seemed to move in the sunshine, and looking down, Dicken frowned. The damn things *were* moving! He looked again, and it dawned on him that what he was looking at was an Aviatik painted in a checkerboard of black and white, which was flying along the river bed so that it was almost indistinguishable from its background.

Moving alongside Trenarworth, he waved and pointed downwards. Trenarworth stared in the direction of the pointing finger but obviously saw nothing and lifted his head to stare inquisitively at Dicken. Gesturing wildly, Dicken pointed again, but Trenarworth still didn't seem to see and, when, a minute or two later he gave the washout signal for the return, Dicken turned away and dived towards the river bed.

He had lost the black and white machine by now, however, and for a moment he wondered if he'd been mistaken. Then he saw it again, flying up and down, keeping carefully to the pebbled banks of the river. Artillery fire was bursting along the Italian lines.

Howling down out of the sky, he came up behind the Aviatik but the Austrian pilot was experienced and swung back underneath him and flew at speed in a south-westerly direction, so that by the time Dicken had turned to follow him, he had begun to head north and was bolting at full speed for the shelter of the Austrian anti-aircraft guns.

With his petrol low, Dicken turned for home, to find a mist settling over the airfield. He put the machine down quickly but by the time it had been wheeled to the hangar, the mist had become a fog that blanketed the field and made further flying impossible. Trenarworth demanded to know why he had left the flight and as Dicken explained what had happened the telephone went.

Trenarworth answered it. When he put it down, he looked curiously at Dicken.

'Artillery, me dear,' he explained. 'Said it's about time somebody chased that black and white bugger away. He's been troubling them for weeks.'

*

It didn't take them long to discover that flying on the Italian Front wasn't as easy as they'd expected and that the Austrian Air Force wasn't as inadequate as their showing at Christmas had indicated. Instead of 'jagdstaffeln', they called their squadrons 'fliegerkompanien', shortened to 'Flik', and until recently had all been flying Hansa-

Brandenburgs, designed by a man called Heinkel, strange high-nosed machines with tall fuselages, which were called Spiders because of their strange strut formation. Now, however, they had gone over to Bergs, Albatroses and Phönixes, small machines with round-ended wings, large scalloped tails and inward-sloping struts, that could out-climb a Camel, and they had been taking a steady toll of the Italian airmen.

There were other difficulties which highlighted the difference from France. Because of the rapid retreat, there were few military telephone lines and the normal telephone system had to be used. But this was very indifferent and, as there was no priority for military signals, when they wished to contact the artillery or the forward positions, they had to take their turn with commercial and private callers.

The mists and fogs that appeared on the Venetian Plain were a further hazard. Occillotti said they were caused by the warm air from the Adriatic striking the bitter winds off the mountains, and the weather changes were sudden. At bewildering speed, sunshine gave way to fog which could rise to five hundred feet. To overcome the difficulty, they set up a forward signal station to indicate by ground markers to returning aircraft which airfields were fogbound and which were clear, but they soon found it didn't work because the signal station was invariably fogbound, too.

With the weather clamped down and the local people insisting it would stay clamped down for several days, the Italians were quick to arrange a public ceremony to announce the arrival of their allies. They didn't think much of the British Government because they felt they should have sent troops to the Italian front months before, but now that they'd arrived they were determined not to miss the opportunity for an occasion. The whole Aubrey family was excited at the prospect of a march past and Nicola was allowed a new coat and hat, which she shyly brought to show Dicken.

'They'll ruin the march past,' he said gallantly. 'Everybody will be too busy looking at you.'

'Our Father said she wanted a new coat and hat especially for you,' Marie-Gabrielle pointed out.

Nicola tried to shoo her away but she refused to go, a

miniature version of Nicola herself and, like all the Aubrey children, attractive to look at.

'Blue suits her,' she pointed out in matter-of-fact tones. 'Last year she went in for red. Our Father said it was because she was a bit gone on a French officer who wore red trousers.'

Despite the close proximity of Venice, they were not allowed to fly within five miles of it because the Italians there didn't want to fire their anti-aircraft guns in case the vibration damaged the fragile buildings. They had already discovered at Issora that the Italian gunners weren't very particular and shot at anything that appeared. The Italians were nervous in every way about Venice, in fact, and cameras were not allowed, even in Issora, and the sending home of picture postcards which might fall into Austrian hands was forbidden, as was the purchase of spirits, wine or bread from local shops because of the shortages.

Despite the blue skies and the beauty of the countryside, Italy seemed in the end to have less to recommend it than they'd expected. It was riddled with rickets, tuberculosis, illiteracy, inertia, corruption, unemployment, charms, churches, absentee landlords, bailiffs, floods, debts, bad sanitation, malnutrition and infant mortality. But the Italians themselves were warm-hearted, gregarious and quick to rejoice. But they liked to be dramatic about things and their sudden glows of warmth had their reciprocals in sudden bursts of histrionic rage, though they soon caught on to the fact that British troops delighted in egg and chips, and small cafés opened all along the road to Capadolio, each with its little group of tables and its wired-in chicken run with laying hens.

Even Italian humour was different, uproarious and bawdy, and they seemed to spend a large part of every day singing. Foote's gramophone was of a type they had never seen before and the air was full of 'Oohs' and 'Ahs' and 'Mamma mias', and from then on they were constantly on the doorstep with records they wanted playing – all of them, to Foote's disgust, opera. Even the Italian infantrymen camped across the road edged nearer, joining in to outsing the record and indignantly stopping the carts which rattled past so they could hear better.

Without doubt, the war in Italy was a happier, more naïve affair than the war in France where everything was deadly, adult and in earnest. In Italy there wasn't the same intensity. The Italians had been known from time to time to hang their washing on their barbed wire, and when the Austrians had advanced to the Piave they hadn't even cut off the telephone across the river.

'*Ma naturalmente*,' Occillotti explained. 'The people there are Italians and they have paid their subscriptions.'

They were not fools, however, and their uniforms, surely the ugliest in Europe, were also the least visible. 'Their wearers don't even make a shadow,' Occillotti said proudly.

Because of the tree-clad slopes where they fought, they wore what they called grigio-verde – grey-green – known to the British as rat-grey, and it was quite uncanny how difficult it was to see them against the background.

'Take mud from the Nile,' Foote said, 'rub in a couple of pounds of ship-rat's hair, then paint a roan horse with it and you'll understand why the Austrians can't see an Italian at fifty yards.'

The bersaglieri were always popular and were always being asked to swop headgear, but the carabinieri, their famous cocked hats covered with grey linen for the war, were totally uncompromising. You didn't argue with them and you didn't ask them to change hats.

Seeing what was provided for off-duty British troops in the way of YMCA canteens and bars, Occillotti was indignant that the Italian politicians had done nothing for their men.

'Because we can sing,' he said, 'they expect us to sing all the time.'

For the celebration of the arrival of the allies, British infantry appeared from the north, to be followed shortly afterwards by a battery of artillery and a French alpine battalion. Drawn up on a patch of empty ground outside the town, they shivered with the rest of the squadron as they waited for the word to march in. Having arrived first, 28 and 45 Squadrons had opted out with a claim that they were too busy defending the sacred soil of Italy.

An Italian band marched up, resplendent with brilliant uniforms and cocks' feathers in their hats, and while the musicians licked the mouthpieces of their instruments, a civilian photographer with a camera on a three-legged stand manoeuvred blindly under his black cloth.

As they approached the Town Hall the streets were crowded. Bunting had been hung up and there were banners at every window – Italian, British and French – but, with the band playing an impossible marching tune, it was difficult to keep the step.

'I think it's a valeta,' Foote murmured out of the corner of his mouth.

The crowd seemed to love it nevertheless. Schoolchildren waved miniature flags and the streets were full of cheering. Every window was crammed with people and photographers were stationed at every corner. Among the crowd round the mayor were delegations from all three countries, and among the British contingent Dicken could see the Aubreys, Nicola in her bright blue coat and hat.

They remained at attention while the band played *God Save the King*, the *Marseillaise*, the *Marcia Reale*, the *Brabançonne*, *Tipperary* and the *Marcia dei Alpini*. By the end of it their knees were trembling with the effort of standing still.

As the band finished, there was a yell of '*Evvivano i Liberatori! Evvivano gli Inglesi! Evvivano i Francesi!*' and everybody began to sing *La Campana di San Guista*, the song of the Italians who had fought for generations to free Northern Italy from Austrian domination.

> '*O Italia, O Italia del mio core,*
> *Tu ci vien' a liberar'.*'

The mayor made a speech, to which a British staff officer replied in halting Italian. The crowd was entranced.

'They speak the language of Dante,' the mayor crowed.

For some reason, an elderly man with long white hair delivered an oration on behalf of the Italian Teachers' Association. Speaking a little English, he bored them silly with references to Gladstone, Palmerston, Garibaldi and Cavour, and announced that he was proud to see them there because his wife was also 'an Englishman.' Italian banners were presented to the commanding officers, to be flown alongside their national flags, and women moved along the lines of men, giving short lengths of red, white and green ribbon for good luck. Among them was Mrs Aubrey, who handed Dicken not only a red, white and green ribbon, but also a red, white and blue one.

'My brave brother in France,' she announced, 'has always worn one as a good luck charm and he is still safe after three years of fighting.'

Since he was Railway Transport Officer at Dieppe, his safety, Dicken decided, probably owed less to his scrap of ribbon than to the fact that he was eighty miles from the front line.

He had been informed by this time that in future he was to live with the rest of the squadron on the aerodrome and the Aubreys decided that the parting merited another dinner. It was the usual mixture of solemnity and gaiety, with prayers for Dicken's safety alongside Mrs Aubrey's boasts that 1918 would see the end of German domination in Europe.

'By then,' she said, 'gallant France will have asserted her mastery over the treacherous Boche.'

While the younger children were whipped off to bed and Aubrey disappeared to his study to work on papers for the next day, Nicola played the piano softly for Dicken. He sat alongside her, trying to turn the sheet music when she nodded. As their fingers touched, her playing faltered and, as she stopped, he leaned over and kissed her cheek.

For a second she stared back at him, her eyes huge and starry with long dark lashes.

'You shouldn't have done that,' she whispered.

'Why not?'

'Because kisses have meaning.'

'They're supposed to have.'

'But it's dangerous. We're Catholics. You're a Protestant.'

He smiled. 'Nothing like variety.'

She frowned. 'You're making a joke of it.'

The smile faded. 'Aren't you?'

She was silent for a long time, then she shook her head slowly. 'George has decided that instead of university, he's going to enter a seminary and become a priest. His religion's very important to him. So it is to me.'

Dicken wasn't quite sure what to say. He couldn't imagine Zoë getting steamed up about anything as illogical as religion, and as far as he could remember, he'd never seen her going to church.

From a girl who appeared to have no religion at all, he seemed to have progressed to one with too much.

9

The next day, as the Italians had predicted, the weather shut down. The sky became a steely grey sheet and blizzards began to claw at the hangars. Because there was no coal, the stoves wouldn't have warmed a rat and the mechanics were having to place braziers filled with wood near the aircraft to prevent the oil freezing.

Snow was shovelled from the landing area and the machine that was sent up to check the weather took off dragging a veil of snow, the slipstream blowing rime off the wings into the faces of the men holding down the tail as it swung. It returned with its pilot in agony with frozen hands and feet.

Ice hung on the trees, the sky remained dark, and the wind coming from the mountains cut like a sword. The roads froze so that lorries had difficulties on the hills and for three days Issora was shut in. As it grew colder, they started digging trenches in case the Austrians tried another bombing raid, and huts were sandbagged by soldiers who, finding how much better the Flying Corps lived than they did, tried in droves to transfer as observers and machine gunners.

The fortifications were erected just in time because the next night Austrian bombers, which had been busy for some time over Padua, returned to Capadolio, black-painted machines flying low across the airfield to fill the air with the iron throb of their engines. Wheeling in succession over the hangars, signalling to each other all the time with Morse lamps, they left huts burning, men without equipment, and the field pitted with holes.

On New Year's Eve, to organise the co-operation of the Italian anti-aircraft gunners, Dicken and Foote went with

Trenarworth to the front. After the grimness of Flanders, Italy seemed a little unreal. Occillotti drove the car through a wild rugged country strewn with boulders and crossed by rushing torrents, stopping in the villages they passed through to let them see the churches. Each with its own campanile, they all seemed a little dark, seedy and tumble-down, but at one of them a funeral service was in progress and the interior was ablaze with candles.

'From Caporetto,' Occillotti explained. '*I due fratelli.* Two brothers. Both die of wounds.'

As they came out, watched by a gloomy-looking police-man and a fat Franciscan friar in a mudstained brown habit, a woman trudged by with a bundle of twigs high on her back and two girls slapped at washing in a stream, despite the fact that the air was so thin it caught at the breath and the ground was covered with a coating of ice that made it difficult to walk.

In that sector of the front, the roads were well-engineered but contained a great many hairpin bends all of which Occillotti took at speed despite the ice, cheering himself every time they rounded one safely.

'*Bravo,*' he cried. '*Bravissimo!*'

The troops were living in huts and shacks they'd built with wood from the thick forests that covered the front. In one sector a whole saw mill had been set up to provide planks, logs and fuel for their fires and they looked well established with their own cows and chicken runs. The guns were concealed in bowers of acacia trees whose branches were clipped back to give an arc of fire, there was a waterfall handy, and the area was incredibly beautiful after the stark landscape of the Western Front.

The slopes were festooned with telephone lines and an artilleryman pointed out the problems of communication and supply, gesturing to where they could see the snout of a gun among the rocks above their heads and a long wire reaching up to it. 'Cable railway,' he explained. 'To carry the ammunition.'

Horses were brought forward and they climbed higher. On the Italian side of the Piave, the Montello rose in steep ridges from the river, its forward face exposed to the enemy view so that the slightest movement produced shellfire. It was explained that guns on this slope were too easily found by the enemy but on the rear slope they couldn't range on enemy positions and only howitzers with their high angle of fire could be used. Shallow breastworks had been erected on the summit for observation posts and covered with turf to make them invisible. From them they were able to look down on the river, with its pebbled bed and stretches of stony islands that stood out against the steely water in patches of sharp black and white.

'When the snows melt,' the Italian officer said, 'the river becomes a roaring torrent.'

There was an immense silence about them and the trees below looked like dark cotton wool, falling away from the mountains which rose, ridge on ridge, spire on spire, until the summits pierced the sky. It was ghostly in the stillness, and awesome away from the sound and movement of the streams.

As they watched, the same black and white Aviatik Dicken had chased away flew along the river bed out of sight of the anti-aircraft gunners on the reverse slope, and the Italian artilleryman's eyes bulged with his fury.

'Always,' he said. 'Always he is there!'

They dined with the artillerymen, and as they returned down the steep winding roads, a storm started with unexpected suddenness. A tremendous wind began and the trees started to sway, scattering snow in showers from the branches. On Occillotti's suggestion they halted at an inn and sat drinking while the thunder rolled round the mountains and the lightning lit up their faces. When they continued their journey, the night was bright with millions of stars and mountain air clear as crystal wafted across their faces. Foote and Trenarworth were chattering happily with Occillotti but Dicken was silent. It seemed harder to accept death and mutilation in an area of such outstanding beauty, and the war suddenly seemed a vast conspiracy between the generals to kill everybody off.

*

Work started on the second day of the new year when orders were received for five Camels to escort a raid by ten RE8s on the Austrian Army headquarters at Vittorio. Air battles in Italy, it seemed, were not fought above the trenches as in France but close to where the staffs lived and worked in comfortable quarters.

'I like that,' Foote said enthusiastically. 'Staff against staff. Pity they don't do it more often. Put 'em all in a field with clubs, for instance. If they did, someone might get the idea of calling it a draw and sending us all home.'

It was Trenarworth's view that not enough was being done to win the war on the Italian Front and he decided they would shoot down a captive balloon which hung in the sky five miles inside the enemy lines at Campo Sordo. It seemed he had a cousin with the artillery who'd been complaining it could see everything they did.

Dicken didn't like the sound of it very much but the bombing raid was made without loss. As they drew away, Austrian fighters attempted to attack and Dicken managed to get his sights on a DIII which flew through his fire and continued on without wavering into the mountainside near the town, where it burst into flames and rolled down the steep slopes into the valley, starting an avalanche which roared down after it, bringing down trees, telegraph lines and huts until it swept over a line of trenches.

As the RE8s reached the safety of the British lines, Trenarworth fired a red Very light, and leaving three Camels to see the RE8s home, dropped almost vertically out of the sky with Dicken alongside him. Ears crackling after the descent, they shot across the lines to hedge-hop back to Campo Sordo. There was no machine gun fire as they approached and they could see the men at the winch of the balloon trying to haul it down. The two observers jumped as they roared up and Dicken saw his bullets stitching the surface, then the grey repulsive bag gave off a puff of smoke and slowly dissolved as the gas inside ignited, and began to wriggle down out of the sky like a gigantic diseased caterpillar.

As he lifted his machine away, getting a lungful of acrid black smoke, he heard the clatter of a machine gun just behind him and saw two lines of tracer pass through the gap between his wings. Wrenching the Camel to the right, he found himself following an Albatros round in a frantic ring-a-roses. The Camel's faster turn brought him nearer to the Albatros's tail and the Austrian pilot lost his nerve and pushed his nose down to dive away. Dicken was only fifty yards away when he fired, and the Austrian pilot threw up one arm and the machine immediately nosed over and dived into a field.

Trenarworth was holding up both hands and waving, and just behind the Austrian lines they found an Austrian staff car on which they swooped one behind the other. Instead of stopping dead and allowing them to pass overhead, the driver accelerated, and they caught him as he approached a curve on the hillside. It was Dicken's impression that neither of them hit the car but it careered across the road, smashed through a wooden fence and made a tremendous leap into the valley where it burst into flames.

It was late in the day now and as they reached Capadolio Dicken saw that one of the sudden fogs that infested the northern plain had risen. It was impossible to see the airfield in the shadows below and he visualised them circling until their petrol ran out.

Seeing a pink glow near the top of the fog, he realised that someone below had heard their motors and was firing Very lights to indicate the position of the field. A moment later, one of the flares burst through, shining and pink, to cast a rosy light on the upper surface of the bank of mist.

Trenarworth began to drop down. Dicken followed more warily, and as they entered the mist he lost sight of his companion. Very lights were going up all over the place now, so he flew towards them, able now to see houses below, then a small hill loomed up, on its summit a tree, winter-bare of foliage, and he scraped past with inches to spare. Ahead of him he could see the source of the lights and he glided over the fence and side-slipped in. As he switched off his engine, he realised he could still hear Trenarworth droning about somewhere, trying to get down.

'For God's sake, keep those flares going,' he yelled as Foote appeared, but even as he spoke they heard a crunching sound and the high scream of the engine which stopped almost immediately. In the silence, they peered through the mist at a red glow near the end of the airfield.

'I think,' Foote said heavily as they started to run, 'that somebody's wound the war up out here.'

*

With Trenarworth gone, there was no one else of sufficient experience to lead C Flight but Dicken. But even as he put up his third pip, Morton was killed. As squadron commander, he was not supposed to engage in combat, so, instead of leading patrols, he flew on the pretext of making sure they did their job properly and simply shot at anything that came his way.

A DFW was reported heading south and he shot it down near San Luca. Then, when nothing further was heard of him, it was assumed he'd landed elsewhere; but that afternoon the artillery reported that a machine carrying British markings had fallen out of the clouds, and crashed near Limbragga. Nobody knew what to make of it because Limbragga was well inside the British lines but, late in the evening, information arrived that Morton had been shot down by mistake by an Italian pilot.

'The oily beggars,' Foote raged, his face bleak and angry. 'I suppose the bastard's claimed it as a victory.'

It came as a hard blow to Dicken because Morton had been his commanding officer in his first nervous days as an observer and it had been Morton who had given him his first chance. He had been fighting ever since 1914 and had never taken advantage of the fact that commanding officers were not supposed to fly in action, and it became just one more little jarring reminder that he wasn't invulnerable. If it could happen to Morton it could happen to him.

The mess was seething because Morton had been a popular commanding officer but the following morning as they were waiting for orders, Hallowes, the Recording Officer, an ex-infantryman with a stiff leg, informed Howarth, the commander of A Flight, who was running the squadron until a new CO arrived, that every man was to be on parade, properly dressed, at midday because the Commander-in-Chief, the Earl of Cavan, was to inspect them.

They stared at each other, wondering what it was all about. It soon became clear.

'I have here,' Cavan said, flourishing a piece of paper, 'the Italian report, signed by the colonel commanding XVI Group. He expresses his deepest regret and hopes the incident will not disturb the loyal collaboration between the two air forces.' The C-in-C stared about him. 'There will be no reprisals. Major Morton was the last man in the world to expect his death to start a vendetta. It was an incident without malevolence. A tragic mishap in the course of a war. Let it remain so.'

*

Two days later the whole squadron of eighteen machines were ordered to take on 20lb Cooper bombs to raid the hydro-electric power station at Lugagnano as a diversion while RE8s bombed bridges to the west. It seemed a dubious way to draw the Austrians' attention because they kept their hydro-electric power stations well guarded. No precise instructions were given as to how to make the attack, and Howarth decided they would approach from the west, going in as flights.

'It lies in a deep valley near the river,' he said. 'So we'll dive low and go in close to the ground.'

It was a brilliant day with a sky of burnished gold so that Dicken was caught by the infinity of uncluttered emptiness. He was lucky, he decided, because he did his fighting where the debris of battle disappeared at once and the winds blew the air clear of fumes and the smell of death. They formed up over San Luca in three groups of six machines but as soon as they reached Lugagnano it was obvious Howarth's plan wasn't going to work. Behind the power station was a sheer wall of mountain over which it would be impossible to climb if they went in low, and because of the narrowness of the valley there simply wasn't room to go in any other way but singly, one machine behind the other.

Without any means of communicating with each other, it was impossible to change the plan and, leading the third flight, Dicken watched the machines ahead trying to change position to a line-astern formation. It took time because nobody had been expecting it and he began to wave his own men out of their V-formation while they still had room to manoeuvre. By the time they had regained some order, the machines in front were swooping into the valley one after the other and heading for the power station. It's like flying into a sock, he thought grimly. We shall never get out of this one.

Anti-aircraft and machine guns started to fire and he saw tracer bullets and shells arc into the sky. Howarth's machine wriggled away and started to climb up the face of the mountain behind the power station, but he obviously decided he wasn't going to make it and, under tremendous fire from positions on the mountainside, he turned round at the end of the valley, his wingtips almost scraping the slopes and flew out the way he'd entered.

The second machine was still approaching the target when it burst into flames and Dicken saw it spin down in a column of black smoke to crash into a rocky pinnacle, roll itself into a smoking ball and slither in a mass of wreckage down the face of the mountain. The third and fourth machines, which dropped their bombs short, turned the opposite way from Howarth so that the pilots flying in behind them found themselves facing their own machines flying out. There were several near-collisions and in no time the following flight was entirely without cohesion.

The last to go in, Dicken wondered if he could do the job differently but, no matter which way he considered it, there was always that great wall of rock behind the power station and in the end he had to do the same as everybody else. Though there were no enemy aircraft, the valley seemed to be full of flying bullets, bursting shells and puffs of drifting yellow-brown smoke, with British machines wheeling in all directions.

C Flight all escaped but one, who continued in a shallow dive until he hit a house on the side of a hill. He seemed to go straight in one side and out of the other, the building dissolving in a shower of flying bricks and debris. Following the machine down to see if the pilot were still alive, Dicken recrossed the river close to the ground and was just approaching the Piave when he became aware of a long looping curve of wire almost invisible in front of him and realised it was one of the cables the Austrians strung up to lift ammunition up to their guns.

It sliced off his upper wing as cleanly as a razor stroke and, as the debris fell across the cockpit to trap him in his seat, he decided that his last moment had come. As the machine fell into the river, however, the water absorbed some of its momentum and neatly removed the debris of the wing. Scrambling free, startled to find himself still alive, he managed to get a foot on the bank and tried to cling to the wreckage of the fuselage. But the current was strong enough to sweep the smashed machine downstream and he lost his grip as it swung away from him.

Almost sinking under the weight of his sodden flying clothing, he was swept after it. As he struggled to keep his head above water he saw a group of Italian soldiers running down the snow-covered bank towards him. Two of them leapt in but the current was strong and the water bitterly cold and they, too, were swept away. As he was swirled about, sinking as the last of the air trapped in his flying suit escaped, to leave him with the buoyancy of a house-brick, he saw them washed up on an island nearby and drag themselves to safety.

He had just decided his time had come – and what a way to go, he thought: drowned while flying – when another man jumped into the river and began to swim towards him. As he was whirled round, half-drowned, he felt a hand on his collar dragging him to safety.

They flopped against the bank, the Italian without the strength to push him out, Dicken burdened with the saturated flying suit and unable to help himself. But more soldiers were running down the hill now and, grabbing them, they dragged them from the water and began to run them, shivering, up the hill to a group of abandoned houses where they lived.

Arriving back at Issora, Dicken was still white and unable to control the shuddering that convulsed his body from time to time. It didn't worry him too much because he knew it was only shock and he felt he had enough experience and inner strength to deal with it as he'd dealt with it before, but the battle over the power station at Lugagnano had left the younger pilots of the squadron depressed. Most of them were new to war and a group of them were muttering in the mess, shaken by the casualties. Among them was Foote's brother, his face wearing a look that came from the unexpected discovery that he was mortal after all.

As Dicken threw down his still sodden flying suit, Foote himself appeared, carrying a folding cot and a suitcase.

'I thought you were dead, man. What happened?'

'I nearly got drowned.'

'Flying a Camel?'

Dicken explained what had happened and Foote's face grew grim.

'Five down,' he said. 'One from A Flight, one from yours – two including you – two from mine, including the flight commander. They gave me his job.' He paused and, indicating the folding cot with his foot, managed a twisted smile. 'That makes three of us, because from now on, kid, we've got company.'

As he spoke, the door burst open and a figure appeared in the opening, holding a kitbag. The sun was behind it, dazzling on the snow outside. Squinting against it, Dicken frowned, then he leapt to his feet.

'Willie! What are you doing here?'

Hatto threw the kitbag at him. 'Been sent out to give you a hand, old fruit,' he said. 'A flight of Bristol Fighters. X Flight. Unknown quantity, I suppose. Six pilots. Six observers. Me leading. We're attached to you lot for orders. Probably because we weren't very good and could easily be spared.'

'Now we've all got flights,' Dicken said soberly. 'In spite of Diplock's machinations.'

'C'est la guerre. But –' Hatto's face changed '– hold your water, lad. That's what might be called the good news. Stand by for the bad. You've got a new CO. Speaks good Italian. He's on his way from Verona. It's Cecil Arthur Diplock. Parasol Percy himself.'

Part Three

I

There he was, with his bulging forehead and protruding ears and the smooth, self-confident look of the well-patronised. He'd grown a small moustache that looked as if a mouse had died on his upper lip, and his uniform was immaculate, his breast decorated with the ribbon of the DSO he had gained from staying close to the Wing colonel.

'Confounds the theory that it means Duke's Son Only,' Foote observed. 'Here we have somebody who's a bastard and *he*'s got one.'

'What's he doing here?' Dicken asked. 'His string-pulling must have gone wrong. He'd never choose an operational squadron.'

'That's just what he would choose,' Hatto said. 'Because he won't be expected to fly and it pushes him smartly up another notch to major. I told you he was crafty and ambitious.'

There was a feeling already that the top officers in Italy lacked the magic touch of Trenchard in France, who despite his insistence on an aggressive policy, had the gift of compassion for his pilots. Magnetism was missing and everybody felt they were risking their lives merely to make up charts of statistics – patrols flown, bombs dropped, enemy machines destroyed. The arrival of Diplock added to the feeling.

His first action was to get them all in the mess and give them a pep talk.

'There's a rumour that the Germans are going to start a push in France,' he said. 'We've got to give it all we can here so they can't draw reserves from this front.'

'Will you be flying, sir?' Hatto asked innocently.

A small frown crossed Diplock's face. 'Commanding officers aren't expected to engage in combat.'

'Morton did,' Foote growled.

Diplock frowned again. 'Have no fear,' he said. 'I shall be going up.'

As they were dismissed, he called the flight commanders back – Howarth of A Flight, Dicken, Foote and Hatto of the attached Bristol Flight. He spoke to Howarth about trivial things, then dismissed him and turned to the others.

'We all know each other,' he said slowly. 'We've met before. Well, let it be understood that, as far as I'm concerned, I don't remember things that happened in England and in France, and I expect you to forget them, too. However, I have a long memory and I ought to make it clear that I shall brook no attempt to drag up old quarrels.'

'I'm not sure,' Hatto said as they grouped together outside the mess, 'whether that was a friendly chat, an effort to let bygones be bygones, or just a veiled threat.'

As they turned away, Hallowes, the Recording Officer, put his head out of the door. 'Dick!'

Diplock was still standing near his desk. 'I brought a message from home for you,' he said stiffly. 'It's from my sister-in-law. She's still being seen about with that Canadian of hers. They appear to be constant companions.' There was an element of satisfaction in the way he spoke, and Dicken wondered if there really had been a message or whether he was merely seeking to be malicious.

'She sent her regards,' Diplock went on. 'All her time nowadays is spent at Shoreham aerodrome. My wife doesn't approve at all and neither do I. Before I left England, we tried talking to her.'

And I hope, Dicken thought, that she told you to mind your own bloody business.

The new régime started with a flurry of orders. More attention was to be paid to dress and smartness, and saluting was to be less perfunctory. Nobody had bothered a great deal with it before because respect was mutual between the men who flew the planes and the men who cared for them, but Diplock had spent most of his career at headquarters where things were different. With the weather growing warmer, he also tried to institute physical training but the flight sergeants quickly got their heads together and managed to

prove that aeroplanes, being the tricky, uncertain, inflammable things they were, there was always something to be done
on them, and the unhappy corporal Diplock appointed to
conduct the physical training sessions could never find a
quorum.

'No matter how much the powers that be think up ways
and means to harass the lower orders,' Hatto smiled, 'the
lower orders always find a way of dodging them. Except, of
course, when the authorities fall back on the charge of
"dumb insolence", which can't really be defined and should
be classed as cheating.'

It was noted that though, true to his word, Diplock flew,
he was careful not to go over the lines. His excuse was that,
like Morton, he was watching his patrols but it was noticeable that he never went far enough forward for it to be of
much value, and returning from one of them, his engine cut
and he had to put his machine down inside the local sewage
works.

'That's the second time,' Hatto pointed out gleefully. 'And
God knows, there aren't all that many sewage works in this
part of Italy.'

The following week, Dicken shot down a buff-coloured
Aviatik. No two patrols were ever alike and the sky was
empty except for a patch of cirrus high above, blank and
blue. He was enjoying himself, catching the warm smell of
the engine, his lungs rasped by the cold purity of the thin air,
when he saw it below, almost invisible against the pattern of
the earth. Diving out of the sun, he saw his bullets entering
the fuselage and watched as it began to descend in a slow
gliding turn towards the Italian lines. About 2000 feet above
the ground there was a flash and an explosion and the
machine simply vanished, with the two dark shapes of the
crew hurtling earthwards, followed by the wings curving
down for all the world like falling leaves.

That same evening, they were attacked by a flight of
Albatros DVs which overshot without hitting anyone so that
the Camels found themselves above. Dropping down in their
turn, for ten minutes they manoeuvred and circled and
Dicken found himself following a green-nosed machine with
a chequered tail surface. As he fired it erupted into flames. A

second DV was shot down by a newcomer called Bolitho who was immediately pounced on by another DV as he was watching his victim. In its turn, the second DV was caught by Dicken and followed the first one down, trailing a stream of black smoke. They crashed within half a mile of each other just behind the Austrian lines, and had already been confirmed by the artillery observers on the Montello when they returned.

'Three!' Hatto said, staring at Dicken. 'What a bad-tempered little man you are! How do you do it?'

'I don't know,' Dicken admitted. 'I just suddenly seem to have the knack.'

It seemed to please Diplock. 'A good pilot can run up a big score these days,' he said. 'We must make greater efforts. I think the Hun air force is beginning to run out of steam.'

'Rats, how the hell does *he* know?' Foote demanded furiously. 'He's one of those bastards who think that flying a fighter's like being in a goddam competition with a box of chocolates for the winner.'

The following day, Dicken shot down another two-seater. Two of them crossed the lines at 17,000 feet and, spotting them against a herring-boning of cloud, he stalked them from below, positioning himself so that their wings hid him from view. As he fired, the nearer of them started circling, while the second went into a shallow dive for home. The first machine was still circling as Dicken swung round again and, watching it, he was wondering what in God's name the pilot thought he was doing when he saw that the observer was leaning over the front cockpit and realised he'd hit the pilot who was either dead or wounded and the controls were jammed. Remembering his own horrifying experience with Hatto, he pulled away even as he was about to fire, and watched. The observer saw him but he waved to indicate that the observer should look after himself and the Austrian waved back. For a while, he struggled to climb into the forward cockpit but his changed position altered the trim of the machine and as Dicken watched, the two-seater's bank became steeper and steeper until it had turned over on to its back. The observer fell clear and the machine followed him in a dive which grew steeper until the centre section collapsed. The wings folded back and it dropped like a stone, the fuselage wagging from side to side with the speed of its fall. For a long time, Dicken watched it, tears in his eyes, until it disappeared into a patch of woodland in a flower of flame.

He was subdued when he landed and in no mood to celebrate. 'It comes no easier to see men die,' he admitted. 'I wanted like hell for him to get down safely.'

Two days later, he caught the Aviatik that so troubled the Italian artillery. He had flown a patrol with Foote's brother but, separated by a skirmish with three Albatroses, he was heading home alone along the Piave when his eye caught a movement beneath him and he realised he was looking down on the chequered machine flying over the pebbled patches of the river. Swinging into a gentle glide, he dropped down on it, firing as soon as he was within range. As the Aviatik swung violently southwards, he followed and its manoeuvres grew more desperate. As he forced it closer and closer to the steep sides of the Montello, the pilot, realising he was losing space to manoeuvre, tried to climb away but the machine hit the side of the hill and, as wings and spars crumpled, it slid along the ground on its belly, crashing through a stone wall and finally standing on its nose in a rainwater gully.

During the afternoon an artillery officer arrived in a car with a soldier carrying a large bunch of flowers which was handed over with a great many smiles and kisses on the cheek to indicate their gratitude. During the evening a colonel from Wing arrived and, a little like a conjuror producing a rabbit from a hat, Diplock produced the pilot of the Aviatik. He was a Hungarian called Ferenc who had got away with nothing more than a broken arm, though his observer had died in the crash. He seemed relieved to be alive but, as nobody could speak his language, the meeting produced very little, though the colonel seemed suitably impressed.

'Five in two days,' Diplock told him. 'Nobody can say we aren't pulling our weight.'

*

The news had reached the Aubreys when Dicken went to see them that Sunday. They were about to leave for church and Aubrey was standing in the hall brushing his top hat with his sleeve.

'My dear boy,' he said. 'I've heard you've been risking your life again. Five in two days I hear. The fiancé of our maid works at the airfield and he brings the news.'

As they talked, the children crowded round, yelling to be noticed, and Marie-Gabrielle swung on Dicken's arm.

'Nicola saw you coming,' she said. 'She's gone upstairs to put stuff on her face. They say you've killed a lot of Austrians. Is it difficult?'

'Not really. You just point the aeroplane at them and pull the trigger and they fall down.'

'Could you make one fall outside our house so we could see?'

Dicken frowned. 'I don't think you'd like it very much if you did.'

'Our Father says he wouldn't either. And so does Nicola. But she's a bit soppy. Are you going to marry her?'

'I hadn't thought of it.'

'If you don't marry her, will you marry me?'

Dicken grinned down at the pair of huge dark eyes staring up at him. 'I'll make a note of it for when you're old enough.'

'How old do you have to be?'

'A bit older than you.'

Marie-Gabrielle considered. 'I suppose I could wait a bit,' she said.

Mrs Aubrey arrived with a rush, to embrace him and kiss him on both cheeks and a moment later, Nicola appeared, wearing the blue outfit made for the parade.

'You were wearing green a minute ago,' Marie-Gabrielle accused.

'Sssh!' Mrs Aubrey shooed her away with the others but she clung to the door as she was dragged outside.

'If you're going to church with Nicola,' she asked, 'can I sit behind and watch what happens?'

'Dick doesn't go to church with us,' Nicola said shortly. 'We're Catholic and he's not.'

'I shouldn't think God would mind, would he?' Dicken chided gently.

'Protestants can't take Communion with us. And that's important, especially when my brother's to become a priest.'

Dicken was disappointed. He could think of nothing pleasanter than sitting alongside Nicola in a quiet church, letting himself be absorbed into the ancient ritual. The fact that it wasn't his church or his ritual seemed to matter very little.

'Still,' she smiled at him, 'I'd be happy if you'd walk there with us.'

They spoke very little as they headed along the street between the old brown houses, surrounded by Italian women in the inevitable black. Aubrey and his wife walked behind with the other children in a small crocodile.

As Dicken sat on a bench alongside the church, Italian soldiers tramped northwards past him, with here and there small groups of lorries, mule carts and waggons piled with hay, lumber, wine casks, flour, shells, barbed wire and ammunition. The weather had changed and the sun was warm as he sat smoking. Overhead he could hear an aeroplane droning away in the distance beyond the acacias.

Marie-Gabrielle was the first to reappear, hurtling out of the church like something shot from a gun to fling herself into Dicken's arms.

'I pretended I felt sick,' she said.

'And did you?'

'Not really. Our Father says I take a lot of looking after. I'm delicate, you see.'

'You look as tough as an old seaboot.'

'I've got a wasting disease. Listen.' She coughed energetically. 'Here's Nicola. She was praying for you. I heard her.'

Being prayed for was a new sensation to Dicken. He assumed his mother prayed for him but he couldn't somehow imagine Zoë doing it. She probably didn't even believe in God.

As they walked back to the house – 'In formation,' Dicken said – with the family just ahead, Nicola slipped a small packet into his hand.

'What is it?'

'You wear it round your neck. Promise you will. It's a St. Anthony medal. To keep you safe.'

'Even though I'm not a Catholic?'

He was teasing but there was a hurt look in her eyes and later in the garden she asked him if Protestants ever thought of becoming Catholics.

'*I*'ve never thought of it,' he said honestly.

'It would make things more easy if they did.'

'What sort of things?'

She blushed. 'I don't think mother approves of Catholics marrying non-Catholics.'

Dicken smiled. 'Who's going to get married?'

She blushed and stumbled lamely over an excuse, trying to pretend it concerned a cousin of hers. It was transparent, however, and she'd clearly been entertaining private hopes. When he considered the idea, it didn't seem a bad one. Because of the war and the life a pilot lived, girls seemed especially important, gentle and tender and twice as precious despite all the smutty talk in the mess, and this one was the beauty of the family.

He looked at Nicola with new interest, conscious of her naïvety and innocence. He'd been aware from the moment he'd first met her of her interest in him, but this was something different. Marriage had never crossed his mind and he'd regarded her just as part of a warm-hearted, friendly family, but the idea had begun to take root by the time he returned to camp and was given an extra fillip by the fact that mail had arrived and there were several letters on his bed from England. One was from Zoë and announced that she was learning to fly.

'Casey takes me up on the pretence of testing,' she wrote, 'and lets me handle the controls. He says I'm a natural pilot.'

The letter bubbled over with excitement and it was impossible not to feel her enthusiasm.

'The sky's so big and so blue,' she said. 'I feel when I'm up there that I'm like Columbus journeying into the unknown.'

Her delight made him smile, but when he looked at the letter again, he realised it was remarkably short of affection and barely mentioned him.

2

It was growing apparent that the Austrians were preparing for an offensive. Since everybody who arrived from France said the Germans were preparing for an offensive there, too, it was probable the two would start together so that allied reserves could not be moved from one front to the other.

The number of aircraft opposite increased and, as they grew more aggressive, Diplock's visits to the line to watch his patrols at work noticeably grew less frequent and he made a great deal of the amount of paperwork which kept him chained to his desk. As the days grew longer, continuous air cover was ordered with more patrols but, since they couldn't increase their strength, they could only increase the number of patrols by reducing the number of aircraft flying together.

Hatto's flight was having a bad time. Because the Bristol Fighter had proved itself a redoubtable aircraft, they were expected to fly without escort and, sent out singly, had lost several, so that Camels finally had to be provided to see them safely to and from their targets. Just when they were growing a little desperate, however, more machines arrived and they became a two-flight squadron, still under Diplock's general command, and began to provide their own escorts.

The increased activity set Foote worrying about his brother. Like all newcomers, young Foote had been hotheaded, eager to win the war and inclined to do foolish things and, though the attack on the power station at Lugagnano had shaken him, he still seemed to consider it his duty to do better than his brother and was always coming back with his machine shot full of holes.

'Look, you crazy kid,' Foote stormed at him. 'Why don't you listen to what a guy with experience tells you? The war isn't going to end tomorrow! Beginners don't see things the same way the old hands do. Get some flying hours in first. Give yourself time to get used to things.'

Young Foote smiled bleakly and slapped his brother on the back. It was obvious he thought he was slow and unaggressive.

'I reckon you're nuts,' Foote said. 'I'm going to have a word with Parasol Percy not to use you on the long patrols.'

'Don't you goddam dare!'

Foote's good-natured face was troubled as he watched his brother walk away, his shoulders stiff with hurt pride. 'Aw, hell,' he said unconvincingly. 'The guy's old enough to take care of himself.'

Another attempt was made to bomb the Lugagnano power station, this time by the Bristols, and with the same results as before. Three failed to return.

'Don't those bloody people at Wing ever come and see for themselves what's going on?' Hatto said.

The next day, in a sky vivid with thousands of little clouds like puffy dumplings which would burn off as the sun grew stronger, Dicken led his five Camels over the line. Catching a faint movement against the checkered ground below him, like insects moving in long grass, he realised it was caused by ten camouflaged DVs escorting three Aviatik two-seaters along the river where they were taking photographs of the Italian positions.

With an Austrian push just in the future, every reconnaissance machine shot down meant one more small item of information unfurnished, one more portion of the line not surveyed; and, to Dicken, people like young Foote, who considered it unsporting to attack slow two-seaters when there were fast and dangerous fighters about, had got it all wrong. Falling out of the sun, he drove for the centre of the formation so that the Austrian machines were obliged to leap apart like a flock of startled birds. As they scattered, he headed for the nearest of the two-seaters and, firing a burst, saw it lift upwards then stall and fall over to one side in a flop-winged dive.

The other two-seaters had dived away, escorted by two of the DVs, and were trying to continue their reconnaissance further west. Wrenching the Camel round in a tight bank, so that the blood drained from his face, he overhauled the rearmost of them near Roda. The Aviatik went down in a dive, a thin plume of escaping petrol trailing behind. A minute red glow appeared underneath the fuselage, gradually changing to smoke which grew thicker to become a black banner curving through the air behind the stricken machine. There was a flash of flame and he saw the pilot's mouth open in a cry of fear and pain, and the aeroplane, a mass of flames from wingtip to wingtip, fell away, small burning fragments of canvas detaching themselves as it went. Catching a whiff of oily smoke, he watched it fall to pieces, the burning front half separating from the tail and falling like a bright spark across the sky.

For a second, he stared at the drifting smoke with narrowed eyes, then one of the DVs flashed past him and dived away north at full speed. As he followed it up the valley and took up a position behind it, it began to manoeuvre wildly, trying to lift out of what was rapidly becoming a trap. But, with Dicken sitting above it, it had to dive away again and again until it finally flew into the rising ground.

Diplock was over the moon, and the Wing colonel appeared at dinner again that night. Congratulating Dicken, he told him he'd put him in for a medal and that the Italians had awarded him the Croce di Guerra for his earlier victories.

'With all that metal hanging on your chest,' Foote said, 'you'll jangle like a goddam Clerget with a broken ball race.'

The Wing colonel also told them that the Russians, torn by revolution and with the Tsar a Bolshevik prisoner, had signed surrender terms at Brest-Litovsk. There were long faces at once, because it meant the Germans had not only secured access to new supplies of oil and food and cleared the way to Central Asia so that they could join up with the Turks and threaten India, but had also disposed of the dangerous Eastern Front and could transfer troops to France for a new drive to the sea.

'The bloody war will probably go on for ever,' Foote said.

'One did once,' Dicken pointed out. 'The Hundred Years War.'

'Hundred Years War?' Foote looked shocked. 'I bet business went down a bit. What were they fighting about?'

'I think they forgot long before it finished. If this one goes on for a hundred years, we'll be flying aeroplanes at three hundred miles an hour.'

'They couldn't make aeroplanes to go that fast. They'd fall apart.'

Hatto smiled. 'They once said,' he pointed out, 'that motor cars couldn't go faster than twelve miles an hour.'

The following week news reached them of a massive German offensive in France. Helped by fog, the Germans had broken through the British lines and had split the allied armies in two.

'Here we go,' Foote said. 'Year one of the new Hundred Years War.'

By the end of the week they'd heard that half the ground captured with such sacrifice in 1916 had been lost and that the Germans were almost back to the positions they had held in 1914.

'It makes you wonder what all the last three years were for,' Hatto said.

When Dicken visited the Aubreys that night, they had lost a lot of their gaiety and Nicola was in a sombre mood. She'd just come from the hospital and was still wearing her uniform. Because of the impending Austrian offensive, they had been told to prepare wards for the arrival of wounded.

Sitting in the music room in front of the piano, she played for a while, her expression blank, while Dicken turned the sheets over, then she dropped her hands in her lap and looked at him.

'Shall we ever defeat the Germans?' she asked.

'Bound to.' Dicken entered the argument briskly, though he honestly didn't believe what he said. He had long since come to the conclusion that the war would go on for ever and that he and Foote and Hatto and all the others would never live to see the end of it. The thought lay like a spectre at the back of all his waking hours but it was something they none of them ever mentioned and he tried to sound enthusiastic and confident. 'In the end,' he said, 'we can't fail. The

Americans are arriving in France in their thousands. It's bound to make a difference.'

She sat silently for a little while and he leaned over and kissed her cheek.

'Are you in love with me, Dick?' she asked.

'Yes.'

'And I with you. It's very difficult.'

He stared at her in frustration. His own views on religion were vague. To him God was a sort of benign Wing colonel who not only didn't expect his subjects to go out and get killed but actually looked after them. He decided it was time to take a firmer grip on the situation and without a word he leaned forward and kissed her on the mouth. Up to that moment, his kisses had all been decorous salutations on the cheek and for a second she stared back at him, her eyes huge. Then, impulsively, she reached out for him and kissed him back. He put his arms round her and she clung to him, warm and trembling and feminine, and he wondered what he had ever seen in Zoë, with her brash manner and liberated approach to life.

Then he saw her eyes were full of tears. As they spilled over and ran down her cheek, her expression became lost and a little afraid so that he wanted only to bring happiness back to it.

'What are you crying about?' he asked. 'Your mother and father don't seem to mind me being a non-Catholic.'

'They're very broadminded.'

'And you're not?'

'I'm jealous when anyone looks at you,' she said with heartbreaking simplicity. 'Even Marie-Gabrielle. I mustn't be. I've admitted it at confession and I pray often to the Virgin when I go to bed. But she gives me no guidance and I'm bewildered.'

She was struggling through a wilderness of emotions, all of which seemed to be a little out of control, and he felt a unique tenderness towards her.

'Bewildered about what?' he asked gently.

She looked up, her eyes moist. 'I want to love you,' she said. 'But I mustn't.'

*

Towards the end of the month, it seemed the German advance in France was slowing down. They were now suffering from the problem that had plagued the allies ever since the war began: they were attacking across the ground their own artillery had shattered and were trying to bring up supplies across the devastated area where fighting had taken place for nearly four years. Eventually they learned that the Germans had been held.

'Us next,' Hatto observed. 'They're bound to try on the Piave now.'

Sure enough, Diplock gave orders that the offensive against enemy aircraft was to be pursued with increased vigour.

'He sure is an aggressive sonofabitch behind that desk,' Foote said.

On April 1st, they found that the RFC and the RNAS had been united under one command, to be called the RAF.

'It sounds to me like a forced marriage,' Hatto commented. 'And April Fool's Day's hardly a happy augury for the future. I suppose we'll become known as the Royal Air Farce.'

The new régime seemed to have affected Diplock's sense of balance because he started once more going out on what he called his supervisory patrols, though it was noticeable that they were all south of the Piave and most were in the direction of headquarters.

'Buttering up the brigadier,' Hatto said as they filled in their reports in the empty squadron office.

As the telephone rang, Foote answered it. His face changed abruptly as the telephone crackled and he grinned and made signs to Dicken. 'It's himself,' he whispered.

'You want a tender sending over?' he went on. 'Because your engine's giving trouble?' His voice rose to a high falsetto. 'My dear fellow, who do you think you are?'

'This is Major Diplock.' The voice on the telephone rose until they could all hear it. 'Who's that?'

'Don't you know?'

'No.'

'And a damn good job, too,' Foote said, slamming down the telephone.

No tender was sent and Diplock arrived back in the afternoon in such a bad temper, he put his machine down too far up the field so that it buried its nose in a pile of manure the Italian farmer, his wife and daughters were about to spread across their land.

'Oh, Jesus,' Foote said. 'That stuff sure has a fatal fascination for him.'

As Diplock stalked towards the mess, Foote made a great show of moving to windward so that the Italian farmer and his family began to cackle with laughter, and it was good enough for Hatto to head for the mess piano and begin to play 'Dan, Dan, the Lavatory Man'. A binge started; any excuse was good enough and they didn't come often, because there was too much flying to do and nobody fancied bumping into an enemy formation while still sluggish after a heavy night.

The attempt at humour rebounded a few days later when Foote was called to the office after a patrol. Diplock had suspected all along who'd been responsible for answering the telephone and Foote reappeared, looking shaken and furious.

'He said I wasn't pulling my weight,' he spluttered. 'Because I've only got five and a half Huns down – mostly in bits shared with other guys. He said he was over the lines today and had a bunch of DVs dive on him when his guns were jammed, and I should have seen 'em and driven 'em away. He said he had to splitarse to frighten 'em off.'

'He couldn't splitarse a Camel to save his life,' Dicken growled.

'I doubt if he could splitarse a bicycle,' Hatto observed. 'Just hang on, darlings. Your Uncle Willie's had thoughts.'

He returned half an hour later, smiling. 'The armourer sergeant said no jam was reported to him. He even inspected the guns while I was there and couldn't find anything wrong with them.'

'Jesus,' Foote said. 'Is he like that?'

'He's exactly like that,' Hatto pointed out. 'I told you long ago. This is a dangerous type, and spite forms a large part of his make-up. You made too much of the smell, Walt, old fruit, when he ploughed into the cowshit.'

*

193

Towards the end of the month, a replacement from France brought them the news that Richthofen had been killed.

In the fiercer furnace of the Western Front, enormous flights of machines were taking the air daily against each other. The big squadron ideas of Richthofen had taken root so that it was nothing, the man from France said, to see the sky full of aeroplanes. He was glad to be out of it where the fighting was done in smaller numbers by what was virtually an independent air force.

'It was ground fire that got him,' he explained.

Foote shrugged. 'I expect there are plenty of others,' he said.

'Sure.' The newcomer seemed anxious to frighten them to death. 'Udet. Löwenhardt. Baumer. They haven't run out of 'em by a long way. And, in spite of the death of the proprietor, the Richthofen mob's still in business.'

*

It was growing much warmer now and on the southern slopes of the mountains there were millions of gentians and buttercups among the grass, and massed clumps of dwarf hydrangea and soldanella between the rocks and the cushions of moss. By this time they felt they were old Italy hands, used to spaghetti, chianti, red tiles and swallows against the blue sky; even the awful *Macedonia* cigarettes which were so loosely packed one good drag finished them off in a puff of smoke, a shower of sparks and a fit of coughing.

As the heat increased, Diplock issued orders that nobody was to be in the sun without suitable head cover and pith helmets were issued. They were useless for flying and the ground crews complained they were always knocking them off against the bracing wires. When mosquitoes began to appear, netting was erected over the beds and the sentries had to wear gloves and veils sprayed with repellent. Nobody thought very highly of it.

'They use it as a sauce when they bite,' Hatto complained.

With the creation of the RAF, a whole new set of regulations had been issued.

'Most of the bloody things have nothing to do with the war,' Hatto objected. 'I expect they were worked out by people like Parasol Percy who have nothing better to do.'

Certainly Diplock was involved in a flurry of paperwork about uniforms and ranks. In the past, RFC and RNAS pilots had lived and worked together, while ex-infantry, cavalry and artillery officers had all worn their own uniforms, with the direct-entry people like young Foote wearing the double-breasted maternity jacket of the RFC. Now, they were informed, anyone buying a new uniform had to buy the RAF style, which, Hatto claimed, had been designed by an admiral with the assistance of a girl friend.

'Probably the Hon. Maud,' he said.

Diplock himself was the first to appear in one. It was of light blue with gold stripes on the cuffs.

'Oh, Mother,' Hatto said. 'Look at Dick!'

Foote almost collapsed. 'Those little gold things at the side of the badge!' he crowed. 'I think they're bananas!'

'It should go a long way to heighten the dullness of wartime streets,' Hatto admitted. 'Is he going to meet the Pope or something?'

'More likely the Wing colonel,' Dicken said. 'He's probably aiming at a new gong to go with it.'

The only good thing that emerged from the change was an increased freedom to travel about the countryside and the institution of leave to places away from the front for anybody who could afford it.

'You must join us in Venice,' Nicola said. 'We always take a house there before the weather grows too hot.'

With an Austrian offensive clearly in the air, they were occupied escorting the bombers and reconnaissance machines trying to find out where it was to come. Against Santa Giustina airfield, where a new Austrian squadron had been reported, they accompanied eleven Italian Capronis, sitting above, screened by a fringe of cloud, to watch for fighters. As the columns of smoke began to rise, Dicken saw a flash of light below him which he knew was the sunshine catching the doped wings of aeroplanes. Five Phönixes, sporting German crosses and the Austrian national colours, were sliding in beneath.

The Capronis were speeding across the field, through the plumes of yellow smoke that leapt up from hidden gun positions. The Phönixes followed, totally unaware of the Camels falling out of the sky on them. Within seconds two of them were twisting to earth, and the Camels were howling after the Capronis to open fire on a line of Bergs just beginning to taxi across the front of a hangar. One of the Bergs was hit by an Austrian shell as it took off and slithered along the ground in a mass of wreckage, throwing debris in all directions like a chicken taking a dust bath.

The Capronis were flying boldly backwards and forwards now, dodging by inches each others' wheels and wingtips, while the Camels held off the Austrian fighters. Diving on a waggon-wheel gun mounting, Dicken saw the crew roll away like collapsed dolls, their gun swinging impotently, then, as he lifted upwards, something big and ugly with three tails staggered across his vision. It was a Caproni and, as the pilot misjudged his pull-up, it disappeared into the open maw of a hangar which promptly burst into flames. A truck came tearing across the field towards it and a Camel swung round low down to fire at it so that it slid into a ditch and turned over. As it did so, the Camel touched a wingtip against the ground and cartwheeled across the field, so that a Berg which was just taking off, slammed into it and burst into flames.

His heart in his mouth, he saw a green Very light flare up, and thankfully swung away as the remaining planes re-formed and fell in behind the Capronis to scurry through the smoke for the south.

The increased reconnaissance brought in what seemed to be growing evidence of the impending offensive and the Camels were occupied with machine gunning grey columns and bombing waggons and trucks moving towards the front.

'They can't win the battle even if it comes,' Diplock insisted. 'They'll be advancing over the ground abandoned after Caporetto, and the Italians know all the holes and corners where they're likely to hide.'

It didn't seem as easy as that to everybody else, and the following day Hatto was wounded again in another attempt to bomb the power station at Lugagnano. They knew something was wrong as soon as the Bristols returned. Only two out of the three which had taken off had appeared and, as the first one landed, the pilot jumped out and started shouting at the flight sergeant who turned and yelled into the hangar. Almost immediately, the ambulance hurtled out of its shed and began to roar towards the far end of the field. Men began to run, and the tender appeared round the end of the headquarters hut, with Foote clinging to the side. As it slowed down, Dicken jumped aboard.

'Willie's in trouble,' Foote yelled.

As Hatto's Bristol turned above the trees, they could hear the engine making a strange whirring noise, and could see wires hanging loose. There was no sign of the observer.

Its wheels skimmed a hut, then it slammed down hard, bouncing into the air. Settling again, it swung in a ground loop and jerked to an abrupt stop. The ambulance roared up alongside and the tender stopped with such a jerk both Dicken and Foote were flung to the grass.

The aeroplane was canted to one side and Dicken saw that the tyre had been shot away and the tyreless wheel had collapsed. They were hoisting Hatto out and lowering him to the grass.

'Never mind me,' he kept saying. 'It's getting to be a habit. Look after Henry.'

Dicken had scrambled on to the wing to peer into the after cockpit but the observer was huddled in a heap on the floor, his face grey, a thin trickle of blood across his cheek.

'It's too late, Willie,' he said. 'Henry's dead.'

Hatto scowled. 'What's so special about a bloody power station?' he snarled. 'Sending three of us in is like sending a bunch of gnats.'

Foote looked towards the headquarters hut, where Hallowes, the Recording Officer, stood outside the door with Diplock, who was using a pair of binoculars to see what had happened.

'You'd think the sonofabitch could be bothered to come across to see what had happened,' he said. 'Instead of using goddam glasses.'

Hatto's wound wasn't serious, but was made to look worse by the amount of blood it shed, and he sat on his bed, his leg bandaged, glaring at the floor in a way Dicken had never seen before, his eyeglass screwed in as if it were the single orb of a cyclops.

'Hallowes told me,' he said harshly, 'that these bloody bombings are Diplock's idea. He's after another gong or something. Top marks for efficiency.'

The Bristol crews were silent in the mess that night and when Diplock arrived with orders for the following day, they pointedly didn't bother to look up.

'Visual and photographic evidence,' Diplock said, 'shows the growing scale of the Austrian preparations for a ground offensive. We've made preparations to counter it, though. Camel squadrons will make a combined bombing attack on troops concentrated in hutments in the Val D'Oro. Three squadrons will provide thirty-five machines loaded with Cooper bombs. X Flight will attack the Lugagnano power station again.'

'Why?' Hatto's word snapped out and Diplock's eyebrows lifted.

'Because it supplies electricity to the Austrian armies,' he said. 'That should be obvious. We all regret the losses, of course, but there seems to be no alternative. However, Headquarters express their appreciation and I'd like to, also —'

'Why?' It was Foote this time. 'Why should *you* be so bloody pleased, you sonofabitch? You've done nothing to-wards the goddam war except buy a new uniform that makes you look like a Hungarian Hussar. You've no right to be pleased about anything, you Limey bastard. *Your* experience of war flying is nil.'

There was a dead silence. Diplock stared at Foote for a while, then, without a word, he turned and walked out of the mess. For a moment, Hallowes remained, uneasy and embarrassed, then he followed.

Foote stared about him. Nobody spoke and he looked faintly ashamed.

'You're Limeys, too,' he mumbled. 'You're all bloody Limeys! But at least you're not bastards.'

3

News from France indicated that the German push had been held. The forward movement had been halted north of the Somme and, at long last, instead of each allied army fighting as and when it pleased, a commander-in-chief had been appointed to co-ordinate the whole allied effort.

'What was obvious to every fighting soldier from the day the war started,' Hatto observed, 'seems at last to have filtered through to the generals.'

With nothing happening on the Italian front, it began to look as if the Austrians were having second thoughts about their offensive, especially since they were considered to be in no condition to launch anything without German help, and with the general easing off of tension, leave was allowed. Dicken took advantage of it to accept the Aubreys' invitation to visit them in Venice.

The city was like a beautiful playhouse closed for repairs. The gondolas had vanished because the gondoliers had gone into the army, and there were no lights and no merriment and, because of the frequent air raids, everybody disappeared at dusk. The narrow streets were lit only by purple bulbs, and most of the great tourist hotels had been turned into hospitals. There had been some damage, and one or two churches had been destroyed, while St. Mark's looked like a warehouse, sheathed from top to bottom in planking and asbestos, the bronze horses removed.

'Napoleon said they weren't any good for cavalry, anyway,' Aubrey smiled, 'and were far too light for artillery.'

One or two theatres were still open, giving performances during the afternoon, and Nicola managed to drag Dicken to a performance of *Tosca*. The soprano spent most of the first act manoeuvring the tenor's back to the audience, but in the second, the tenor, no less powerful, rebelled and did the same to the soprano, so that for the rest of the performance they struggled together in the centre of the stage like Japanese wrestlers. When the tenor gallantly kissed the soprano's hand after the final curtain, to Nicola's disgust Dicken almost collapsed. 'I think he's taking a bite out of it,' he said.

The pavement cafés were full as everybody crowded in for a drink before darkness came. There was no wind and the smell of the stagnant water was strong. But there was a violinist who played *Addio, mia Napoli* and *Ciri-Biri-Bi* and Nicola was won round sufficiently to suggest a visit to Murano.

'The glass and lace factories are having to close down because of the war,' she said. 'If we don't go now, there'll be nothing to see.'

'I don't want to visit anything,' Dicken said. 'I just want to be with you.'

He had a feeling somehow that time was growing short. When they sang their bawdy ballads about dying in the mess they were scoffing at the possibility of a messy end, but they were nevertheless well aware that the likelihood of suffering one was great. Every week brought news of someone else they knew who'd been killed – Roode had gone, they'd heard, shot down flying an SE5 in France, and Lewis had collided with a DH9 in mid-air – and they were well aware that only sheer chance prevented it being them. And Dicken had been in the war almost from the beginning so that his chances of survival grew less, by the sheer weight of the odds against it, with every day it continued. At that moment, the only thing he wanted was to remain within the aura of gentleness that surrounded Nicola and the idea of sharing it with other people was one he couldn't bear.

Nicola seemed disappointed, but Dicken's leave was almost over now and while they were still arguing over it the sirens went and everybody started to run. There was a sign – *Rifugio* – outside one of the hotels and they sat in the basement listening for the bombs. It turned out to be a false alarm and, deciding they were safer at the Aubreys, they hurried through the narrow streets and over the humped-back bridges.

Marie-Gabrielle was in the hall when they arrived. 'I thought you might have got blown up,' she said cheerfully.

'There weren't any bombs,' Nicola said. 'It was a false alarm.'

She was quiet through the meal as the family made Dicken tell them of the aerial fighting on the Piave front.

'What about the ones that burst into flames?' Marie-Gabrielle asked. 'It must be jolly exciting to see them.'

Dicken shook his head. 'No,' he said. 'It isn't exciting. It never is.'

'Do they sometimes fall out?'

'Oh, do shut up,' Nicola snapped. 'Dick's here to forget the fighting for a while.'

As they sat on the balcony holding hands in the warm night air, there was a moon and the stars were glinting on the water of the canal. The whole city was in darkness and there was no sound save for the slap and chatter of the water as it was stirred by the wind from the Adriatic.

Nicola's fingers moved in Dicken's, tense and hard. 'When will things be normal again?' she asked. 'When will it end?'

Dicken gave a small defeated shrug. 'It probably won't end,' he said. 'It'll probably just die of old age.'

She seemed to want to dig again into the problem of their differing religions but he refused to let her, and though she allowed him to kiss her, their mouths seeking each other in the darkness, somehow something had gone from the evening.

The following morning, he took his leave and caught the train to Capadolio. Arriving at Issora, he found the squadron had disappeared and was informed by the Italians that they'd been moved to Schia Piccola, north of Vicenza. The rumours had been wrong and the Austrian offensive was on after all.

*

He arrived in Vicenza late at night and telephoned for transport. Hatto was the first person he saw. He was leaning on a stick, his leg still bandaged.

'Where's Walt?'

'Flying. Parasol Percy's not forgotten what he said and he's pushing him hard. His kid brother too.'

'They told me at Issora the offensive's on.'

'Not half,' Hatto said. 'That's why we've been moved here. We were going to make a push towards Val Sugana but now the Austrians are expected to move first.'

Bad visibility, he said, had prevented normal observation but it had become apparent that the Austrians were concentrating astride the River Brenta and were even dropping leaflets on the British troops there.

'Their aircraft are about in much larger numbers,' he ended. 'It doesn't pay to sing or play the piano much.'

When Foote arrived, his heavy thigh-boots flapping round his knees, his eyes sore from flying, he looked worn out and sat on his bed staring at the floor. The grey cordite marks on his cheeks made his face look ghostly, his expression empty of everything but weariness, a shapeless hunched bulk in his flying suit, his hair flattened by his flying cap.

'I think I'll transfer to our own air force,' he said. 'Me and the kid brother both. At least it'll get us away from Parasol Percy.'

'Don't they have Parasol Percys in your lot?' Hatto asked.

'I guess they've got 'em in everybody's air force. But maybe I could start afresh. Maybe, even, the war'll end before I open my big mouth again.'

He lit a cigarette. 'I worry about the kid,' he said. 'My mother wrote asking me to look after him. But how in bejesus do you look after a guy in a different aeroplane flying on a different patrol?' He calmed down abruptly. 'I've got the wind up,' he admitted. 'We've been making too many low attacks on troops and reserves. Us trying to stop this goddam push's like a flea trying to stop a mad elephant. There aren't enough of us and you can't dodge. Some of these goddam staff types ought to come and try it themselves. I notice Parasol Percy never does.'

He took a drag at his cigarette and let the smoke come from his nostrils. 'It wouldn't be so bad if the country was flat,' he went on. 'But when you're flying in and out of these goddam valleys you find they're firing *down* at you from the mountains as well as up from the ground.' He tossed the cigarette away and managed a painful smile. 'How did the leave go?'

'All right.'

'Get married?'

'Not even engaged.'

'What's wrong with her? Rats, doesn't she know she's got a four-square, gold-plated hero for a boy friend? Didn't you even go to bed with her?'

Dicken smiled. 'It's not that sort of thing.'

'You mean, there's another sort?'

'We're not all like Walter C. Foote, of Boston.'

'It's a goddam good job, boy. If everybody were as scared as I am, we'd never win the war.' Foote jerked a hand at the medal ribbons under Dicken's wings. 'Those are goddam pretty, kid,' he went on, 'and I'm glad I've got my one. But I'm sure not aiming to win any more.' His smile came again as he looked round at them. 'What a goddam lot we are ! Willie's full of holes. I'm full of heeby-jeebies. The kid here's the only one who's full of fight.'

After the evening meal, Diplock appeared in the mess with the orders for the next day.

'Lugagnano power station,' he said.

'What, again?' The words burst out of Foote involuntarily.

'It has to be destroyed,' Diplock insisted.

'Then why don't they get the Capronis to do it?'

Diplock drew a deep breath as if he found the interruption irritating. 'The Capronis are attacking Austrian airfields and railway junctions,' he said. 'We're all who can be spared. 28, 45 and 66 Squadrons are engaged in shooting up the Austrian troop movements.' He looked hard at Foote. 'At least we're not going down to the ground.'

'*He*'s not going down anywhere,' Foote growled as Diplock turned away. 'He doesn't even go *up* these days.'

As the mess emptied, he stood smoking for a while, then he headed for Diplock's office. Diplock seemed surprised to see him. Foote drew a deep breath. It was a great effort he was making.

'I guess – I –' Foote frowned. 'I'm asking you, Major, to leave my kid brother out of this one. He's only nineteen.'

'I was only just over nineteen when I first put on uniform,'

Diplock pointed out. 'So were many others.'

'I'm trying to look after the kid, sir. I promised his mother.'

'Hardly the way to fight a war.'

'Leave the kid out of this one,' Foote burst out, 'and I'll fly all the goddam patrols you want! Even the bad ones.'

'It can't be done, Foote.' Diplock was unmoved. 'We've been asked for full support and we're going to give it.'

When Foote appeared in the hut later, he was in low spirits.

'Why don't you just walk out?' Hatto said. 'Take a train to Rome, see your ambassador and say you want to join your own air force. Tell him why, if you like. Parasol Percy couldn't do a thing about it.'

'What about the kid?'

'Take him with you.'

'He doesn't want to go. You don't know my kid brother. He wants a medal of his own and he's determined to get one. Rats, I tried to talk to him but he won't listen and says to mind my own goddam business. He's flying and that's that, so I guess I've got to fly, too, to keep an eye on him.'

*

Because the Bristols were short of pilots, Hatto announced that he was also going to fly. The doctor objected but he refused to listen.

'We've bombed that bloody power station so often,' he said, 'they know we're coming before we set off. They've got machine guns and anti-aircraft guns all round it, to say nothing of a couple of dozen squadrons of DVs, Bergs and Phönixes sitting upstairs. I'm going.'

The Bristols and Foote's flight were to go in as low as possible while the other two flights of Camels were to fend off attacks. The idea was to catch the defences before they were properly awake, and they were to take off as soon as it was light enough to see.

'Why does the stupid sonofabitch think that'll make it easier?' Foote growled. 'They'll have just got up and be full of beans after a good night's sleep. And if they haven't just got up, they'll be mad as wildcats because we've got 'em out of bed. Why not late in the evening when they're tired after a hard day's work?'

He slept badly and when Dicken woke the following morning, he was already sitting on the edge of his bed, smoking, grey-faced and strained.

'Once more into the goddam valley of death,' he growled.

The stars were still shining as they finished their breakfast of coffee, rolls and boiled eggs. No one felt much like chattering and they trudged silently across the field working out the imponderables of the situation with a sense of foreboding as they adjusted gloves and scarves and fastened belts and buckles in the steely half-light beginning to pick out huts and trees.

The machines were lined up ready to take off in groups. Italian photographers were waiting with their heads under the black cloths that covered their cameras, and there was an artist making sketches for an Italian illustrated magazine. Diplock appeared in his light-blue uniform as they gathered round the machines. 'Going to headquarters,' Hatto said. 'Always likes to be properly dressed.'

'Properly dressed,' Foote growled, 'would be in a Sidcot suit and flying helmet.'

As they collected in a group, checking map references and instructions, nobody pretended it was going to be easy. By this time the defences at Lugagnano had grown so used to them there weren't any new tactics. As they climbed into their seats, shouts came across the quiet air, then the engines started in bursts of blue castor oil smoke. Cold blasts slapped into Dicken's face.

The countryside seemed empty, just an occasional column of smoke rising from a farmhouse chimney. The burping of the engines was filling the air and little clouds of moisture were being whipped off the dew-laden grass to hang over the field like patches of mist. Diplock raised a Very pistol and as the flare curved into the air, the Bristols began to lurch forward, their wings swaying as they moved over the uneven ground. As they lifted, hanging stiffly in the air, the Camels began to follow, first Foote's flight, then the other two, well spaced so they wouldn't be in each other's slipstreams.

Italians heading for the countryside with their forks and

hoes, and the Italian airmen on their own half of the airfield, stopped to watch them as they climbed to meet the light. The mountain peaks were touched with red, glowing against the pale sky like broken bloodstained teeth.

Beneath them were all the signs of the coming attack. Every village swarmed with soldiers and there were interminable processions of lorries pushing supplies to the front, mule carts, and waggons piled with hay, lumber, wine casks, flour, shells, barbed wire, ammunition.

As they began to approach the Lugagnano valley, the lower flights formed up into two long lines, one behind the other. Mortano came up, then Spasso, and the Bristols and Foote's Camels began turning in a wide arc to enter the end of the valley. As they became a straight line again, Lugagnano appeared, the houses showing through the mist as a swathe of white boxes clustered round the power station. As they drew nearer, the sun lifted between a gap in the mountains and the dew-wet roofs began to shine like golden squares.

As the Bristols entered the valley, Dicken circled at eight thousand feet, watching as black puffballs of smoke began to appear. Hatto was going low, roaring along the valley at the head of the two long lines of aircraft. A quick glance about him showed Dicken that the two upper flights were in order, then he saw the first flash of a bomb and Hatto's Bristol clawing its way upwards, turning desperately to avoid the mountain. As it did so Dicken saw a faint movement to his left and, looking down, caught a glimpse of two flights of DVs coming in from the direction of Caldonazzo, the sun catching their buff-coloured wings. A Flight had seen them, too, and began to drop from the sky. Dicken was just about to take up a position behind them when he glanced upwards and saw a group of tiny glittering dots against the blue at the other side of the valley and made out a swarm of Bergs and Phönixes. Instead of following A Flight, he raised his arm and pointed in the other direction.

As he turned to meet the newcomers, he saw huts burning on the ground, men on foot and on horseback scattering from the rain of bombs, and the last of the Bristols manoeuvring wildly to get out of the way of Foote's Camels. As the

Austrian machines dived across his front, he fired quickly and the leading Phönix lifted abruptly so that the machine behind flew into it. Locked together, they fell like stones. As they vanished, a Berg appeared and, as he fired, the wings snapped back as if the pressing of his triggers had affected some switch. It had been climbing away from the mêlée but, as its nose dropped, it fell past him, the wings folded about it, and he could see the pilot trying to lift himself from his seat against the wreckage that enveloped him.

As he climbed to regain height, the fight broke up into whirling groups of aeroplanes. A Camel went down in a long straight dive, trailing a thin stream of smoke, then dissolved in a flare of flame to fill the sky with flying wreckage, small glittering pieces of burning fabric falling from it as though it were melting. Another Phönix appeared in front of him, standing on its wingtips in a vertical bank. As he fired, the nose dropped slightly and he watched it descend, still turning in tight banks, until it disappeared into the smoke made by the exploding Camel.

By this time the sky was emptying of aircraft. The Bristols were heading out of the valley, followed by Foote's Camels. Dicken tried to count them but could make out only three. On the way back, his engine was blowing back into the carburettor and, afraid of fire, he landed at Issora where the Italian pilots greeted him like a long-lost brother and filled him with wine while the mechanics examined his machine. It was past midday when he landed at Schia Piccola.

'Thought you'd gone west, sir,' one of the mechanics said as he switched off the engine.

'Not this time. What about the others?'

'One of the Bristols didn't come back, sir. New man. Only arrived last week. I heard someone say he hit the hillside.'

'What about the Camels?'

'One missing, sir, from A Flight. Another landed for oil at Sovizzo.'

'What about B?'

The mechanic jerked a thumb. A small group of men were standing by the hangar entrance staring to the north. Dicken counted them: Six. Three fitters. Three riggers. That meant Foote had lost three.

'Who?' he asked.

'Mr MacKay, sir. Mr Blaze.' The mechanic paused and glanced again at his mate. 'And Mr Foote, sir. Young Mr Foote.'

4

'Flew into the goddam power station,' Foote said, his face grim. 'Went down in a straight glide to drop his bombs and seemed to go straight into a window. The wings fell off and you could see the tail sticking out. Then there was the most God-awful explosion and that was that. His bombs must have gone off and set off something inside.' He took out a cigarette with a shaking hand. 'At least he did what he was sent to do.'

Diplock had disappeared to Wing – obviously to wait until things had blown over – and they eventually put Foote to bed very drunk. When they woke in the morning there was no sign of him. Later they learned there was a tender missing and eventually it was found at the station and they heard Foote had been seen boarding a train. When Diplock returned, he seemed relieved to find Foote had disappeared and finally called Dicken into the office to question him about his movements.

'There seems little doubt but that he's deserted,' he said coldly.

Because the Austrian offensive still seemed to be hanging fire, Dicken was able in a week-end of bad weather to slip away to Capadolio thirty miles away. The news of Foote's disappearance threw the whole Aubrey family into gloom. They had got to know him well in the early days before the rest of the squadron had arrived and they seemed to think it portended mass desertions. The imminence of the Austrian offensive was having its effect and the increased patrolling along the front had brought in a batch of Italian wounded.

'We have the wives and girl friends,' Mrs Aubrey said sternly. 'They come to see their men and they ask me '*In nome di Dio*, what am I to do?' *Mon Dieu*, I am more concerned with what their *men* are going to do.'

She seemed more able to cope with the horrors than Nicola who seemed depressed by them. Most of all, she was shocked by the attitude of the city children who waited outside the hospital to see the wounded arrive. ' "He's got no hands," they say,' she pointed out bitterly. 'Or "Look, he's bleeding." Why do people have to get so hurt? Why are there wars?'

'Because there always have been.'

'That's no answer.'

Dicken sighed, feeling old and depressed. 'It's the best I can do,' he said.

*

The bombing of the Austrian troops continued.

The weather was growing hot now and the grey columns were covered with white dust that was stirred up in clouds that settled on leaves, grass, human beings, horses, lorries and houses. Every railway siding was choked with waggons and every village swarmed with men moving north. There were pontoon trains, balloon outfits, searchlights, siege guns hauled by tractors, lighter guns hauled by oxen, even herds of cattle and flocks of sheep on the hoof, and thousands of the bright-eyed, green-caped soldiers. Matting made of corn stalks had been hung across the road to prevent the Austrians seeing anything and in the banks dugouts had been made for the infantry.

Fans were revolving now in the houses and cafés, and ice appeared in the wine. The flies increased a thousandfold and British gunners had begun to wear drill shorts and Australian bush-hats against the heat, while the rations had been changed to check the dysentery that was starting to take its toll.

A new German attack in France had flung the French back but it had then been flung back in its turn by the Americans at Château-Thierry, and a new push near Mondidier had been a total failure. The German lack of success lifted spirits because it meant the expected Austrian offensive would now have to be mounted without German help.

Since Caporetto, the quietness of the front had given the Italians time to get their breath back, and there were even rumours that they might mount their own offensive first after all. Patrols became more intensive and there seemed no time during daylight when machines were not over the lines, denying air space to the Austrian reconnaissance aeroplanes. Hatto lost another Bristol but two days later over Italian territory, Dicken shot down a Rumpler which turned over as it fell, scattering thousands of what proved to be leaflets destined for the British infantry.

Finding out the Austrians' intentions was growing more difficult. They were still concentrating near the River Brenta but their plans seemed to have changed and they were no longer moving in daylight. Diplock ordered his pilots to fly lower to bring back the missing information but it produced nothing but another lost Camel and another lost Bristol. By the middle of June, they still had no real information, then, in the middle of the night, Dicken woke to find Hatto leaning over his bed.

'It's started,' he said.

Sitting up, Dicken was aware of lights flickering in the sky through the open door and the steady thudding of guns.

'Where is it?'

'Everywhere. Along the whole front. Hallowes says it's on a twenty-five mile front from the Adriatic. Wing thinks it'll come everywhere at once, against the Italians on the Piave, the French on Monte Grappa and us on the Asiago plateau.'

The day when it came was overcast and sultry, and flying brought in little information because of mist near the high ground to the north. They learned that the Austrians had broken through part of the British line for a depth of nearly a mile but had then been held by prepared defences. The mist was preventing air support, but patrols were called for nevertheless, and the Camels endeavoured to bomb opposite the beleaguered infantry, marking their position from any momentarily visible landmark seen through the swirling grey curtains. By midday the weather had become so thick all flying was halted.

'Rain's stopped play,' Dicken said. 'Can't see why they can't hold the bloody battle indoors.'

They gathered near the office with their flying clothing, all of them nervously lighting cigarettes and praying the battle would be decided without them having to go down into the haze again. But the Austrians were still forcing their way across the Piave and were now adding smoke screens to the mist to hide their preparations. It was gradually becoming obvious where they were, however, from the positions of their reconnaissance aeroplanes, and finally news came through that they had laid pontoon bridges across the river and were threatening the Montello, the hog's back which had been such a difficult barrier for both sides, and that Venice was in danger.

A letter from Nicola informed Dicken that, because of the threat, the hospital was being evacuated to Bologna and that the Aubreys were going there, too. It was impossible to get into Capadolio because he knew they were going to have to fly, whatever the weather, and Diplock appeared soon afterwards with orders for a patrol northwards. It was led by Dicken and they caught a DFW near Bassano. It fell into the river and, following it down, Dicken suddenly became aware that, beneath him in a gap in the mist, he could see a bridge at Trivizzo that hadn't been there before and that heading across it to the southern bank was a steady stream of men, horses and vehicles. Almost immediately, the mist closed over it again.

As the sun rose higher, the mist began to burn off and the machines were bombed up with 20-lb bombs and took off again in groups of three. The mist had dispersed a lot by the time they reached the river and they howled down out of the sky towards the bridge at Trivizzo. Dicken saw one of his bombs explode in a pontoon filled with soldiers and another in a boat just as it left the northern bank, and circling, drawing the fire of Austrian machine guns as the other two machines went in, he saw more bombs fall into an Austrian trench. Then, as the other two Camels formed up on him once more, they went down through the hail of fire to spray the grey columns advancing towards the bridge. They dispersed abruptly, diving for cover as if someone was drawing a comb through thick grey hair. A lorry went up in flames and a horse-drawn battery dissolved in a kicking heap of animals, men and overturned guns. Flying along the river, they fired at anything that moved and saw other Camels combing the Ponte di Piave on the direct route south, before returning to Schia Piccola with their guns and bomb racks empty.

The Austrians were across the river at several points and as the aircraft were rearmed and refuelled for the next day, the pilots gathered in the mess, still tense and jumpy, and noisy with the explosive excitement of the fighting.

Their maps marked in red, they climbed into the air again at dawn the following morning and flew north, never much more than fifty feet off the ground. Following each other nervously in the mist, they passed over masses of Italian infantrymen waiting by white arrows laid on the ground for some sort of counter-attack and ran into a thick fog made by low cloud mingling with smoke. The air was bumpy with explosions and, flashing overhead at ninety miles an hour, Dicken caught sight of shell bursts below him and groups of men huddled among rocks, then, as they moved further north and the ground rose, he found himself skimming the trees so low the reek from bursting shells made his eyes sting.

Their bombs looked like sunbursts through the mist but added little to what was happening below, and in a split-second glimpse, he saw two Italian Hanriots collide head-on with a smash like the explosion of a shell before dropping like stones into the smoke.

The chances of finding a target in the confusion were negligible. A Phönix shot past him in the murk, and, while his heart was still pounding, he almost flew into a house. Swerving violently, he climbed above the smoke to get his breath. Seeing a column of Austrians in a patch of clear ground, he went down again, alone now because everybody else had disappeared, and bullets cracked by his ears as he was fired at by machine guns on lorries.

He was sweating profusely and had no idea where he was but he managed to spot the railway line south and followed it to pick up Schia Piccola. He was last down and everybody else was chattering noisily with barely restrained fear.

'There are a hell of a lot of them,' Dicken said. 'More than I've ever seen. I thought they'd hit me.'

'If you don't rattle,' Hatto commented, 'you're all right.'

The serviceable machines took off again as soon as they were patched, rearmed and refuelled. With flying halted in the west by the weather, they were now being concentrated along the Piave where the Italians were bearing the full weight of the Austrian attack, and every machine was in the air, often close enough to the sea for the pilots to see Venice with its lagoons, canals and churches.

Along the river and over the Venetian Plain all the way from the mountains to the Piave there were Camels, Bristols and RE8s, as well as Italian Hanriots and Caproni bombers, and Austrian Bergs, Phönixes, Hansa-Brandenburgs, Albatroses and every kind of two-seater imaginable. The targets remained batteries and trenches and moving columns of men. Machines returned with leaves or the remains of telephone wires round their undercarriages and the edginess became more marked.

'They'll do for the lot of us at this rate,' Hatto growled.

There was no rest but the news was that the Austrians were not making much progress and the terrible excitement of feeling that they were achieving something kept them going. The Austrians were still pushing troops across the river at Trivizzo and, as he shot over them in a wild erratic flight, Dicken saw an officer on a horse, yelling at scattered men to reassemble, disappear abruptly from the saddle. As he pulled out of the murk, he almost flew into an Austrian reconnaissance machine. The two aeroplanes passed so close he felt he could have reached out and shaken hands.

There was a lot of confusion along the river now and many of the pontoons were sinking or on fire. Italian shells were falling among the Austrians, who were having difficulty making repairs because of the strong current and, as he went down again, Dicken saw boats and pontoons swept away. Climbing once more, keeping the target always in view, he ruddered over with the engine off in a vibrationless dive, and once again saw men scattering, clawing at the ground and staring over their shoulders in fright at him. As he climbed into the air, an explosion lifted the tail of the Camel. He regained control with difficulty, the motor clattering like a steam traction engine. As the rising ground of the Montello appeared in front, he knew he couldn't hope to clear it and as he swung away, his engine clonking wildly, he found himself facing two small white-painted houses and a brown line of trenches. It was impossible to avoid the houses so he aimed for the gap between them. There was a sound of splintering wood and twanging wires and a shower of tiles as the fuselage, devoid of wings and with Dicken still inside, slid along the ground, its undercarriage gone, until it hit a large grey rock.

For a second he remained in the machine, dazed, then he realised that shells were throwing up dirt and stones around him and, coming to life, scrambled free and leapt for shelter. Italian soldiers were waving to him from their trenches and he ran bent-double in zigzag fashion to dive headlong among them.

For a moment, he huddled among the legs at the bottom of the trench, shocked and exhausted, wanting nothing but to remain there, curled up like a foetus, ignoring the men who were even then reaching down to him, the battle, the war, the whole world even, but he was yanked upright and offered a cigarette and a bottle of Strega.

'You are well?' one of the soldiers asked. It seemed an understatement. He was alive and that was enough.

He was taken to an officer's dugout and offered a brandy, then given a guide to lead him to the rear.

'We are holding them, I think,' the officer said. 'It is difficult, but their progress is very slow and it becomes slower.'

The roads to the rear were choked with wounded, on stretchers, walking, carried in litters on the shoulders of their friends. They were all wet through and looked scared stiff. Men tramped by in the darkness, phantom figures which loomed up for a moment then vanished. Incessantly in the ears was the jingle of harness and the clatter of hooves, the rattle of lampless lorries and the crunch of boots on the road. Blunt-nosed grey ambulances like moving vans were trying to edge against the stream of refugees, but, wailing at their lost properties, the Italian peasants were driving donkey- and mule-carts containing marble clocks, wine casks and canaries in cages, and a furious Italian colonel, a bottle of chianti in his hand, was trying to force them down the side roads.

'*Va via!*' he kept yelling. 'Go away! Get out of our path!'

The town of Pontello, just behind the line, had been bombed, and the bell in the campanile was still jangling as a warning for everybody to take cover. Women were weeping in the street and the church was crowded with people who were overflowing on to the steps. It was growing dark as the day drew to an end and half the village was burning, bright red against the dark background of trees. Up ahead, shells were exploding with a rush of air, a hard bright flash and a shower of sparks like fireworks, leaving a smell of explosive and turned earth. A few young soldiers, their eyes large and scared, were pushing towards the rear but a company of bersaglieri came up at their swift trotting pace to draw a line across the road, and the young soldiers were rounded up and sent forward again.

As he moved further back, Dicken found a British officer with a battery of guns who found him a car to take him back to Schia Piccola. They headed south past an endless stream of motor lorries moving towards the front. Among them were Sicilian mule carts which had been commandeered and brought north to help. There seemed to be hundreds of them, painted in gaudy colours like ice cream carts, with religious pictures on their sides, the mules which pulled them wearing harness studded with brass and hung with scarlet tassels. Behind them were long strings of donkeys so heavily laden all that could be seen were their ears and tails, followed by groups of Austrian prisoners, dirty, depressed and guarded by cavalry, tall men on tall horses with lances that seemed to reach heavens high.

As they fought their way past, an aeroplane skimmed overhead. No one took any notice, assuming it to be allied, and a moment later there was a tremendous explosion as a bomb landed, and men, horses and carts went up into the air in a shower of arms, legs and debris. The bomb had landed in the centre of the road just ahead and around the crater there was a ring of dead and wounded. A mule was dragging itself away, its back broken, its hind legs trailing, its mouth open in a hoarse scream of terror and pain.

It was dark when they reached the airfield. The two-seaters, both RE8s and Bristols, were being loaded with food.

Hatto grabbed him and felt him all over. 'You all right?' he asked. 'We stopped the buggers, but they've been free from air attack since dark and they've rebridged the bloody river at Trivizzo. Rebuilt everything we smashed. The Italians say they're bringing up anti-aircraft guns, too, now. They hadn't got any today. Somebody on the staff forgot, I suppose, because I expect their staff's as stupid as ours. We're going to try to drop supplies to the Italians.'

Snatching a few hours sleep, Dicken was awakened at three o'clock next morning. The mist was so thick he couldn't see how the two-seaters were even going to get off the ground, but almost immediately he heard aircraft starting up and then the drone of motors as they took off.

At six o'clock Diplock sent him up for a weather test and he climbed directly above the airfield. The mist was still thick, a brilliant white haze at 300 feet, and he could see nothing, but by the time the two-seaters returned, it had thinned a little and they got down with only one of the Bristols missing and Hatto edgy with nerves.

The continued low flying was taking its toll of all of them by this time and the mess alternated with the noisy chatter of over-excited frightened young men or the heavy silence as their fears finally caught up with them so that they sat smoking and staring into the distance, held by unimaginable terrors that they couldn't – and didn't wish to – put into words. They looked like ghosts and moved like drugged bees, full of a growing suspicion that the Austrian offensive was going to put the war – and their world – back by years, so that the prospect of peace and living to grow old dwindled to little more than a tiny speck of light in the distance.

About nine o'clock the mist lifted sufficiently for the Camels to get off the ground, but at 800 feet there was still low cloud through which they could see nothing of the ground and they had to drop down and fly north beneath it.

Their reception at the river was much hotter than the previous day and they went down into the hail of bullets to bomb and machine gun along the whole front. Near Miroda, to the east of Trivizzo, the Austrians had constructed a wooden bridge to an island half way across the river and were continuing from the island to the south bank. Dropping his bombs round it, Dicken flew along the river and found three other bridges further along, all in good condition and passing troops to the south bank while their engineers struggled waist-deep in grey and swirling water.

Returning to Schia Piccola for more bombs, he led his flight north again àt once. The bridges had not been destroyed and, as Hatto had said, the Austrians had taken advantage of the night and the early mist to repair everything they'd wrecked the previous day, so that there seemed to be thousands more men and dozens more machines on the south side of the river. Returning for still more bombs, he was sent with two other men to report on what he could see north of the river. There were angry rags of cloud near the mountains and eventually he found himself in a downpour that prevented him seeing anything at all. Ahead of him was just a whirling wall of water and his windscreen was blurred by wind-whipped trickles that flew off the edge and disappeared over his shoulder. Within five minutes he had lost touch with the other machines and decided the search was pointless. Dropping lower, he saw the mountain streams below had changed to white foam that tumbled downwards in an increasing volume of water, and when he landed, all the varnish had been removed from the propeller.

There seemed to be a panic in Diplock's office and Dicken noticed he had a suitcase standing near his desk, packed ready for a quick take-off if the Austrians broke out of their bridgeheads. Already they had pushed a considerable force across the river and were still making progress, and the Italians had so far been unable to mount a counter-attack to stop them. As darkness fell, there was a feeling of frustration. The attempts to drop supplies had not been successful.

The following morning the clouds were low again and it was raining heavily once more.

'I always thought Italy was sunny,' Dicken observed bitterly.

'Pure fallacy, old fruit,' Hatto said. 'Anywhere there are mountains you can expect rain and it stands to reason that where snow falls in winter, rain'll fall in summer. I can't see why they don't up-end the peaks into the valleys and roll 'em flat.'

The rain continued throughout the day, in a steady downpour, the clouds so low it was impossible to see the mountains. During a lull, Dicken was ordered off with two others to bomb the bridge at Trivizzo again. Clinging to the underside of the cloud, they met a hail of anti-aircraft fire as they arrived, but when they went down into it they were unable to find the bridge. Swinging round for another try, wondering if he'd arrived at the wrong spot, Dicken suddenly realised that where the bridge had been were now only the splintered ends of timber and the wreckage of boats and pontoons. The firing was tremendous and it dawned on him that the Austrians were trying to prevent him seeing that the bridge had been destroyed.

He was still wondering who'd done it when he realised that the river had become a raging torrent. The level had lifted with the rain and it was roaring down from the mountains, covering the white pebbles that lined the banks and washing high against the islands in midstream. The bridge had been destroyed not by bombs but by water.

Leading his two companions along the valley, he saw tree trunks that had been washed downstream mingling with the wreckage of the bridge at Miroda and rushing along in a vast battering ram. The next bridge along at Rimanicci had also gone, and he reached the next one just as the wreckage arrived and crashed into it like a massive sledge hammer of timber and fallen trees that set if lifting and swaying.

Returning to Schia, he reported what he'd seen and later in the day the Italians said that only two bridges ten miles from the coast were useable, and that all the Austrian troops on the Italian side of the river near the Montello were cut off.

Suddenly the weather cleared, and relieved of the need to bomb bridges, they took off to drive away the enemy aircraft trying to help the stranded infantry. Bumping into a mixed group of machines near the Montello, Dicken drove down one that he couldn't identify, which crashed in the Austrian trenches, and half an hour later he caught a Berg fighter, whose pilot never knew what hit him. The following morning he caught a two-seater which fell near Arcade.

As the excitement died, it was clear that the Austrians were withdrawing back across the river. All they could see was the debris of disaster, dead horses, dead men, smashed waggons and abandoned guns. The Austrian offensive was over.

5

In the lull that followed the fighting on the Piave, it was possible to sit back and count noses. There were new faces in the mess but there was also a great deal of new confidence because, despite the smallness of the allied air force in Italy, at no time had the Austrians gained command of the air.

There was no Nicola, however. Though it was possible once more to go to Capadolio, the house there was being run only by the servants and Italy suddenly seemed empty, part of another world, part of another war. After six months, they had lost touch with England and Italy seemed more different than ever. Food was different, the way of life was different, the people were different, the backdrop of the mountains different, the thunder of the guns coming from forests carpeted with moss, pine needles and cones, where black-white-and-red woodpeckers tapped and eagles soared against the sky.

With the end of the Austrian offensive, a feeling was even creeping in that the war was coming to an end, too. The newspapers had it that the Austrians would be glad to throw their hands in, and Bulgaria and Turkey were in much the same boat, while in France the German offensive had finished and the allied armies had begun to counter-attack.

A letter arrived from Nicola from Naples. Her father had been transferred to Rome and since overwork at the hospital during the Austrian offensive had resulted in some sort of breakdown, her mother had taken her to the coast to recover.

For a while Dicken felt bereft. Now that she was beyond his reach, his mind was full of her, how she looked, how she spoke, how she worried about her religion, and he had almost forgotten Zoë when he received a letter from her.

'I can fly', she wrote ecstatically. 'I shall take out a licence as soon as the war's over and probably be the first woman to fly the Atlantic. Casey Harmer taught me. He thinks I'm in love with him and he'll do anything for me.'

For a moment, he sat staring at the words, unexpectedly churned by jealousy and wondering what she'd been up to. Since she'd slipped into bed with him without argument, he wondered if in exchange for flying lessons she'd slipped into bed with Casey Harmer with the same ease.

He was still choked with jealousy when he received another letter from Nicola in Naples, telling him in her solemn way that she'd finally decided that their religions shouldn't come between them.

'My brother says if I love you it doesn't matter and that Protestants have married Catholics before without difficulty or shame. He's finally decided to become a missionary and it's this which finally made up my mind. If he can give up his family, so can I.'

It was naïve and gentle in the way that Nicola was naïve and gentle, and it pleased Dicken. He liked the Aubreys who were good, kind, intelligent, attractive and well-brought-up, all the things he'd learned from his mother to expect from a partner. But the idea of marriage brought a head full of new thoughts as he began to wonder what he could do after the war to support a wife. The prospect of going back to the routine of an office held little appeal, he no longer had much love for seafaring, and hadn't used his skills with a wireless set for months. Something would surely turn up, he thought, but he couldn't imagine the cautious Aubrey giving his daughter away without a guarantee that she could expect a stable future.

*

The squadron had moved now to a field at Sottanunga and were living in a mansion full of marble busts owned by an Italian count who preferred to remain in Rome. The Austrians, showing little fight after the failure of their push, had withdrawn towards the mountain barrier to the north. It was clear they had been weakened by the failure of their offensive, which seemed to have knocked the stuffing out of them so that the possibility of the war ending became an intriguing question mark.

Dicken was still considering his future when Hallowes took him aside in the mess.

'You're for home,' he said. 'You're to take over a Snipe Squadron in France.'

Dicken was flattered. The tragedy in France still held a terrible fascination and Snipes were the latest thing. The natural development of the Camel, they were of advanced design and increased performance, and had been built to take advantage of a much bigger Bentley engine. With their excellent climb and manoeuvrability and the absence of the Camel's viciousness, they were already being considered the best all-round single-seat fighter in service. It was a matter of pride to be given a squadron, too, and with luck it meant he could hope to stay alive until the end of the war.

The following day, however, Hallowes took him on one side again. He was pink-faced and embarrassed. 'I got it wrong, Dick,' he said. 'I'm terribly sorry. I misread it. It's the Major who's going.'

Dicken couldn't think what use Diplock could be to a Snipe squadron and he was disappointed, but since he had never expected to have his own squadron, the blow was not too heavy.

He went up early to lead a patrol beyond the river, where he caught a Hansa-Brandenburg that fought and wriggled to escape but ended up flying into the side of a hill. Before lunch he was told to provide an escort in the afternoon for the Bristols who were doing a reconnaissance over the railway junction at Vittorio.

Hatto met him as he headed for his machine. He looked tired these days. 'Sorry to drag you out,' he said. 'But it'll be the last job before you go home.'

Dicken shrugged. 'I'm not going home,' he said. 'Hallowes misread the signal.'

Hatto frowned. 'He didn't seem to have misread it when I spoke to him,' he said. 'He seemed very pleased. And it certainly seemed to me to indicate you were going home.'

They made their arrangements over a map resting on the wing of Hatto's machine but Hatto was late appearing as Dicken headed for his machine after lunch.

'Tried to get another look at that signal,' he said. 'But Hallowes says Parasol Percy's got it in the safe, which,' he added, 'is unusual. Signals of that sort are usually stuck on the notice board for everybody to see and crow about.'

The target was heavily guarded by anti-aircraft guns but the photographs were safely made. As Hatto climbed back to take station alongside Dicken's flight, three Austrian aeroplanes appeared from between the mountains, their blue and green camouflage making them hard to see against the slopes. They were a new type Dicken hadn't seen before and they could outclimb the Camels, so he turned for the lines and increased speed, only to see Hatto dropping behind with engine trouble.

Waving him on, he swung north to guard his rear. As the leading Austrian came in close, he yanked on the stick and went up in the first part of a loop, then fell over sideways to drop into position behind, his guns clattering. The Austrian immediately started going down in a flicking spin and after a few turns began to shed pieces of wing before finally dropping like a stone, a blue-and-green-blotched coffin rapidly disappearing against the blue of the earth. The other two machines vanished.

In the region of Monte Campolo, they were attacked again, this time by five Bergs. Turning to meet them, Dicken headed for the centre of the formation and, aiming at the right-hand machine at close range, saw it roll on to its back and dive vertically into the hills at Peralto. As the other Bergs swung away, he dropped into position behind the rearmost and it began to go down in an erratic glide towards a patch of wood in the Val Freddo. Almost immediately, he found himself face to face with yet another Berg, but the Austrian lost his nerve and, as he tried to pass above, he presented the belly of his machine. Raked from one end to the other, it caught fire and exploded and when Dicken looked down there was nothing except two red-and-white-striped wings fluttering down into the mountains. As the Camels reformed, he saw three long columns of smoke and his companions were both waving their arms wildly and pointing at themselves to indicate that they, too, had each downed an enemy.

Hatto's Bristol was only a speck in the distance now and as they headed after it, red Italian anti-aircraft fire rose near the lines to draw attention to an Aviatik near Disina. As Dicken fired, the observer disappeared inside his cockpit and the Aviatik began to go down in a long dive towards the south.

Dicken's motor was giving trouble now and, waving his companions on, he landed on a Caproni aerodrome near Remido and telephoned to Sottonunga.

As he put the instrument down, the Italian colonel appeared, full of smiles. He was a big man, as if he'd been chosen to go with the large machines he commanded, and he suggested Dicken should return with him and dine with his family.

He had a house alongside the River Remo, which was a tributary of the Piave, and since the weather was hot, he suggested they should swim. As they were heading towards the water, the colonel's wife and daughter appeared. The daughter was pretty and dark-eyed, and it turned out that the colonel was a count, which made her a contessa because in Italy everybody in the family carried the title, too.

After dinner they danced on a marble-floored verandah to music from a gramophone, and the colonel offered him a bed for the night. The evening was warm enough to sit outside, the sky pearly with a cold moon; and, as the colonel and his wife and two other guests who'd turned up, went inside, Dicken managed to kiss the girl, who kissed him back with marked enthusiasm.

He left after breakfast and reached Sottonunga in the middle of the morning. Hatto was flying and, as he arrived, Diplock greeted him with a smile. He couldn't understand why until he realised Diplock had read the report made out by his companions.

'Five!' he said. 'The whole flight! This is remarkable!'

He didn't seem to know whether to be pleased or jealous but in the end, obviously deciding it was going to do him a lot of good, too, he added his praise and congratulations, and offered Dicken two or three days off to get information on the Austrian flight.

'Go up to the Val Freddo,' he said. 'Find out where they came from. This sort of thing looks good in my reports.'

6

Driving the tender himself, Dicken promptly headed back to the home of the colonel of the Caproni squadron. His daughter was delighted to see him and he used the tender to take her on a picnic in the mountains.

The day was warm, the woods were silent and the girl clearly had a crush on Dicken. Conversation was none too easy because she didn't speak much English, so they overcame the problem by holding hands as they walked and kissing when they sat down.

Girls, he decided, seemed to fall for him much more easily than they once had and he wondered why until he looked at himself in the mirror. Then he realised that, with dark hollows under his eyes, his face was leaner and older, even with a grittier, more assured look about it. Like aeroplanes, which had grown from uncertain box-kites of dubious quality and inflammable intensity to strong, fast, reliable machines with an obvious future, he had been matured by the war, fired, steeled and made into a man.

He spent the night at the colonel's house and the following morning was given a flight in a Caproni bomber. It had two fuselages and three engines and carried a crew of two for daytime bombing and four for night bombing. The colonel was delighted with his interest and gave him several of the leaflets they were engaged in dropping on Vienna. Since they were printed in Italian, they seemed to Dicken to have a somewhat limited value. Eating lunch in the Italian mess, he decided Italian pilots were very much the same as British pilots – just better-looking on the whole, more excitable and noisy, and with a greater tendency to burst into song.

It was late when he continued his journey north. Troops

were passing the airfield and the dust they raised drifted through the woods, catching the sunshine as it went. Near Adiero he found a Berg spread across the side of a hill. Parts of it were scattered across a distance of fifty yards and the Italians had laid the pilot's body in a hut. His scalp had been torn off in the crash and somebody had picked it up and placed it on the bent engine cowling so that it lay like a fur mitten, blond and curling, with the parting still in place.

Accepting the pilot's papers and the serial number of the machine, which had been cut from the fuselage, Dicken drove on to Runduda where he found a second Berg, almost intact. The pilot, who had been wounded, had been taken to hospital.

At Barstole, he found the remains of a third Berg and the Italians once more offered the papers and said they had taken photographs of the debris and would send him one.

The unknown type he'd shot down turned out to be a Siemens-Schuckert, but it couldn't be salvaged because it was within machine gun range from the Austrian lines. An Italian sottotenente who had lived in New York and spoke English with an American accent told him that the pilot had fallen out.

'We've got him under a tarpaulin down the hill,' he said. 'He's a bit of a mess. Would you like to see him?'

'No, thanks. I'll take your word for it.'

As the Italian produced the identity card of the dead pilot, Dicken found himself staring at the portrait of a man who looked exactly like Foote. He stuffed it hurriedly back into the envelope the Italian held out, wondering if it could somehow *be* Foote who had changed sides in disgust and started flying for the Austrians. But the young man's name was there alongside the picture, Jozséf Mikzsáth, and it set him wondering if Jozséf Mikzsáth was like Foote in temperament and character as well as in looks. Then he began wondering if he ought to write to Jozséf Mikzsáth's mother. But how do you write to a woman and tell her you had just ended her son's life? 'Dear Frau Mikzsáth, I have just killed your son. I didn't look at the body because I was told it was a bit of a mess.' He decided to forget the idea.

It was a brilliant day and the clouds had disappeared

except for mist drifting among the mountains with the hint of an afternoon storm so that the outer bastions sparkled against the deep blue of the sky. All round him was the silence of the countryside, quite still except for the chirp of crickets and the distant song of a soldier in an orchard. The silence caught at his throat and he decided he'd had enough. The silence and the photograph of Jozséf Mikzsáth had finished him.

It was something he had been aware of growing in him for some time, though he had constantly thrust it out of sight behind him into the darkest recesses of his mind. Now, suddenly, it was as if he no longer had the strength to combat it, as if his muscles no longer belonged to him. His mind had grown sluggish and could think of nothing but getting away from the killing. Jozséf Mikzsáth hadn't asked to die and he, Dicken, hadn't asked to kill him, and suddenly the whole war seemed a huge, ignoble plot hatched by politicians, generals and financiers to destroy his generation. Aware of a sudden lost yearning for something he couldn't define – a missed youth, frustrated hopes, the ever-present possibility of death – he came to the conclusion that he was emotionally spent and needed leave. He needed to go home. He certainly needed something badly. Until that moment, he had never accepted that he was tired, but suddenly he realised that if he carried on he would probably start doing silly things. He had passed his peak and begun to grow over-confident, certain there was nothing he couldn't do, and it was that point that was the most dangerous.

As he descended the mountain, he stopped for a meal at a small bar with a garden. An Italian artillery officer wearing ribbons of the Libyan campaigns joined him and, as they talked, a cloud covered the mountain and the sun disappeared. A shutter slammed and the leaves started rattling, then the dust started to whirl. As they went inside the air turned liquid and drops of rain as big as half-crowns began to fall.

'Rain,' the Italian said, gesturing to the north. 'Austrian rain. The sun's Italian. The summer is coming to an end. And then the politicians in Rome will once more start saying "Not another winter in the trenches." ' He shrugged. 'What do they know of it, these patriots? They have never been in the trenches. Not even in summer.'

By the time Dicken returned to Sottanunga he had been away nearly a week. He knew that had not been Diplock's intention, but it had calmed him and he felt the sharp edges of his nerves had been soothed. Hallowes told him he'd been awarded the Italian Medaglia ad Valore Argenta, which was a high award for bravery, but he wasn't interested, wishing only that the Aubreys were not in Naples so that he could visit them.

When he reached his room, he found Hatto there, smoking a cigarette.

'Made it, I see.' He fished in his pocket and brought out a letter. It carried a Rome postmark and was addressed to them both. It was from Foote who had joined his own air force.

'I've got over it now,' he wrote. 'Thanks for everything. I'll always remember you two – the Glass-Eyed Bastard and the Kid Who Could Shoot.'

Dicken refolded the letter and put it back in the envelope. 'I'm glad he made it,' he said.

Hatto seemed in a strange mood and Dicken studied him with a frown. Then he realised he was wearing his best uniform, and raised his eyebrows.

'What's on? Are we celebrating something?'

'I think we might be. I've been given a squadron of Bristols in France.'

'Bit sudden, isn't it?'

Hatto smiled. 'Uncle Willie's been a naughty boy,' he said. 'Parasol Percy was told he had to supply someone and wanted to send Fosdyck who's senior to me. When I got back he was having lunch in Capadolio with the mayor. The Wing colonel's gone home so he's got nobody else to crawl to. I went into Hallowes' office and demanded to see the signal about him going to the Snipe Squadron. Hallowes didn't want to show me but I said I'd already seen it once on his desk and it was no bloody use trying to hide it from me.'

'Hide what from you?'

'All that about Diplock being ordered to France is a load of cock, old fruit. The signal had your name on it. I made him fish it out of the safe. The name had been altered and the alteration was in Diplock's writing. A new gong and a squadron of Snipes would be useful when the war ends, wouldn't it?'

'And Diplock?'

'When he returned from his lunch I was sitting in his chair. I told him he was a slimy bastard. He went red and blustered a bit, but I said I'd seen the signal before he'd altered it, so then he said it had been a mistake and that the promotion and the gong *were* yours. The wretched little tyke was trying to cover up, and the next thing I knew, a message came to the mess for me to say I was going to France. That makes me a major, also, y'see. What's more it makes you one, too.'

'Since when?'

'Immediate. Both of us.'

'Then we can go together.'

Hatto smiled. 'And Parasol Percy will once more have got rid of everybody who's aware of his dirty tricks department. First Foote, then me, now you.'

Dicken was silent for a moment. 'He'd never have got away with it, Willie,' he said slowly.

'No. And it might have been nice to see him led away in chains. But, y'know, Italy *is* different, the colonel's gone home, and documents have a habit of going astray. Possession's nine points of the law, and he might just have wangled it. In fact, I dare bet he would. He's a staff type by instinct and would know how to do it.' Hatto smiled. 'What he probably hasn't noticed, though, is that we're now the same rank as he is and can tell him what we think of him. I suggest we have a go.'

*

Diplock was keeping out of their way and their railway warrants were made out by Hallowes. Dicken managed to telephone the Aubreys' house in Capadolio but the maid said the family were still in Naples, so he spent the afternoon writing a long letter explaining what had happened, and that evening he and Hatto headed for the town in a tender to celebrate.

'We'll work our way through the alphabet,' Hatto suggested. 'Starting with absinthe. For A.'

'And then?'

'Benedictine. Or beer. Or brandy.'

'Christ! And for C?'

'Chianti, of course. All the way to vermouth and whisky.'

'X, Y and Z'll make you think a bit.'

They were unable to pass H and their journey home was uncertain. Rounding a corner outside the town, Hatto put the front wheel of the tender in a ditch and they decided it was safer to walk. The transport sergeant grinned and offered to have the tender pulled out and brought back, and they gave him a bottle of Strega for his trouble.

'We'll pack first,' Dicken said. 'Get everything in the tender ready for off. That way we'll have left before he has time to think what to do in reply.'

The plan didn't work out as expected because they fell asleep and didn't wake up until the following morning. As the tender appeared, they threw everything aboard, feeling as if the sides of their heads were about to drop off.

Hatto managed a wan smile. 'It'll put us in a nice bad temper,' he said. 'And if you've got something unpleasant to say, I always think you should say it as unpleasantly and as loudly as possible. People understand better then.'

Hallowes seemed to guess why they'd come when they asked to see Diplock and a nervous look crossed his face. He gestured at the door and, as they pushed it open, Diplock was reading a sheaf of reports.

'Came to say goodbye,' Hatto said.

Diplock's expression was uncertain but he managed a nervous smile.

'Also came to say what we think of you,' Dicken added, and the smile vanished at once. 'It isn't much, of course,' he added. 'But I suppose you guessed that long since.'

'In fact,' Hatto went on, 'we think you're a low-life bastard.'

Diplock's face went red. 'How dare you?'

Hatto tapped the new crown on his shoulder. 'Oh, we dare,' he said. 'Discussion's permitted between officers of equal rank. Not that there's anything to discuss, really.

Nothing would change what we think. We consider you a bit of a shit.'

'Mean little gadget,' Dicken added.

'Dirty tricks expert.'

'Hope you choke.'

'Hope your right leg drops off.'

'Or that you break out all over in warts.'

While Diplock was still struggling to find words, they clicked to attention, saluted and turned away. Outside, they climbed into the tender and gestured to the driver to start up. As it lurched away from the office, Hatto beamed.

'Feel much better now,' he said.

Dicken grinned. 'I think he'll have got the message,' he said.

'Not that it matters,' Hatto smiled. 'Because he's got another shock coming to him shortly. While I was looking at that signal of yours, Hallowes was called away and I got my hands on the personal files. I put a little insert into Diplock's and signed it "William Wymarck Wombwell Hatto, Major." Looked rather good, I thought.' He shrugged. ' 'Course, he'll take it out but, you never know, somebody might get a look at it first.'

'What *is* in it? What did you put?'

'Nothing much, old fruit.' Hatto smiled a ruminative smile. 'Just "I would not breed from this officer." '

7

France was very different from the previous year. The Germans were being steadily pushed back and there was a feeling in the air that victory wasn't far in the future.

Appearing before a full colonel at St. Omer, Dicken and Hatto were informed of what was expected of them.

'It's no good you going home to form your squadrons without some knowledge of what it's become like out here,' he explained. 'Get some flying in and find out how things are done these days.'

They tried to appear enthusiastic while looking forward to a long spell in England and, because, after Cambrai, they didn't believe anything anybody told them, they were careful to obtain the view from lower down the scale. Almonde, who'd been flying with them as an observer in Strutters and was now at St. Omer, clarified things.

'We're not human beings any more,' he said. 'Just units in a bloody great machine they've built for killing Germans.'

All the big names – McCudden, Mannock, Ball – were all dead, but there were a whole lot of new men coming along. A lanky New Zealander called Keith Park had run up a score with a Bristol squadron, and a South African called Beauchamp-Proctor, who stood about four-foot-nothing in his socks and had to sit on a cushion to see out of the cockpit, but had extraordinary eyesight, was knocking the German planes down in droves. There were also a few obvious leaders like Collishaw, Douglas, Tedder and one or two more, and the German air force was being outfought and outflown.

'They've got a new high-winged monoplane,' Almonde said. 'And the new Fokker DVII's a tremendous machine, but there's a feeling it's not as dangerous as it ought to be because some of the stuffing's leaked out of the German pilots and you spend half your time trying to tempt them to have a go.'

The Richthofen Circus was now being led by a Bavarian called Goering but, though he personally was said to be good, it was no longer the dread name it used to be.

'All the same,' Almonde ended, 'there are still a few to watch out for. Löwenhardt's gone but Udet's still around. He flies a red Fokker with white stripes like a setting sun on the upper wing. It has "Lo" on the fuselage – the name of his girl friend, they say – and if you should get behind him, which I doubt, because he's a hot stuff pilot, you'll know who he is straight away because he also has "Du doch nicht" on the upper surface of his tailplanes. Means "Balls to you" or something.'

*

There seemed to be enormous numbers of Americans about, all of them tall and strong and fit. Their enthusiasm was infectious and their air force was doing splendid work round St. Mihiel. They met a Princeton man called John Winant, who looked like Abraham Lincoln, tall, black-haired, earnest and handsome, and a former racing motorist with a name that sounded like Richthofen who was said to have started as the general's chauffeur but was now making a tremendous name as an air fighter. They were flying French Spads because, as Foote had warned, the idea of a sky black with American machines had never materialised.

The squadron to which they were attached consisted of a number of new types – improved Bristol fighters, Snipes, Dolphins, Martynsides, De Havillands – and men were constantly arriving for conversion courses. It was run by a major called Norman with, holding a watching brief over his head, Rivers, who had commanded the 1½-Strutters at Ste. Marie. He was now a lieutenant-colonel, and recovered from his gloom at the thought of an end to the killing.

After the backwater of Italy, it was exciting to be back in France, and the feel of being part of a new service was tremendous. The RAF was a broad-minded organisation and thoroughly cosmopolitan because it had often taken the

235

best men from the other services and from the colonies, and like all air forces, because it was new and young, it was free of snobbery and self-importance and was never parochial in outlook, despite the occasional misfit like Diplock. Even the American Air Force, young as it was, was vigorous and unpredictable.

The whole service had élan, style, dash, cheek if you liked, and a lack of formality that was detested by the army and the navy. It hadn't a hint of stodginess, and for the most part everybody in it was full of the excitement of youth, believing in the future of flying with an unbelievable intensity. There were no old men in the RAF and, though they sometimes died young – heartbreakingly young at times – they also sometimes reached command while young.

Dicken felt he should have been entirely happy because the sense that the war was approaching its end was even more marked in France than in Italy, but it was clear that, though the squadrons were hard and tough, they were also like ancient garments which had been darned and darned again. The shape remained the same but little of the original was left.

Then Foote appeared. He was wearing American uniform with a high stiff collar and the wings of his own air force.

Dicken touched the insignia on his shoulders. 'What do they mean?' he asked. 'Did they make you a major?'

Foote laughed. 'Did they hell! There are so many goddam desk fliers, you can't get near the higher ranks.'

They had a wild night out on the town and parted full of nostalgia, all a little maudlin and swearing they'd never lose touch with each other. Dicken wondered if they would.

Handiside was at St. Omer, too, wearing the crown of a flight sergeant now.

'Makes you wonder what it was all for, sir, don't it?' he said. 'This is roughly where I started in 1914.'

Finally, like a bolt from the blue, came the news that Diplock had also arrived in France. Hatto arrived in the mess, a shocked look on his face. 'I've just seen him,' he said.

It didn't take long to find out that, sensing that, with the war ending, his place was in France, he had wangled his way north despite his original setback and was once more under the old Wing colonel's protection and expecting promotion. Though they saw him from time to time, it was obvious he was carefully avoiding them. He had clearly expected them to be in England and the fact that three men who knew of his trickery in St. Omer had unnerved him.

'What a bloody life,' Dicken growled. 'Spending all his time dodging round corners.'

Diplock, in fact, seemed to be a symbol of the future. Idealism had died long since in France but as the war approached its end, in England the enthusiasm seemed to be increasing. The newspaper barons were demanding that the Germans should pay for what they'd done and the generals, pushing hard as they scented victory, were killing men, it seemed, merely to get their names in the honours lists when hostilities ceased.

Not only the generals. *Everybody* seemed to be wondering what they were going to do when peace came. Those who hoped to return to civilian life were concentrating on staying alive so they could go home and carve a career out of what was left after the best jobs had been taken by those who'd dodged military service. Those who hoped to stay in uniform were busy feathering their nests, manoeuvring themselves into good jobs they hoped to hang on to, so that, just when there was a need for increased comradeship, there was less than there had ever been. Everybody was wondering what lay ahead and it started once more Dicken's worry of what he was going to do after it was all over.

'Why not stay in the RAF?' Hatto suggested. 'Parasol Percy's staying in. That's why he's out for all the promotion he can get before it ends. Why do you think he's so maty with the Wing colonel? Why do you think he got himself that DSO? The fact that he got it pushing a pen won't make a scrap of difference in five years time.'

Dicken pondered the idea. 'Think they'd have him?' he asked.

'Dear old lad –' Hatto looked at him pityingly '– before the war there *wasn't* an air force. Now we've got one, the people who're running it won't part with it in a hurry, and Trenchard will be girding up his loins already to make sure the army and the navy don't arrange for it to die a pauper's death. If there's no air force, y'see, there'll be more money in the old coffers for *them* and more money means more generals and admirals.' He smiled. 'We'll survive, of course, but it's going to need a few chaps with intelligence to run the show.'

'Surely there's somebody better than Parasol Percy?'

'Think so? When peace comes, all the Hostilities Only people will rush back to their nine-to-fives, and the ones who stay in will get what promotion's going, because there won't be anyone else. And think what that means. They'll be the ones who'll be running the show in the next war. A château to live in, champagne to drink, French chefs, women of heartbreaking loveliness. It sounds all right to me.'

As he thought about it, Dicken realised that the idea of turning his back on the sky appalled him. Never again to see the blue haze that covered the earth, never to see the sun disappearing when the land was already in darkness, never to see the fabric of the wings rippling, or smell petrol, hot oil and dope – it seemed impossible.

'There's another way of looking at it, too.' Hatto sounded uncharacteristically sombre. 'As a civilian, you'll be as out of place as a pterodactyl in a parrot house. Your glory's already departing, old lad. That idealism that made us join up in 1914's long since vanished and it's no good trying in a disintegrating world to hold on to it. We've been living sixty seconds to the minute for the last four years and you'll never see eye-to-eye with those chaps who're too young to have put on uniform, and you're separated by a lifetime from those who were too old. All the bright ideas we had for when it ended seem to have got lost somewhere, because the standards we've been living by don't exist any more. Sometimes it seems very lonely.'

Dicken smiled affectionately. 'Sometimes, Willie,' he said, 'I realise you're not as stupid as you look. I think perhaps I *will* stay in. Flying seems to be the only thing I can do well. What about you? Are you going back to being a lord? Horse shows, race meetings, society balls, patting the heads of the deserving poor?'

Hatto grinned. 'You've got a bloody funny idea of what the landed gentry do with their time, old fruit,' he said. 'My lot spend most of it with bits of paper on the dining room table wondering if they've got enough in the bank to repair the roof or stop the stables falling down. These days, old lad, it's the profiteers who've got the money. Lloyd George's friends. They'll be in the honours lists when the war's over and, because they've got the money, within ten years half the country houses in England will be owned by brand-new barons and the old lot will be living in the lodges on a pension to give a little tone to the parties they throw. I'm staying in, too.'

*

The bright summer gold was changing to bronze and the trees were showing a rusty tint. Leaves began to fall and suddenly there was a winter chill in the evening air and mist in the valleys.

There had been no reply from Nicola and Dicken had come to the conclusion that she'd forgotten him. Then he received a letter from, of all people, Marie-Gabrielle. It was post-marked Genoa, written in a full round hand and shockingly spelled, but she pointed out that they all missed him and were sorry he'd disappeared. It raised his hopes but since she'd forgotten to include the Genoa address, he had no idea where to reply to and could only send his letter to the house in Capadolio, which, he felt sure, was standing empty and echoing by this time.

There was still no news of moving to England and he decided the postings home were hanging fire because the authorities thought the war might end. He and Hatto were flying only occasionally and were spending the rest of their time visiting squadrons and learning RAF methods with reports, records, returns and repairs.

'I think they just wanted a couple of spare adjutants,' Hatto complained.

October came with the countryside beginning to look shabby, with heavy dews, steel helmets wet with rain, and the Germans going backwards faster and faster. They began to think they were never going to fly in war again, but just when they were least expecting it and when they had come to the conclusion they were permanent fixtures, they heard that Rivers had gone home and that they were going home, too.

Diplock took over the squadron, and it wasn't entirely unexpected that late in the evening Dicken was presented with a demand for a full-length report on the Snipe.

'Why?' he asked. 'The damn' thing's been around since early in the year.'

The Recording Officer seemed puzzled. 'The Major wants one written in the light of cold weather conditions. He says 201 Squadron's complaining that the Bentley doesn't give the power output it's supposed to.'

It sounded an odd sort of request but the German Air Force was said to be regrouping for the final assault on the German frontier, because nobody seemed to have seen anything of them for days, and he rather fancied a last look at the sky where he'd fought so long.

The wind was cold and there was a smoky autumn smell in the air as he climbed into the Snipe and taxied across a muddy field marked by wheels and tailskids. He liked the Snipe despite the habit it shared with its feathered namesake of darting from side to side as it took off. Both were endowed with a high power-weight ratio and the zigzags were caused by the pilot trying to counteract the gyroscopic kick of the huge Bentley rotary.

The evening was heavy with low-bellied clouds that looked like the wet sails of ships-of-the-line, majestic and threatening and, with the sun blood-red in the west, full of threatening purple valleys and glistening pink pinnacles. As he lifted towards them, he could see fragmentary glimpses of the patterned earth, squared hedgerows and patched fields, and the black ruins of the fighting zone, its buildings like broken teeth near the zigzag lines of the trench system.

Climbing higher, enjoying flying after so long, he felt he belonged among God's chosen few. It wasn't given to many men to experience the joy of being alone in the upper air, looking, it seemed, on the face of the Almighty himself. It was a heady sensation, especially with the war ending. For four years thousands of young men like himself had known no future, but in all that time, apart from small cuts and bruises, he had not been much hurt. He'd been luckier than Hatto, lucky to have been sent to Italy. Staying in the fiercer flames of France, he might well have been dead.

His thoughts busy, his eyes roved restlessly about him, moving instinctively, alert for the slow-moving specks above or the brief shadows below that could mean death. The Snipe climbed easily and he reached 20,000 feet without much trouble, breathing in great gasps through his mouth in the thin air. As he levelled off, he saw a two-seater Rumpler to the west of him against the light, its wings and spars outlined with fire. Unable to resist the temptation, he swung the Snipe round on its wingtips, the motor crackling, the wires howling, the earth revolving, and went down in a shallow dive. The German observer clearly hadn't seen him and, as he came up beneath it and fired, the Rumpler shuddered and began to break up.

He was still watching it, curiously saddened by its fall, when something smashed against his right thigh with a force that made him cry out. It lifted his foot from the rudder bar and, for a moment, unable to make out what had happened, he thought something had broken from the wing and shot through the side of the fuselage. It was only as the pain came that he realised he'd been hit by a bullet.

He was shocked and wondering where in God's name it had come from because the observer of the two-seater couldn't possibly have hit him, but as he looked frantically round, he saw a square-bodied machine disappearing below in a flash of vermilion. He recognised it from the comma-shaped tail as a Fokker DVII and realised it must have been guarding the two-seater.

Automatically, he swung to face it. It was sitting on his tail, waiting to kill him, and, lifting the nose of his machine as if to climb, he saw the Fokker follow suit. As it did so, he kicked hard with his good leg at the rudder bar and slithered sideways to put the machine in a vertical bank. As the Fokker appeared alongside and then in front, so close he could see the streaks of oil on the engine cowling, he saw the pilot look round in alarm, the sun catching his goggles so that they were like two huge red eyes. As he pressed the trigger, the German's head lifted, then the machine began to slide away in a long slow dive, the sun glinting redly on the curve of the wings. At first he couldn't tell whether he'd hit it or not, but then he saw a thin white trail coming from beneath it that he knew was petrol and, as he watched, there was a flash that became flame and the machine curled away beneath him, trailing a thick column of smoke.

Half-fainting from the pain of his wound, he was on the point of turning for home when he saw aeroplanes all round him, like a cloud of flashing butterflies in the crimson sky. In a half-daze, he couldn't imagine where they'd come from because they hadn't been there when he'd spotted the two-seater or even the Fokker. At first, he thought they were British machines, then that it was a dogfight that had somehow drifted his way, because they seemed to be all different. He recognised Albatros DVs, Pfalzes, Fokker DVIIs and triplanes, even a high-winged monoplane he'd never seen before which seemed to have an incredible rate of climb.

The air about him was filled with the smoke trails of tracers and he decided the Germans had been deliberately keeping quiet to lure him to where they could fall on him. The Snipe was already showing the effects of their firing, little flags of fabric flapping on the wings, and just behind his head he could hear a crack-crack-crack which at first he thought was a machine gun but finally realised was a strip of canvas torn from the fuselage and clattering in the slip-stream.

A Fokker swam past in a pink glow that came through the purple clouds and he saw a red and white sunburst on the upper wings and the letters, *LO*, on the fuselage. Somewhere, he remembered, someone had told him about this machine. As it slithered away, avoiding him, he saw the moving elevators were lettered, and though he couldn't recognise what they said, he knew without doubt that he was up against Udet and his group.

Pressing the trigger, he saw his bullets go into the red Fokker's fuselage, then it slipped away expertly and he had to concentrate on another machine that appeared in front. Somehow, the very number of enemies had revived him. His right leg was agony but it still moved and he realised the bullet had not broken his thigh but had simply gone through the thick part of the flesh. But as he wrenched the Snipe round, congratulating himself that with luck he might still get away with it, a second bullet tore into his left calf like a sledge hammer.

Half-fainting and nauseated by fear, aware that his only hope was to keep the Snipe going round in tight circles, he held on, clinging desperately to consciousness and firing every time anything came within his sights. Preserve your ammunition. Keep circling. Then something hit his head and, as blood filled his eyes, he decided he was dying. But even through fading consciousness he instinctively kept the machine in a tight bank. Keep turning. Keep turning. Don't panic.

For a moment he lost consciousness but, as he came round again, he forced himself to concentrate and wrenched off his goggles so that he could see better. Vaguely he saw a triplane going past like a set of shelves burst into flames and wondered if someone had come to his help. But the rest kept pecking at him and he had to assume that it had been his own bullets which had sent it down. A DVII appeared in front of him and, as he fired, it seemed to stagger in the air and fall away, its rudder hanging off, its pilot head-down in the cockpit. Still he kept on going round and round and suddenly the machines about him vanished.

When he came round, the Snipe was falling in a flat spiral like a falling leaf and automatically he pulled it out and started to turn again as he saw the Germans close in once more. By this time he had decided he was as good as dead and found himself, even as he forced himself to hold the machine in its turns, wondering what it would be like. So many of his friends had died, he wondered if there would be a party when he joined them or whether it would just be darkness, like going into a room without windows, without light, or sense or smell.

Several times he saw the red Fokker with the word *LO* on the fuselage and was once near enough to read the jeering comment on the elevators, 'Du doch nicht!' But he couldn't hit it, though the Germans – because there were too many of them and they were getting in each other's way – also seemed able to do no more than put odd bursts into the Snipe. Two of

243

them directly in front of him missed each other by inches as they swung away from his bullets and he saw the pilots give him a horrified look.

Another Albatros fell away then he saw a gap and headed for it in the hope of diving for home. But his left hand jerked as a bullet ripped into his forearm and he saw blood pouring down his sleeve. Oh Christ, he thought, this is really *it* this time.

Still the Germans came at him, making a final effort to kill him as if determined to avenge their friends. It was Voss all over again, he thought. Even the same time of day. Everybody in the RFC had felt admiration for the young German who'd taken on a whole flight of SE5s led by, of all people, the great McCudden. But the SEs had killed him in the end for the simple reason that one into seven didn't go and, though the Germans were reputed to be no longer as good as they were, it was clear that one into thirty didn't go either.

Knowing his petrol was low, he managed to switch to the reserve tank. Then he realised he was no longer being nagged by the Germans and saw that a squadron of SE5s had appeared above him and the Germans had bolted for home. The clouds had closed over the sun at last and the brilliant blood-red in the sky had given way to a pale pink with, beyond it, the rising purple of the night, and he was alone, a minute speck in the immensity of the heavens.

He could barely see now for the blood in his eyes and he was barely conscious, but in front of him he could make out the road that led to Ypres and realised he was safe behind the British lines. Certain he couldn't make it home, he looked round for somewhere to put the machine down. Through a blur of pain he saw his wings in tatters, wires hanging loose and one of the centre section struts almost shot through. If he didn't put it down soon, the Snipe would fall down of its own accord.

He was low now but how he'd got there he had no idea and as he saw a darkened field, he quickly put the machine down in it. Half way across, he saw a dip approaching, but there was nothing he could do about it, and as the Snipe touched the ground, an incredible lassitude swept over him. The wheels dropped into a ditch, the nose went down with a twanging of wires and the groaning of strained struts and the tail came up. Fortunately the Snipe's forward momentum had almost finished and it didn't break up, but, thrown forward as the machine nosed over, he felt the crunch as his nose broke. The world went red and unrecognisable and he decided for a moment he was in hell; then he realised he was hanging upside down from his straps. Forcing himself to move, he released his safety belt and fell out.

His nostrils full of the smell of petrol, he pulled himself to his knees, aware of men pounding across the grass to him, and was just on the point of crawling away when there was a flash and a great gust of flame that seemed to belch up at him. Feeling himself being dragged away, he heard himself shrieking for them to put him down because too many things were hurting at once. The flame died quickly and they had him on his feet now, unaware of his injuries, and were hurrying him into the dusk away from the machine.

'Made it, lad,' someone with a Red Cross brassard said. 'You're going to be all right. Where's all the blood on your face come from? Have you banged your nose?'

Dicken shook his head feebly, almost devoid of the strength to do so. 'I think it's more than that,' he said. 'I think I've been wounded as well.'

They stared at him, startled, then the man who had spoken saw the blood on his legs and immediately began wrenching at his coat. The pain was more than he could bear and he slid through their hands and sat down. He was just conscious as he flopped back in the grass.

'But thanks all the same,' he whispered. 'It was kind of you to try.'

8

The first real awareness that he was still alive came with Hatto's voice.

For some time he had been lying in darkness, certain he was dead but puzzled because he didn't seem to be in Heaven, nor yet in Hell. Around seemed to be the blackness of nothing, with a numb ache in legs, arms and head, though the pain also seemed to overlap and include the whole of his body. After a while he decided that he was in a type of half-way house, somewhere beyond life while the authorities, whom he saw as a sort of Railway Transport Officer, decided where he should go.

Then a voice spoke to him. It sounded worried. 'You all right, old fruit? This is Willie, your old chum.'

'Where are you?' Dicken's lips were cracked and stiff and he found difficulty in speaking. 'Are you dead, too?'

'I beg your pardon.'

'Aren't we dead?'

'Not by a long chalk, old fruit. I'm fine, and they say you'll be fine, too, before long. I've brought you a bottle of champagne for when you're feeling better. Nothing like champers for an operation, a military disaster or taking a girl to bed.'

Dicken was silent for a long time. 'I felt certain I was dead,' he said eventually.

'The pill-roller says you're going to be all right. An SE crowd said you'd taken on a bunch of about thirty Huns and were knocking hell out of them.'

'Don't you believe it! They took *me* on and they were knocking hell out of *me*. Where did I get hit?'

'Both legs, one arm, and across the top of the skull. You're lucky to be alive.'

246

Not long before, Dicken recalled, he'd been priding himself on never having been much hurt. He'd certainly made up for it. Four wounds in as many minutes.

'Still,' Hatto went on. 'They're all flesh wounds, though you got a bit burned, too. That's why you can't see so well. It's a good job I was handy when they brought you in. The surgeon wanted to have your leg off.'

'Oh, God, don't let him, Willie!'

Hatto laughed. 'Not likely. But you know what army surgeons are like. They get into a rhythm. Slap a man on the table, off with his leg – or his arm or even his head – then "Next please. Pass down the car." He asked if you were a friend of mine and I said that after four years you were the only one I'd got left and if he took your leg off I'd have his to go with it. Knowing how you like your grub, I told him the best thing would be to plug up the holes so you didn't leak and hang a feed bag on you and you'd start getting better at once.'

There was another long silence before Dicken spoke again. 'How long have I been here?'

'Two days. Or getting on that way.'

'Shouldn't you be in England?'

'Bugger England. They won't need me, anyway. The Germans are said to be thinking of chucking their hands in.'

'You mean the war's over?'

'Not yet. But it's beginning to look as if it will be by Christmas. The writing seems to be on the wall.'

Slowly, Dicken began to learn what had happened. After the two-seater, it seemed he had destroyed three other Germans, though, since two of them had fallen on the German side of the line, it was difficult to confirm them. It didn't matter much. Killing people was no longer important, and he was sick of it, anyway.

A little while later a doctor came to dress his face with picric-acid solution. He examined his eyes which were tight-shut with the burnt stubs of his eyelashes and there was a great pink weal across his nose and cheeks.

'You were lucky,' the doctor said. 'Your flying helmet and scarf stopped it being worse. It'll look unpleasant for a while but the tissue's not destroyed.'

'Will I be able to see?'

There was a moment's silence then the doctor's voice came again. 'Left eye's fine,' he said. 'Right eye we're not sure about. So you won't be flying for a while. The cold could attack them while they're not protected by lashes.'

For the next day or two Dicken slept and, when he wasn't asleep, he pretended to be. For the first time he realised how tired he was and, as he tried to recall some of the men he'd flown with, he found his mind rejected the memories so that all he could see were dead faces, and hear voices that didn't seem to be earthly.

There were questions, too. His mind was full of questions. Why had Diplock sent him up? Had he had prior knowledge that Udet was about? It didn't seem possible, but when Hatto reappeared the thoughts came out. Hatto listened in silence.

'Could he have known, Willie?'

Hatto was a long time replying. 'It's strong meat, old fruit,' he said at last. 'But I see your point. I suppose we'll never know the truth.'

'Perhaps it's as well.'

'Perhaps it is. Either way, you came out of it alive and, apart from a little wear and tear, in reasonable shape. They say you were arsing about with Udet and his boys and think you deserve another medal for your cheek.'

'Can't see the point now the war's nearly over.'

Hatto chuckled. 'Don't delude yourself, old son. The more the merrier. Anybody with a few gongs and a good record'll do very well for themselves. I've got a modest one or two and you've got a modest two or three. They'll count. Reinforcements against the Parasol Percies of the world.'

Dicken shook his head. 'Air fighting's sheer luck,' he said. 'There must be dozens who could have done just as well if they'd been given a Camel instead of one of those bloody awful BEs.'

There was a pause, then Hatto touched his hand. 'Last I'll be seeing of you for a bit, old fruit,' he said. 'They say if I don't go home I'll be court-martialled. Look me up when you arrive.'

'Give my love to the Hon. Caroline, Willie. Are you going

to marry her? She's been writing to you since 1915.'

'Might at that. She seems to want to and you should never stand in the way of an express train or a determined woman.'

There was a moment's silence, then Hatto put a couple of letters in Dicken's hand. 'Picked 'em up for you,' he said. 'Female handwriting. Want me to read 'em to you or are they too private?'

Dicken shook his head. 'They won't be important. One from Nicola to say "Come home. All is forgiven." And one from Zoë to say she's going to Canada with that chap Harmer.'

The following day, they took the bandages from his eyes and the doctor examined him carefully, before announcing he wouldn't be losing the sight of his right eye.

One of the nurses brought a mirror and held it up. The face that stared out at him was a mixture of red, blue, yellow and green. His nose was swollen and listed slightly to the left, his forehead was all the colours of the rainbow, his cheeks seemed unable to make up their mind whether to be burned or bruised, and the yellow stains of picric made him look even more battered than he was.

'Can I read?' he asked. 'Just a couple of letters.'

The nurse opened the letters and held them up. She looked a little like Nicola and, in her starched apron and cap, seemed so clean, so decent, so honest, so pure, he almost wept. The letters startled him because they were not at all what he'd expected. Nicola's letter was from Madras.

'Father's been posted to Delhi,' she wrote. 'We had to leave almost immediately. It's sad we haven't seen each other to say goodbye but I don't think now that we ever shall again. My parents send their affection and so do the smaller children, particularly Marie-Gabrielle, who always seemed to have a warm feeling for you.'

Particularly Marie-Gabrielle, who always had a warm feeling for you. No mention about Nicola's warm feeling. No reference to the fact that she'd talked of marriage.

He drew a deep breath like a sigh and looked up at the nurse. 'Now the other one, please.'

Once more he was startled by the contents. 'Casey's gone back to Canada,' Zoë wrote. 'I think he's let me down,

249

because he said he'd find me a job in his business. At least, though, he taught me to fly so I can always get a job in aviation. In the meantime, you'd better come home and make an honest woman of me . . .'

As he finished reading, the nurse put the letter back in the envelope.

'Good news, I hope?'

'Bit of both. I can cope with it.'

He decided he could. He'd almost forgotten what Zoë looked like. All he could remember was her bounding energy. Then he remembered Nicola's gentleness and decided it would never have worked. Perhaps she was right. Perhaps Zoë was right, too. He'd have to wait and see.

Max Hennessy is the pseudonym of John Harris, author of many acclaimed historical novels, including *The Sea Shall Not Have Them* and *Covenant with Death,* and the *Lion at Sea* and *Soldier of the Queen* trilogies, written under the name of Max Hennessy. Ex-sailor, ex-airman, ex-newspaperman, ex-travel courier, he went to sea in the Merchant Navy before the war, and during the war served with two air forces and two navies.

D-9600-5-846

1646-5-0096 D.